Eisenhower Middle School
10200 25th Ave. S.E.
Everett, WA 98208

Also by Ray Bradbury

NOVELS

The Martian Chronicles
Fahrenheit 451
Dandelion Wine
Something Wicked This Way Comes
Death Is a Lonely Business
A Graveyard for Lunatics
Green Shadows, White Whale
From the Dust Returned
Let's All Kill Constance
Farewell Summer
Ahmed and the Oblivion Machines: A Fable

SHORT STORY COLLECTIONS

Dark Carnival
The Illustrated Man
The Golden Apples of the Sun
The October Country
A Medicine for Melancholy
R is for Racket
The Machineries of Joy
The Autumn People
The Vintage Bradbury
S is for Space
Twice 22
I Sing the Body Electric
Long After Midnight
The Small Assassin
The Mummies of Guanajuato
Beyond 1984: Remembrance of Things Future
The Attic Where the Meadow Greens

Fahrenheit 451

Fahrenheit 451—
The temperature at which
book paper catches
fire and burns . . .

Ray Bradbury

Introduction by Neil Gaiman

Simon & Schuster Paperbacks

New York London Toronto Sydney New Delhi

Simon & Schuster Paperbacks
A Division of Simon & Schuster, Inc.
1230 Avenue of the Americas
New York, NY 10020

This Simon & Schuster trade paperback edition June 2013

SIMON & SCHUSTER PAPERBACKS and colophon are registered
trademarks of Simon & Schuster, Inc.

For information about special discounts for bulk purchases,
please contact Simon & Schuster Special Sales at
1-866-506-1949 or business@simonandschuster.com.

The Simon & Schuster Speakers Bureau can bring authors to
your live event. For more information or to book an event,
contact the Simon & Schuster Speakers Bureau at
1-866-248-3049 or visit our website at www.simonspeakers.com.

Designed by Nancy Singer

Manufactured in the United States of America

20   19   18   17   16   15   14   13   12

Library of Congress Cataloging-in-Publication Data
Bradbury, Ray.
    Fahrenheit 451 / Ray Bradbury.
        p. cm.
        1. State-sponsored terrorism—Fiction. 2. Totalitarianism—Fiction.
        3. Book burning—Fiction. 4. Censorship—Fiction. I. Title:
        Fahrenheit four hundred fifty-one. II. Title.
PS3503.R167F3 2003
813'54—dc22   2003066160

ISBN 978-1-4516-7331-9

Permission credits can be found on page 251.

This one, with gratitude,

is for Don Congdon

Contents

Introduction

Sometimes writers write about a world that does not yet exist. We do it for a hundred reasons. (Because it's good to look forward, not back. Because we need to illuminate a path we hope or we fear humanity will take. Because the world of the future seems more enticing or more interesting than the world of today. Because we need to warn you. To encourage. To examine. To imagine.) The reasons for writing about the day after tomorrow, and all the tomorrows that follow it, are as many and as varied as the people writing.

This is a book of warning. It is a reminder that what we have is valuable, and that sometimes we take what we value for granted.

There are three phrases that make possible the world of writing about the world of not-yet (you can call it science fiction or speculative fiction; you can call it anything you wish) and they are simple phrases:

What if . . . ?

If only . . .

If this goes on . . .

"What if . . . ?" gives us change, a departure from our lives. *(What if aliens landed tomorrow and gave us everything we wanted, but at a price?)*

"If only . . ." lets us explore the glories and dangers of tomorrow. *(If only dogs could talk. If only I were invisible.)*

"If this goes on . . ." is the most predictive of the three, although it doesn't try to predict an actual future with all its messy confusion. Instead, "If this goes on . . ." fiction takes an element of life today, something clear and obvious and normally something troubling, and asks what would happen if that thing, that one thing, became bigger, became all-pervasive, changed the way we thought and behaved. *(If this goes on, all communication everywhere will be through text messages or computers, and direct speech between two people, without a machine, will be outlawed.)*

It's a cautionary question, and it lets us explore cautionary worlds.

People think—wrongly—that speculative fiction is about predicting the future, but it isn't; or if it is, it tends to do a rotten job of it. Futures are huge things that come with many elements and a billion variables, and the human race has a habit of listening to predictions for what the future will bring and then doing something quite different.

What speculative fiction is really good at is not the future but the present—taking an aspect of it that troubles or is dangerous, and extending and extrapolating that aspect into something that allows the people of that time to see what they are doing from a different angle and from a different place. It's cautionary.

Fahrenheit 451 is speculative fiction. It's an "If this goes on . . ." story. Ray Bradbury was writing about his present, which is our past. He was warning us about things; some of those things are obvious, and some of them, half a century later, are harder to see.

Listen.

If someone tells you what a story is about, they are probably right.

If they tell you that that is *all* the story is about, they are very definitely wrong.

Any story is about a host of things. It is about the author; it is about the world the author sees and deals with and lives in; it is about the words chosen and the way those words are deployed; it is about the story itself and what happens in the story; it is about the people in the story; it is polemic; it is opinion.

An author's opinions of what a story is about are always valid and are always true: the author was there, after all, when the book was written. She came up with each word and knows why she used that word instead of another. But an author is a creature of her time, and even she cannot see everything that her book is about.

More than half a century has passed since 1953. In America in 1953, the comparatively recent medium of radio was already severely on the wane—its reign had lasted about thirty years, but now the exciting new medium of television had come into ascendancy, and the dramas and comedies of radio were either ending for good or reinventing themselves with a visual track on the "idiot box."

The news channels in America warned of juvenile delinquents—teenagers in cars who drove dangerously and lived for kicks. The Cold War was going on—a war between Russia and its allies and America and its allies in which nobody dropped bombs or fired bullets because a dropped bomb could tip the world into a Third World War, a nuclear war from which it would never return. The senate was holding hearings to root out hidden Communists and taking steps to stamp out comic books. And whole families were gathering around the television in the evenings.

The joke in the 1950s went that in the old days you could tell who was home by seeing if the lights were on; now you knew who was home by seeing who had their lights off. The televisions were small and the pictures were in black and white and you needed to turn off the light to get a good picture.

"If this goes on . . ." thought Ray Bradbury, "nobody will read books anymore," and *Fahrenheit 451* began. He had written a short story once called "The Pedestrian," about a man who is incarcerated by the police after he is stopped simply for walking. That story became part of the world he was building, and seventeen-year-old Clarisse McLellan becomes a pedestrian in a world where nobody walks.

"What if . . . firemen burned down houses instead of saving them?" Bradbury thought, and now he had his way in to the story. He had a fireman named Guy Montag, who saved a book from the flames instead of burning it.

"If only . . . books could be saved," he thought. If you destroy all the physical books, how can you still save them?

Bradbury wrote a story called "The Fireman." The story demanded to be longer. The world he had created demanded more.

He went to UCLA's Powell Library. In the basement were typewriters you could rent by the hour, by putting coins into a box on the side of the typewriter. Ray Bradbury put his money into the box and typed his story. When inspiration flagged, when he needed a boost, when he wanted to stretch his legs, he would walk through the library and look at the books.

And then his story was done.

He called the Los Angeles fire department and asked them at what temperature paper burned. Fahrenheit 451, somebody told him. He had his title. It didn't matter if it was true or not.

The book was published and acclaimed. People loved the book, and they argued about it. It was a novel about censorship, they said, about mind control, about humanity. About government control of our lives. About books.

It was filmed by Francois Truffaut, although the film's ending seems darker than Bradbury's, as if the remembering of books is perhaps not the safety net that Bradbury imagines, but is in itself another dead end.

I read *Fahrenheit 451* as a boy: I did not understand Guy Montag, did not understand why he did what he did, but I understood the love of books that drove him. Books were the most important things in my life. The huge wall-screen televisions were as futuristic and implausible as the idea that people on the television would talk to me, that I could take part if I had a script. *Fahrenheit* was never a favorite book: it was too dark, too bleak for that. But when I read a story called "Usher II" in *The Silver Locusts* (the UK title for *The Martian Chronicles*), I recognized the world of outlawed authors and imagination with a fierce sort of familiar joy.

When I reread it as a teenager, *Fahrenheit 451* had become a book about independence, about thinking for yourself. It was about treasuring books and the dissent inside the covers of books. It was about how we as humans begin by burning books and end by burning people.

Rereading it as an adult, I find myself marveling at the book once more. It is all of those things, yes, but it is also a period piece. The four-wall television being described is the television of the 1950s: variety shows with symphony orchestras and low-brow comedians, and soap operas. The world of fast-driving, crazy teenagers out for kicks, of an endless cold war that sometimes goes hot, of wives who appear to have no jobs or identities save for their husbands', of bad men being chased by hounds (even mechanical hounds) is a world that feels like it has its roots firmly in the 1950s.

A young reader finding this book today, or the day after tomorrow, is going to have to imagine first a past, and then a future that belongs to that past.

But still, the heart of the book remains untouched, and the questions Bradbury raises remain as valid and important.

Why do we need the things in books? The poems, the essays, the stories? Authors disagree. Authors are human and fallible and foolish. Stories are lies after all, tales of people who never existed and the things that never actually happened to them. Why should we read them? Why should we care?

The teller and the tale are very different. We must not forget that.

Ideas—written ideas—are special. They are the way we transmit our stories and our thoughts from one generation to the next. If we lose them, we lose our shared history. We lose much of what makes us human. And fiction gives us empathy: it puts us inside the minds of other people, gives us the gift of seeing the world through their eyes. Fiction is a lie that tells us true things, over and over.

I knew Ray Bradbury for the last thirty years of his life, and I was so lucky. He was funny and gentle and always (even at the end, when he was so old he was blind and wheelchair-bound, even then) enthusiastic. He cared, completely and utterly, about things. He cared about toys and childhood and films. He cared about books. He cared about stories.

This is a book about caring for things. It's a love letter to books, but I think, just as much, it's a love letter to people, and a love letter to the world of Waukegan, Illinois, in the 1920s, the world in which Ray Bradbury had grown up and which he immortalized as Green Town in his book of childhood, *Dandelion Wine*.

As I said when we began: If someone tells you what a story is about, they are probably right. If they tell you that that is *all* the story is about, they are probably wrong. So any of the things I have told you about *Fahrenheit 451*, Ray Bradbury's remarkable book of warning, will be incomplete. It is about these things, yes. But it is about more than that. It is about what you find between its pages.

(As a final note, in these days when we worry and we argue about whether ebooks are real books, I love how broad Ray Bradbury's definition of a book is at the end, when he points out that we should not judge our books by their covers, and that some books exist between covers that are perfectly people-shaped.)

—Neil Gaiman
April 2013

If they give you ruled paper, write the other way.

—*Juan Ramón Jiménez*

one
The Hearth
and the Salamander

It was a pleasure to burn.

It was a special pleasure to see things eaten, to see things blackened and *changed*. With the brass nozzle in his fists, with this great python spitting its venomous kerosene upon the world, the blood pounded in his head, and his hands were the hands of some amazing conductor playing all the symphonies of blazing and burning to bring down the tatters and charcoal ruins of history. With his symbolic helmet numbered 451 on his stolid head, and his eyes all orange flame with the thought of what came next, he flicked the igniter and the house jumped up in a gorging fire that burned the evening sky red and yellow and black. He strode in a swarm of fireflies. He wanted above all, like the old joke, to shove a marshmallow on a stick in the furnace, while the flapping pigeon-winged books died on the porch and lawn of the house. While the books went up in sparkling whirls and blew away on a wind turned dark with burning.

Montag grinned the fierce grin of all men singed and driven back by flame.

He knew that when he returned to the firehouse, he might wink at himself, a minstrel man, burnt-corked, in the mirror. Later, going to sleep, he would feel the fiery smile still gripped by his face muscles, in the dark. It never went away, that smile, it never ever went away, as long as he remembered.

He hung up his black beetle-colored helmet and shined it; he hung his flameproof jacket neatly; he showered luxuriously, and then, whistling, hands in pockets, walked across the upper floor of the fire station and fell down the hole. At the last moment, when disaster seemed positive, he pulled his hands from his pockets and broke his fall by grasping the golden pole. He slid to a squeaking halt, the heels one inch from the concrete floor downstairs.

He walked out of the fire station and along the midnight street toward the subway where the silent air-propelled train slid soundlessly down its lubricated flue in the earth and let him out with a great puff of warm air onto the cream-tiled escalator rising to the suburb.

Whistling, he let the escalator waft him into the still night air. He walked toward the corner, thinking little at all about nothing in particular. Before he reached the corner, however, he slowed as if a wind had sprung up from nowhere, as if someone had called his name.

The last few nights he had had the most uncertain feelings about the sidewalk just around the corner here, moving in the starlight toward his house. He had felt that a moment prior to his making the turn, someone had been there. The air seemed charged with a special calm as if someone had waited there, quietly, and only a moment before he came, simply turned to a shadow and let him through. Perhaps his nose detected a faint perfume, perhaps the skin on the backs of his hands, on his face, felt the temperature rise at this one spot where a person's standing might raise the immediate atmosphere ten degrees for an instant. There was no understanding it. Each time he made the turn, he saw only the white, unused, buckling sidewalk, with perhaps, on one night, something vanishing swiftly across a lawn before he could focus his eyes or speak.

But now tonight, he slowed almost to a stop. His inner mind, reaching out to turn the corner for him, had heard the faintest whisper. Breathing? Or was the atmosphere compressed merely by someone standing very quietly there, waiting?

He turned the corner.

The autumn leaves blew over the moonlit pavement in such a way as to make the girl who was moving there seem fixed to a sliding walk, letting the motion of the wind and the leaves carry her forward. Her head was half bent to watch her shoes stir the circling leaves. Her face was slender and milk-white, and in it was a kind of gentle hunger that touched over everything with tireless curiosity. It was a look, almost, of pale surprise; the dark eyes were so fixed to the world that no move escaped them. Her dress was white and it whispered. He almost thought he heard the motion of her hands as she walked, and the infinitely small sound now, the white stir of her face turning when she discovered she was a moment away from a man who stood in the middle of the pavement waiting.

The trees overhead made a great sound of letting down their dry rain. The girl stopped and looked as if she might pull back in surprise, but instead stood regarding Montag with eyes so dark and shining and alive, that he felt he had said something quite wonderful. But he knew his mouth had only moved to say hello, and then when she seemed hypnotized by the salamander on his arm and the phoenix-disc on his chest, he spoke again.

"Of course," he said, "you're our new neighbor, aren't you?"

"And you must be—" she raised her eyes from his professional symbols "—the fireman." Her voice trailed off.

"How oddly you say that."

"I'd—I'd have known it with my eyes shut," she said, slowly.

"What—the smell of kerosene? My wife always complains," he laughed. "You never wash it off completely."

"No, you don't," she said, in awe.

He felt she was walking in a circle about him, turning him end for end, shaking him quietly, and emptying his pockets, without once moving herself.

"Kerosene," he said, because the silence had lengthened, "is nothing but perfume to me."

"Does it seem like that, really?"

"Of course. Why not?"

She gave herself time to think of it. "I don't know." She turned to face the sidewalk going toward their homes. "Do you mind if I walk back with you? I'm Clarisse McClellan."

"Clarisse. Guy Montag. Come along. What are you doing out so late wandering around? How old are you?"

They walked in the warm-cool blowing night on the silvered pavement and there was the faintest breath of fresh apricots and strawberries in the air, and he looked around and realized this was quite impossible, so late in the year.

There was only the girl walking with him now, her face bright as snow in the moonlight, and he knew she was working his questions around, seeking the best answers she could possibly give.

"Well," she said, "I'm seventeen and I'm crazy. My uncle says the two always go together. When people ask your age, he said, always say seventeen and insane. Isn't this a nice time of night to walk? I like to smell things and look at things, and sometimes stay up all night, walking, and watch the sun rise."

They walked on again in silence and finally she said, thoughtfully, "You know, I'm not afraid of you at all."

He was surprised. "Why should you be?"

"So many people are. Afraid of firemen, I mean. But you're just a man, after all. . . ."

He saw himself in her eyes, suspended in two shining drops of bright water, himself dark and tiny, in fine detail, the lines about his mouth, everything there, as if her eyes were two miraculous bits of violet amber that might capture and hold him intact. Her face, turned to him now, was fragile milk crystal with a soft and constant light in it. It was not the hysterical light of electricity but—what? But the strangely comfortable and rare and gently flattering light of the candle. One time, as a child, in a power failure, his mother had found and lit a last candle and there had been a brief hour of rediscovery, of such illumination that space lost its vast dimensions and drew comfortably around them, and they, mother and son, alone, transformed, hoping that the power might not come on again too soon. . . .

And then Clarisse McClellan said:

"Do you mind if I ask? How long've you worked at being a fireman?"

"Since I was twenty, ten years ago."

"Do you ever *read* any of the books you burn?"

He laughed. "That's against the law!"

"Oh. Of course."

"It's fine work. Monday burn Millay, Wednesday Whitman, Friday Faulkner, burn 'em to ashes, then burn the ashes. That's our official slogan."

They walked still further and the girl said, "Is it true that long ago firemen put fires *out* instead of going to start them?"

"No. Houses have *always* been fireproof, take my word for it."

"Strange. I heard once that a long time ago houses used to burn by accident and they needed firemen to *stop* the flames."

He laughed.

She glanced quickly over. "Why are you laughing?"

"I don't know." He started to laugh again and stopped. "Why?"

"You laugh when I haven't been funny and you answer right off. You never stop to think what I've asked you."

He stopped walking. "You *are* an odd one," he said, looking at her. "Haven't you any respect?"

"I don't mean to be insulting. It's just I love to watch people too much, I guess."

"Well, doesn't this mean *anything* to you?" He tapped the numerals 451 stitched on his char-colored sleeve.

"Yes," she whispered. She increased her pace. "Have you ever watched the jet cars racing on the boulevards down that way?"

"You're changing the subject!"

"I sometimes think drivers don't know what grass is, or flowers, because they never see them slowly," she said. "If you showed a driver a green blur, Oh yes! he'd say, that's grass! A pink blur? That's a rose garden! White blurs are houses. Brown blurs are cows. My uncle drove slowly on a highway once. He drove forty miles an hour and they jailed him for two days. Isn't that funny, and sad, too?"

"You think too many things," said Montag, uneasily.

"I rarely watch the 'parlor walls' or go to races or Fun Parks. So I've lots of time for crazy thoughts, I guess. Have you seen the two-hundred-foot-long billboards in the country beyond town? Did you know that once billboards were only twenty feet long? But cars started rushing by so quickly they had to stretch the advertising out so it would last."

"I didn't know that!" Montag laughed abruptly.

"Bet I know something else you don't. There's dew on the grass in the morning."

He suddenly couldn't remember if he had known this or not, and it made him quite irritable.

"And if you look"—she nodded at the sky—"there's a man in the moon."

He hadn't looked for a long time.

They walked the rest of the way in silence, hers thoughtful, his a kind of clenching and uncomfortable silence in which he shot her accusing glances. When they reached her house all its lights were blazing.

"What's going on?" Montag had rarely seen that many house lights.

"Oh, just my mother and father and uncle sitting around, talking. It's like being a pedestrian, only rarer. My uncle was arrested another time—did I tell you?—for being a pedestrian. Oh, we're *most* peculiar."

"But what do you *talk* about?"

She laughed at this. "Good night!" She started up her walk. Then she seemed to remember something and came back to look at him with wonder and curiosity. "Are you happy?" she said.

"Am I *what?*" he cried.

But she was gone—running in the moonlight. Her front door shut gently.

o o o

"Happy! Of all the nonsense."

He stopped laughing.

He put his hand into the glove hole of his front door and let it know his touch. The front door slid open.

Of course I'm happy. What does she think? I'm *not?* he asked the quiet rooms. He stood looking up at the ventilator grill in the hall and suddenly remembered that something lay hidden behind the grill, something that seemed to peer down at him now. He moved his eyes quickly away.

What a strange meeting on a strange night. He remembered nothing like it save one afternoon a year ago when he had met an old man in the park and *they* had talked. . . .

Montag shook his head. He looked at a blank wall. The girl's face was there, really quite beautiful in memory: astonishing, in fact. She had a very thin face like the dial of a small clock seen faintly in a dark room in the middle of a night when you waken to see the time and see the clock telling you the hour and the minute and the second, with a white silence and a glowing, all certainty and knowing what it has to tell of the night passing swiftly on toward further darknesses, but moving also toward a new sun.

"*What?*" asked Montag of that other self, the subconscious idiot that ran babbling at times, quite independent of will, habit, and conscience.

He glanced back at the wall. How like a mirror, too, her face. Impossible; for how many people did you know that refracted your own light to you? People were more often—he searched for a simile, found one in his work—torches, blazing away until they whiffed out. How rarely did other people's faces take of you and throw back to you your own expression, your own innermost trembling thought?

What incredible power of identification the girl had; she was like the eager watcher of a marionette show, anticipating each flicker of an eyelid, each gesture of his hand, each flick of a finger, the moment before it began. How long had they walked together? Three minutes? Five? Yet how large that time seemed now. How immense a figure she was on the stage before him; what a shadow she threw on the wall with her slender body! He felt that if his eye itched, she might blink. And if the muscles of his jaws stretched imperceptibly, she would yawn long before he would.

Why, he thought, now that I think of it, she almost seemed to be waiting for me there, in the street, so damned late at night. . . .

He opened the bedroom door.

It was like coming into the cold marbled room of a mausoleum after the moon has set. Complete darkness, not a hint of the silver world outside, the windows tightly shut, the chamber a tomb-world where no sound from the great city could penetrate. The room was not empty.

He listened.

The little mosquito-delicate dancing hum in the air, the electrical murmur of a hidden wasp snug in its special pink warm nest. The music was almost loud enough so he could follow the tune.

He felt his smile slide away, melt, fold over and down on itself like a tallow skin, like the stuff of a fantastic candle burning too long and now collapsing and now blown out. Darkness. He was not happy. He was not happy. He said the words to himself. He recognized this as the true state of affairs. He wore his happiness like a mask and the girl had run off across the lawn with the mask and there was no way of going to knock on her door and ask for it back.

Without turning on the light he imagined how this room would look. His wife stretched on the bed, uncovered and cold, like a body displayed on the lid of a tomb, her eyes fixed to the ceiling by invisible threads of steel, immovable. And in her ears the little Seashells, the thimble radios tamped tight, and an electronic ocean of sound, of music and talk and music and talk coming in, coming in on the shore of her unsleeping mind. The room was indeed empty. Every night the waves came in and bore her off on their great tides of sound, floating her, wide-eyed, toward morning. There had been no night in the last two years that Mildred had not swum that sea, had not gladly gone down in it for the third time.

The room was cold but nonetheless he felt he could not breathe. He did not wish to open the drapes and open the French windows, for he did not want the moon to come into the room. So, with the feeling of a man who will die in the next hour for lack of air, he felt his way toward his open, separate, and therefore cold bed.

An instant before his foot hit the object on the floor he knew he would hit such an object. It was not unlike the feeling he had experienced before turning the corner and almost knocking the girl down. His foot, sending vibrations ahead, received back echoes of the small barrier across its path even as the foot swung. His foot kicked. The object gave a dull clink and slid off in darkness.

He stood very straight and listened to the person on the dark bed in the completely featureless night. The breath coming out the nostrils was so faint it stirred only the furthest fringes of life, a small leaf, a black feather, a single fiber of hair.

He still did not want outside light. He pulled out his igniter, felt the salamander etched on its silver disc, gave it a flick. . . .

Two moonstones looked up at him in the light of his small hand-held fire; two pale moonstones buried in a creek of clear water over which the life of the world ran, not touching them.

"Mildred!"

Her face was like a snow-covered island upon which rain might fall, but it felt no rain; over which clouds might pass their moving shadows, but she felt no shadow. There was only the singing of the thimble-wasps in her tamped-shut ears, and her eyes all glass, and breath going in and out, softly, faintly, in and out her nostrils, and her not caring whether it came or went, went or came.

The object he had sent tumbling with his foot now glinted under the edge of his own bed. The small crystal bottle of sleeping tablets which earlier today had been filled with thirty capsules and which now lay uncapped and empty in the light of the tiny flare.

As he stood there the sky over the house screamed. There was a tremendous ripping sound as if two giant hands had torn ten thousand miles of black linen down the seam. Montag was cut in half. He felt his chest chopped down and split apart. The jet bombers going over, going over, going over, one two, one two, one two, six of them, nine of them, twelve of them, one and one and one and another and another and another, did all the screaming for him. He opened his own mouth and let their shriek come down and out between his bared teeth. The house shook. The flare went out in his hand. The moonstones vanished. He felt his hand plunge toward the telephone.

The jets were gone. He felt his lips move, brushing the mouthpiece of the phone. "Emergency hospital." A terrible whisper.

He felt that the stars had been pulverized by the sound

of the black jets and that in the morning the earth would be covered with their dust like a strange snow. That was his idiot thought as he stood shivering in the dark, and let his lips go on moving and moving.

They had this machine. They had two machines, really. One of them slid down into your stomach like a black cobra down an echoing well looking for all the old water and the old time gathered there. It drank up the green matter that flowed to the top in a slow boil. Did it drink of the darkness? Did it suck out all the poisons accumulated with the years? It fed in silence with an occasional sound of inner suffocation and blind searching. It had an Eye. The impersonal operator of the machine could, by wearing a special optical helmet, gaze into the soul of the person whom he was pumping out. What did the Eye see? He did not say. He saw but did not see what the Eye saw. The entire operation was not unlike the digging of a trench in one's yard. The woman on the bed was no more than a hard stratum of marble they had reached. Go on, anyway, shove the bore down, slush up the emptiness, if such a thing could be brought out in the throb of the suction snake. The operator stood smoking a cigarette. The other machine was working, too.

The other machine, operated by an equally impersonal fellow in nonstainable reddish-brown coveralls. This machine pumped all of the blood from the body and replaced it with fresh blood and serum.

"Got to clean 'em out both ways," said the operator, standing over the silent woman. "No use getting the stomach if you don't clean the blood. Leave that stuff in the blood and the blood hits the brain like a mallet, bang, a couple thousand times and the brain just gives up, just quits."

"Stop it!" said Montag.

"I was just sayin'," said the operator.

"Are you done?" said Montag.

They shut the machines up tight. "We're done." His anger did not even touch them. They stood with the cigarette smoke curling around their noses and into their eyes without making them blink or squint. "That's fifty bucks."

"First, why don't you tell me if she'll be all right?"

"Sure, she'll be okay. We got all the mean stuff right in our suitcase here, it can't get at her now. As I said, you take out the old and put in the new and you're okay."

"Neither of you is an M.D. Why didn't they send an M.D. from Emergency?"

"Hell!" The operator's cigarette moved on his lip. "We get these cases nine or ten a night. Got so many, starting a few years ago, we had the special machines built. With the optical lens, of course, that was new; the rest is ancient. You don't need an M.D., case like this; all you need is two handymen, clean up the problem in half an hour. Look"—he started for the door— "we gotta go. Just had another call on the old ear-thimble. Ten blocks from here. Someone else just jumped off the cap of a pillbox. Call if you need us again. Keep her quiet. We got a con-trasedative in her. She'll wake up hungry. So long."

And the men with the cigarettes in their straight-lined mouths, the men with the eyes of puff adders, took up their load of machine and tube, their case of liquid melancholy and the slow dark sludge of nameless stuff, and strolled out the door.

Montag sank down into a chair and looked at this woman. Her eyes were closed now, gently, and he put out his hand to feel the warmness of breath on his palm.

"Mildred," he said, at last.

There are too many of us, he thought. There are billions of us and that's too many. Nobody knows anyone. Strangers come and violate you. Strangers come and cut your heart out. Strangers come and take your blood. Good God, who *were* those men? I never saw them before in my *life!*

Half an hour passed.

The bloodstream in this woman was new and it seemed to have done a new thing to her. Her cheeks were very pink and her lips were very fresh and full of color and they looked soft and relaxed. Someone else's blood there. If only someone else's flesh and brain and memory. If only they could have taken her mind along to the dry cleaner's and emptied the pockets and steamed and cleansed it and reblocked it and brought it back in the morning. If only . . .

He got up and put back the drapes and opened the windows wide to let the night air in. It was two o'clock in the morning. Was it only an hour ago, Clarisse McClellan in the street, and him coming in, and the dark room and his foot kicking the little crystal bottle? Only an hour, but the word had melted down and sprung up in a new and colorless form.

Laughter blew across the moon-colored lawn from the house of Clarisse and her father and mother and the uncle who smiled so quietly and so earnestly. Above all, their laughter was relaxed and hearty and not forced in any way, coming from the house that was so brightly lit this late at night while all the other houses were kept to themselves in darkness. Montag heard the voices talking, talking, talking, giving, talking, weaving, reweaving their hypnotic web.

Montag moved out through the French windows and crossed the lawn, without even thinking of it. He stood outside the talking house in the shadows, thinking he might even tap on their door and whisper, "Let me come in. I won't say anything. I just want to listen. What is it you're saying?"

But instead he stood there, very cold, his face a mask of ice, listening to a man's voice (the uncle?) moving along at an easy pace:

"Well, after all, this is the age of the disposable tissue. Blow your nose on a person, wad them, flush them away, reach for another, blow, wad, flush. Everyone using everyone else's coattails. How are you supposed to root for the home team when you don't even have a program or know the names? For that matter, what color jerseys are they wearing as they trot out on the field?"

Montag moved back to his own house, left the window wide, checked Mildred, tucked the covers about her carefully, and then lay down with the moonlight on his cheekbones and on the frowning ridges in his brow, with the moonlight distilled in each eye to form a silver cataract there.

One drop of rain. Clarisse. Another drop. Mildred. A third. The uncle. A fourth. The fire tonight. One, Clarisse. Two, Mildred. Three, uncle. Four, fire. One, Mildred, two, Clarisse. One, two, three, four, five, Clarisse, Mildred, uncle, fire, sleeping tablets, men, disposable tissue, coattails, blow, wad, flush, Clarisse, Mildred, uncle, fire, tablets, tissues, blow, wad, flush. One, two, three, one, two, three! Rain. The storm. The uncle laughing. Thunder falling downstairs. The whole world pouring down. The fire gushing up in a volcano. All rushing on down around in a spouting roar and rivering stream toward morning.

"I don't know anything anymore," he said, and let a sleep lozenge dissolve on his tongue.

At nine in the morning, Mildred's bed was empty.

Montag got up quickly, his heart pumping, and ran down the hall and stopped at the kitchen door.

Toast popped out of the silver toaster, was seized by a spidery metal hand that drenched it with melted butter.

Mildred watched the toast delivered to her plate. She had both ears plugged with electronic bees that were humming the hour away. She looked up suddenly, saw him and nodded.

"You all right?" he asked.

She was an expert at lip reading from ten years of apprenticeship at Seashell ear-thimbles. She nodded again. She set the toaster clicking away at another piece of bread.

Montag sat down.

His wife said, "I don't know *why* I should be so hungry."

"You—"

"I'm *hungry*."

"Last night," he began.

"Didn't sleep well. Feel terrible," she said. "God, I'm hungry. I can't figure it."

"Last night—" he said again.

She watched his lips casually. "What about last night?"

"Don't you remember?"

"What? Did we have a wild party or something? Feel like I've a hangover. God, I'm hungry. Who was here?"

"A few people," he said.

"That's what I thought." She chewed her toast. "Sore stomach, but I'm hungry as all get-out. Hope I didn't do anything foolish at the party."

"No," he said, quietly.

The toaster spidered out a piece of buttered bread for him. He held it in his hand, feeling obligated.

"You don't look so hot yourself," said his wife.

∘ ∘ ∘

In the late afternoon it rained and the entire world was dark gray. He stood in the hall of his house, putting on his badge with the orange salamander burning across it. He stood looking up at the air-conditioning vent in the hall for a long time. His wife in the TV parlor paused long enough from reading her script to glance up. "Hey," she said. "The man's *thinking!*"

"Yes," he said. "I wanted to talk to you." He paused. "You took all the pills in your bottle last night."

"Oh, I wouldn't do that," she said, surprised.

"The bottle was empty."

"I wouldn't do a thing like that. Why would I do a thing like that?" she said.

"Maybe you took two pills and forgot and took two more, and forgot again and took two more, and were so dopey you kept right on until you had thirty or forty of them in you."

"Heck," she said, "what would I want to go and do a silly thing like that for?"

"I don't know," he said.

She was quite obviously waiting for him to go. "I didn't do that," she said. "Never in a billion years."

"All right if you say so," he said.

"That's what the lady said." She turned back to her script.

"What's on this afternoon?" he asked, tiredly.

She didn't look up from the script again. "Well, this is a play comes on the wall-to-wall circuit in ten minutes. They mailed me my part this morning. I sent in some box tops. They write the script with one part missing. It's a new idea. The homemaker, that's me, is the missing part. When it comes time for the missing lines, they all look at me out of the three walls and I say the lines. Here, for instance, the man says, 'What do you think of

17

this whole idea, Helen?' And he looks at me sitting here center stage, see? And I say, I say—" She paused and ran her finger under a line on the script. " 'I think that's fine!' And then they go on with the play until he says, 'Do you agree to that, Helen?' and I say, 'I sure do!' Isn't that fun, Guy?"

He stood in the hall looking at her.

"It's sure fun," she said.

"What's the play about?"

"I just told you. There are these people named Bob and Ruth and Helen."

"Oh."

"It's really fun. It'll be even more fun when we can afford to have the fourth wall installed. How long you figure before we save up and get the fourth wall torn out and a fourth wall-TV put in? It's only two thousand dollars."

"That's one-third of my yearly pay."

"It's only two thousand dollars," she replied. "And I should think you'd consider me sometimes. If we had a fourth wall, why it'd be just like this room wasn't ours at all, but all kinds of exotic people's rooms. We could do without a few things."

"We're already doing without a few things to pay for the third wall. It was put in only two months ago, remember?"

"Is that all it was?" She sat looking at him for a long moment. "Well, goodbye, dear."

"Goodbye," he said. He stopped and turned around. "Does it have a happy ending?"

"I haven't read that far."

He walked over, read the last page, nodded, folded the script, and handed it back to her. He walked out of the house into the rain.

∘ ∘ ∘

The rain was thinning away and the girl was walking in the center of the sidewalk with her head up and the few drops falling on her face. She smiled when she saw Montag.

"Hello!"

He said hello and then said, "What are you up to now?"

"I'm still crazy. The rain feels good. I love to walk in it."

"I don't think I'd like that," he said.

"You might if you tried."

"I never have."

She licked her lips. "Rain even tastes good."

"What do you do, go around trying everything once?" he asked.

"Sometimes twice." She looked at something in her hand.

"What've you got there?" he said.

"I guess it's the last of the dandelions this year. I didn't think I'd find one on the lawn this late. Have you ever heard of rubbing it under your chin? Look." She touched her chin with the flower, laughing.

"Why?"

"If it rubs off, it means I'm in love. Has it?"

He could hardly do anything else but look.

"Well?" she said.

"You're yellow under there."

"Fine! Let's try *you* now."

"It won't work for me."

"Here." Before he could move she had put the dandelion under his chin. He drew back and she laughed. "Hold still!"

She peered under his chin and frowned.

"Well?" he said.

"What a shame," she said. "You're not in love with anyone."

"Yes, I am!"

"It doesn't show."

"I am, very much in love!" He tried to conjure up a face to fit the words, but there was no face. "I am!"

"Oh, please don't look that way."

"It's that dandelion," he said. "You've used it all up on yourself. That's why it won't work for me."

"Of course, that must be it. Oh now I've upset you, I can see I have; I'm sorry, really I am." She touched his elbow.

"No, no," he said, quickly, "I'm all right."

"I've got to be going, so say you forgive me, I don't want you angry with me."

"I'm not angry. Upset, yes."

"I've got to go see my psychiatrist now. They *make* me go. I make up things to say. I don't know what he thinks of me. He says I'm a regular onion! I keep him busy peeling away the layers."

"I'm inclined to believe you need the psychiatrist," said Montag.

"You don't mean that."

He took a breath and let it out and at last said, "No, I don't mean that."

"The psychiatrist wants to know why I go out and hike around in the forests and watch the birds and collect butterflies. I'll show you my collection some day."

"Good."

"They want to know what I do with all my time. I tell them that sometimes I just sit and *think*. But I won't tell them what. I've got them running. And sometimes, I tell them, I like to put my head back, like this, and let the rain fall in my mouth. It tastes just like wine. Have you ever tried it?"

"No, I—"

"You *have* forgiven me, haven't you?"

"Yes." He thought about it. "Yes, I have. God knows why. You're peculiar, you're aggravating, yet you're easy to forgive. You say you're seventeen?"

"Well—next month."

"How odd. How strange. And my wife thirty and yet you seem so much older at times. I can't get over it."

"You're peculiar yourself, Mr. Montag. Sometimes I even forget you're a fireman. Now, may I make you angry again?"

"Go ahead."

"How did it start? How did you get into it? How did you pick your work and how did you happen to think to take the job you have? You're not like the others. I've seen a few; I *know*. When I talk, you look at me. When I said something about the moon, you looked at the moon, last night. The others would never do that. The others would walk off and leave me talking. Or threaten me. No one has time any more for anyone else. You're one of the few who put up with me. That's why I think it's so strange you're a fireman, it just doesn't seem right for you, somehow."

He felt his body divide itself into a hotness and a coldness, a softness and a hardness, a trembling and a not trembling, the two halves grinding one upon the other.

"You'd better run on to your appointment," he said.

And she ran off and left him standing there in the rain. Only after a long time did he move.

And then, very slowly, as he walked, he tilted his head back in the rain, for just a few moments, and opened his mouth. . . .

The Mechanical Hound slept but did not sleep, lived but did not live in its gently humming, gently vibrating, softly illuminated kennel back in a dark corner of the firehouse. The dim light of one in the morning, the moonlight from the open sky framed through the great window, touched here and there on the brass and the copper and the steel of the faintly trembling beast. Light flickered on bits of ruby glass and on sensitive capillary hairs in the nylonbrushed nostrils of the creature that quivered gently, gently, its eight legs spidered under it on rubber-padded paws.

Montag slid down the brass pole. He went out to look at the city and the clouds had cleared away completely, and he lit a cigarette and came back to bend down and look at the Hound. It was like a great bee come home from some field where the honey is full of poison wildness, of insanity and nightmare, its body crammed with that over-rich nectar and now it was sleeping the evil out of itself.

"Hello," whispered Montag, fascinated as always with the dead beast, the living beast.

Nights when things got dull, which was every night, the men slid down the brass poles, and set the ticking combinations of the olfactory system of the Hound and let loose rats in the firehouse areaway, and sometimes chickens, and sometimes cats that would have to be drowned anyway, and there would be betting to see which of the cats or chickens or rats the Hound would seize first. The animals were turned loose. Three seconds later the game was done, the rat, cat, or chicken caught half across the areaway, gripped in gentling paws while a four-inch hollow steel needle plunged down from the proboscis of the Hound to inject massive jolts of morphine or procaine. The pawn was then tossed in the incinerator. A new game began.

Montag stayed upstairs most nights when this went on. There had been a time two years ago when he had bet with the best of them, and lost a week's salary and faced Mildred's insane anger, which showed itself in veins and blotches. But now nights he lay in his bunk, face turned to the wall, listening to the whoops of laughter below and the pianostring scurry of rat feet, the violin squeaking of mice, and the great shadowing, motioned silence of the Hound leaping out like a moth in the raw light, finding, holding its victim, inserting needle and going back to its kennel to die as if a switch had been turned.

Montag touched the muzzle.

The Hound growled.

Montag jumped back.

The Hound half rose in its kennel and looked at him with green-blue neon light flickering in its suddenly activated eye bulbs. It growled again, a strange rasping combination of electrical sizzle, a frying sound, a scraping of metal, a turning of cogs that seemed rusty and ancient with suspicion.

"No, no, boy," said Montag, his heart pounding.

He saw the silver needle extend upon the air an inch, pull back, extend, pull back. The growl simmered in the beast and it looked at him.

Montag backed up. The Hound took a step from its kennel. Montag grabbed the brass pole with one hand. The pole, reacting, slid upward, and took him through the ceiling, quietly. He stepped off in the half-lit deck of the upper level. He was trembling and his face was green-white. Below, the Hound had sunk back down upon its eight incredible insect legs and was humming to itself again, its multifaceted eyes at peace.

Montag stood, letting the fears pass, by the drop-hole. Behind him, four men at a card table under a greenlidded light in the corner glanced briefly but said nothing. Only the man with the Captain's hat and the sign of the Phoenix on his hat, at last, curious, his playing cards in his thin hand, talked across the long room.

"Montag . . . ?"

"It doesn't *like* me," said Montag.

"What, the Hound?" The Captain studied his cards. "Come off it. It doesn't like or dislike. It just 'functions.' It's like a lesson in ballistics. It has a trajectory we decide on for it. It follows through. It targets itself, homes itself, and cuts off. It's only copper wire, storage batteries, and electricity."

Montag swallowed. "Its calculators can be set to any combination, so many amino acids, so much sulphur, so much butterfat and alkaline. Right?"

"We know all that."

"All of those chemical balances and percentages on all of us here in the house are recorded in the master file downstairs. It would be easy for someone to set up a partial combination on the Hound's 'memory,' a touch of amino acids, perhaps. That would account for what the animal did just now. Reacted toward me."

"Hell," said the Captain.

"Irritated, but not completely angry. Just enough 'memory' set up in it by someone so it growled when I touched it."

"Who would do a thing like that?" asked the Captain. "You haven't any enemies here, Guy."

"None that I know of."

"We'll have the Hound checked by our technicians tomorrow."

"This isn't the first time it's threatened me," said Montag. "Last month it happened twice."

"We'll fix it up. Don't worry."

But Montag did not move and only stood thinking of the ventilator grill in the hall at home and what lay hidden behind the grill. If someone here in the firehouse knew about the ventilator then mightn't they "tell" the Hound . . . ?

The Captain came over to the drop hole and gave Montag a questioning glance.

"I was just figuring," said Montag, "what does the Hound think about down there nights? Is it coming alive on us, really? It makes me cold."

"It doesn't think anything we don't want it to think."

"That's sad," said Montag, quietly, "because all we put into it is hunting and finding and killing. What a shame if that's all it can ever know."

Beatty snorted, gently. "Hell! It's a fine bit of craftsmanship, a good rifle that can fetch its own target and guarantees the bull's-eye every time."

"That's why," said Montag, "I wouldn't want to be its next victim."

"Why? You got a guilty conscience about something?"

Montag glanced up swiftly.

Beatty stood there looking at him steadily with his eyes, while his mouth opened and began to laugh, very softly.

One two three four five six seven days. And as many times he came out of the house and Clarisse was there somewhere in the world. Once he saw her shaking a walnut tree, once he saw her sitting on the lawn knitting a blue sweater, three or four times he found a bouquet of late flowers on his porch, or a handful of chestnuts in a little sack, or some autumn leaves neatly pinned to a sheet of white paper and thumbtacked to his door. Every day Clarisse walked him to the corner. One day it was raining, the next it was clear, the day after that the wind blew strong, and the day after that it was mild and calm, and the day after that calm day was a day like the furnace of summer and Clarisse with her face all sunburnt by late afternoon.

"Why is it," he said, one time, at the subway entrance, "I feel I've known you so many years?"

"Because I like you," she said, "and I don't want anything from you. And because we know each other."

"You make me feel very old and very much like a father."

"Now you explain," she said, "why you haven't any daughters like me, if you love children so much?"

"I don't know."

"You're joking!"

"I mean—" He stopped and shook his head. "Well, my wife, she . . . she just never wanted any children at all."

The girl stopped smiling. "I'm sorry. I really thought you were having fun at my expense. I'm a fool."

"No, no" he said. "It was a good question. It's been a long time since anyone cared enough to ask. A good question."

"Let's talk about something else. Have you ever smelled old leaves? Don't they smell like cinnamon? Here. Smell."

"Why, yes, it *is* like cinnamon in a way."

She looked at him with her clear dark eyes. "You always seem shocked."

"It's just I haven't had time—"

"Did you look at the stretched-out billboards like I told you?"

"I think so. Yes." He had to laugh.

"Your laugh sounds much nicer than it did."

"Does it?"

"Much more relaxed."

He felt at ease and comfortable. "Why aren't you in school? I see you every day wandering around."

"Oh, they don't miss me," she said. "I'm antisocial, they say. I don't mix. It's so strange. I'm very social indeed. It all depends on what you mean by social, doesn't it? Social to me means talking to you about things like this." She rattled some chestnuts that had fallen off the tree in the front yard. "Or talking about how strange the world is. Being with people is nice. But I don't think it's social to get a bunch of people together and then not let them talk, do you? An hour of TV class, an hour of basketball or baseball or running, another hour of transcription history or painting pictures, and more sports, but do you know, we never ask questions, or at least most don't; they just run the answers at you, bing, bing, bing, and us sitting there for four more hours of film-teacher. That's not social to me at all. It's a lot of funnels and a lot of water poured down the spout and out the bottom, and them telling us it's wine when it's not. They run us so ragged by the end of the day we can't do anything but go to bed or head for a Fun Park to bully people around, break windowpanes in the Window Smasher place or wreck cars in the Car Wrecker place with the big steel ball. Or go out in the cars and race on the streets, trying to see how close you can get to lampposts, playing 'chicken' and 'knock hubcaps.' I guess I'm everything they say I am, all right. I haven't any friends. That's supposed to prove I'm abnormal. But everyone I know is either shouting or dancing around like wild or beating up one another. Do you notice how people hurt each other nowadays?"

"You sound so very old."

"Sometimes I'm ancient. I'm afraid of children my own age. They kill each other. Did it always use to be that way? My uncle says no. Six of my friends have been shot in the last year alone. Ten of them died in car wrecks. I'm afraid of them and they don't like me because I'm afraid. My uncle says his grandfather remembered when children didn't kill each other. But that was a long time ago when they had things different. They believed in responsibility, my uncle says. Do you know, I'm responsible. I was spanked when I needed it, years ago. And I do all the shopping and housecleaning by hand.

"But most of all," she said, "I like to watch people. Sometimes I ride the subway all day and look at them and listen to them. I just want to figure out who they are and what they want and where they're going. Sometimes I even go to the Fun Parks and ride in the jet cars when they race on the edge of town at midnight and the police don't care as long as they're insured. As long as everyone has ten thousand insurance everyone's happy. Sometimes I sneak around and listen in subways. Or I listen at soda fountains, and do you know what?"

"What?"

"People don't talk about anything."

"Oh, they *must!*"

"No, not anything. They name a lot of cars or clothes or swimming pools mostly and say how swell! But they all say the same things and nobody says anything different from anyone else. And most of the time in the cafés they have the joke-boxes on and the same jokes most of the time, or the musical wall lit and all the colored patterns running up and down, but it's only color and all abstract. And at the museums, have you *ever* been? *All* abstract. That's all there is now. My uncle says it was different once. A long time back sometimes pictures said things or even showed *people.*"

"Your uncle said, your uncle said. Your uncle must be a remarkable man."

"He is. He certainly is. Well, I got to be going. Goodbye, Mr. Montag."

"Goodbye."

"Goodbye. . . ."

o o o

One two three four five six seven days: the firehouse.

"Montag, you shin that pole like a bird up a tree."

Third day.

"Montag, I see you came in the back door this time. The Hound bother you?"

"No, no."

Fourth day.

"Montag, a funny thing. Heard tell this morning. Fireman in Seattle, purposely set a Mechanical Hound to his own chemical complex and let it loose. What kind of suicide would you call *that?*"

Five, six, seven days.

And, then, Clarisse was gone. He didn't know what there was about the afternoon, but it was not seeing her somewhere in the world. The lawn was empty, the trees empty, the street empty, and while at first he did not even know he missed her or was even looking for her, the fact was that by the time he reached the subway, there were vague stirrings of dis-ease in him. Something was the matter, his routine had been disturbed. A simple routine, true, established in a short few days, and yet . . . ? He almost turned back to make the walk again, to give her time to appear. He was certain if he tried the same route, everything would work out fine. But it was late, and the arrival of his train put a stop to his plan.

The flutter of cards, motion of hands, of eyelids, the drone of the time-voice in the firehouse ceiling ". . . one thirty-five, Thursday morning, November 4th, . . . one thirty-six . . . one thirty-seven A.M. . . ." The tick of the playing cards on the greasy table top, all the sounds came to Montag, behind his closed eyes, behind the barrier he had momentarily erected. He could feel the firehouse full of glitter and shine and silence, of brass colors, the colors of coins, of gold, of silver. The unseen men across the table were sighing on their cards, waiting. ". . . one forty-five. . . ." The voice clock mourned out the cold hour of a cold morning of a still colder year.

"What's wrong, Montag?"

Montag opened his eyes.

A radio hummed somewhere. ". . . war may be declared any hour. This country stands ready to defend its . . ."

The firehouse trembled as a great flight of jet planes whistled a single note across the black morning sky.

Montag blinked. Beatty was looking at him as if he were a museum statue. At any moment, Beatty might rise and walk about him, touching, exploring his guilt and self-consciousness. Guilt? What guilt was that?

"Your play, Montag."

Montag looked at these men whose faces were sunburnt by a thousand real and ten thousand imaginary fires, whose work flushed their cheeks and fevered their eyes. These men who looked steadily into their platinum igniter flames as they lit their eternally burning black pipes. They and their charcoal hair and soot-colored brows and bluish-ash-smeared cheeks where they had shaven close; but their heritage showed. Montag started up, his mouth opened. Had he ever seen a fireman that *didn't* have black hair, black brows, a fiery face, and a blue-steel shaved but unshaved look? These men were all mirror images of himself! Were all firemen picked then for their looks as well as their proclivities? The color of cinders and ash about them, and the continual smell of burning from their pipes. Captain Beatty there, rising in thunderheads of tobacco smoke. Beatty opening a fresh tobacco packet, crumpling the cellophane into a sound of fire.

Montag looked at the cards in his own hands. "I—I've been thinking. About the fire last week. About the man whose library we fixed. What happened to him?"

"They took him screaming off to the asylum."

"He wasn't insane."

Beatty arranged his cards quietly. "Any man's insane who thinks he can fool the government and us."

"I've tried to imagine," said Montag, "just how it would feel. I mean, to have firemen burn *our* houses and *our* books."

"We haven't any books."

"But if we did have some."

"You *got* some?"

Beatty blinked slowly.

"No." Montag gazed beyond them to the wall with the typed lists of a million forbidden books. Their names leapt in fire, burning down the years under his axe and his hose which sprayed not water but kerosene. "No." But in his mind, a cool wind started up and blew out the ventilator grill at home, softly, chilling his face. And, again, he saw himself in a green park talking to an old man, a very old man, and the wind from the park was cold, too.

Montag hesitated. "What—was it always like this? The firehouse, our work? I mean, well, once upon a time. . . ."

"Once upon a time!" Beatty said. "What kind of talk is *that?*"

Fool, thought Montag to himself, you'll give it away. At the last fire, a book of fairy tales, he'd glanced at a single line. "I mean," he said, "in the old days, before homes were completely fireproofed—" Suddenly it seemed a much younger voice was speaking for him. He opened his mouth and it was Clarisse McClellan saying, "Didn't firemen *prevent* fires rather than stoke them up and get them going?"

"That's rich!" Stoneman and Black drew forth their rule books, which also contained brief histories of the Firemen of America, and laid them out where Montag, though long familiar with them, might read:

Established, 1790, to burn English-influenced books in the Colonies. First Fireman: Benjamin Franklin.

RULE 1.　Answer the alarm quickly.
　　　2.　Start the fire swiftly.
　　　3.　Burn everything.
　　　4.　Report back to firehouse immediately.
　　　5.　Stand alert for other Alarms.

Everyone watched Montag. He did not move.

The alarm sounded.

The bell in the ceiling kicked itself two hundred times. Suddenly there were four empty chairs. The cards fell in a flurry of snow. The brass pole shivered. The men were gone.

Montag sat in his chair. Below, the orange dragon coughed to life.

Montag slid down the pole like a man in a dream.

The Mechanical Hound leapt up in its kennel, its eyes all green flame.

"Montag, you forgot your helmet!"

He seized it off the wall behind him, ran, leapt, and they were off, the night wind hammering about their siren scream and their mighty metal thunder!

It was a flaking three-story house in the ancient part of the city, a century old if it was a day, but like all houses it had been given a thin fireproof plastic sheath many years ago, and this preservative shell seemed to be the only thing holding it in the sky.

"Here we are!"

The engine slammed to a stop. Beatty, Stoneman and Black ran up the sidewalk, suddenly odious and fat in their plump fireproof slickers. Montag followed.

They crashed the front door and grabbed at a woman, though she was not running; she was not trying to escape. She was only standing, weaving from side to side, her eyes fixed upon a nothingness in the wall, as if they had struck her a terrible blow upon the head. Her tongue was moving in her mouth, and her eyes seemed to be trying to remember something and then they remembered and her tongue moved again:

"'Play the man, Master Ridley; we shall this day light such a candle, by God's grace, in England, as I trust shall never be put out.'"

"Enough of that!" said Beatty. "Where are they?"

He slapped her face with amazing objectivity and repeated the question. The old woman's eyes came to a focus upon Beatty. "You know where they are or you wouldn't be here," she said.

Stoneman held out the telephone alarm card with the complaint signed in telephone duplicate on the back:

"Have reason to suspect attic; 11 No. Elm, City. E. B."

"That would be Mrs. Blake, my neighbor," said the woman, reading the initials.

"All right, men, let's get 'em!"

Next thing they were up in musty blackness swinging silver hatchets at doors that were, after all, unlocked, tumbling through like boys all rollick and shout. "Hey!" A fountain of books sprang down upon Montag as he climbed shuddering up the sheer stairwell. How inconvenient! Always before it had been like snuffing a candle. The police went first and adhesive-taped the victim's mouth and bandaged him off into their glittering beetle cars, so when you arrived you found an empty house. You weren't hurting anyone, you were hurting only *things!* And since things really couldn't be hurt, since things felt nothing, and things don't scream or whimper, as this woman might begin to scream and cry out, there was nothing to tease your conscience later. You were simply cleaning up. Janitorial work, essentially. Everything to its proper place. Quick with the kerosene! Who's got a match!

But now, tonight, someone had slipped. This woman was spoiling the ritual. The men were making too much noise, laughing, joking, to cover her terrible accusing silence below. She made the empty rooms roar with accusation and shake down a fine dust of guilt that was sucked in their nostrils as they plunged about. It was neither cricket nor correct. Montag felt an immense irritation. She shouldn't be here, on top of everything!

Books bombarded his shoulders, his arms, his upturned face. A book lit, almost obediently, like a white pigeon, in his hands, wings fluttering. In the dim, wavering light, a page hung open and it was like a snowy feather, the words delicately painted thereon. In all the rush and fervor, Montag had only an instant to read a line, but it blazed in his mind for the next minute as if stamped there with fiery steel. "Time has fallen asleep in the afternoon sunshine." He dropped the book. Immediately, another fell into his arms.

"Montag, up here!"

Montag's hand closed like a mouth, crushed the book with wild devotion, with an insanity of mindlessness to his chest. The men above were hurling shovelfuls of magazines into the dusty air. They fell like slaughtered birds and the woman stood below, like a small girl, among the bodies.

Montag had done nothing. His hand had done it all, his hand, with a brain of its own, with a conscience and a curiosity in each trembling finger, had turned thief. Now, it plunged the book back under his arm, pressed it tight to sweating armpit, rushed out empty, with a magician's flourish! Look here! Innocent! Look!

He gazed, shaken, at that white hand. He held it way out, as if he were farsighted. He held it close, as if he were blind.

"Montag!"

He jerked about.

"Don't stand there, idiot!"

The books lay like great mounds of fishes left to dry. The men danced and slipped and fell over them. Titles glittered their golden eyes, falling, gone.

"Kerosene!"

They pumped the cold fluid from the numeraled 451 tanks strapped to their shoulders. They coated each book, they pumped rooms full of it.

They hurried downstairs, Montag staggering after them in the kerosene fumes.

"Come on, woman!"

The woman knelt among the books, touching the drenched leather and cardboard, reading the gilt titles with her fingers while her eyes accused Montag.

"You can't ever have my books," she said.

"You know the law," said Beatty. "Where's your common sense? None of those books agree with each other. You've been locked up here for years with a regular damned Tower of Babel. Snap out of it! The people in those books never lived. Come on now!"

She shook her head.

"The whole house is going up," said Beatty.

The men walked clumsily to the door. They glanced back at Montag, who stood near the woman.

"You're not leaving her here?" he protested.

"She won't come."

"Force her, then!"

Beatty raised his hand in which was concealed the igniter. "We're due back at the House. Besides, these fanatics always try suicide; the pattern's familiar."

Montag placed his hand on the woman's elbow. "You can come with me."

"No," she said. "Thank you, anyway."

"I'm counting to ten," said Beatty. "One. Two."

"Please," said Montag.

"Go on," said the woman.

"Three. Four."

"Here." Montag pulled at the woman.

The woman replied quietly, "I want to stay here."

"Five. Six."

"You can stop counting," she said. She opened the fingers of one hand slightly and in the palm of the hand was a single slender object.

An ordinary kitchen match.

The sight of it rushed the men out and down away from the house. Captain Beatty, keeping his dignity, backed slowly through the front door, his pink face burnt and shiny from a thousand fires and night excitements. God, thought Montag, how true! Always at night the alarm comes. Never by day! Is it because fire is prettier by night? More spectacle, a better show? The pink face of Beatty now showed the faintest panic in the door. The woman's hand twitched on the single matchstick. The fumes of kerosene bloomed up about her. Montag felt the hidden book pound like a heart against his chest.

"Go on," said the woman, and Montag felt himself back away and away out the door, after Beatty, down the steps, across the lawn, where the path of kerosene lay like the track of some evil snail.

On the front porch where she had come to weigh them quietly with her eyes, her quietness a condemnation, the woman stood motionless.

Beatty flicked his fingers to spark the kerosene.

He was too late. Montag gasped.

The woman on the porch reached out with contempt to them all, and struck the kitchen match against the railing.

People ran out of houses all down the street.

They said nothing on their way back to the firehouse. Nobody looked at anyone else. Montag sat in the front seat with Beatty and Black. They did not even smoke their pipes. They sat there looking out the front of the great Salamander as they turned a corner and went silently on.

"Master Ridley," said Montag a last.

"What?" said Beatty.

"She said, 'Master Ridley.' She said some crazy thing when we came in the door. 'Play the man,' she said, 'Master Ridley.' Something, something, something."

"'We shall this day light such a candle, by God's grace, in England, as I trust shall never be put out,'" said Beatty. Stoneman glanced over at the Captain, as did Montag, startled.

Beatty rubbed his chin. "A man named Latimer said that to a man named Nicholas Ridley, as they were being burnt alive at Oxford, for heresy, on October 16, 1555."

Montag and Stoneman went back to looking at the street as it moved under the engine wheels.

"I'm full of bits and pieces," said Beatty. "Most fire captains have to be. Sometimes I surprise myself. *Watch* it, Stoneman!"

Stoneman braked the truck.

"Damn!" said Beatty. "You've gone right by the corner where we turn for the firehouse."

"Who is it?"

"Who would it be?" said Montag, leaning back against the closed door in the dark.

His wife said, at last, "Well, put on the light."

"I don't want the light."

"Come to bed."

He heard her roll impatiently; the bedsprings squealed.

"Are you drunk?" she said.

So it was the hand that started it all. He felt one hand and then the other work his coat free and let it slump to the floor. He held his pants out into an abyss and let them fall into darkness. His hands had been infected, and soon it would be his arms. He could feel the poison working up his wrists and into his elbows and his shoulders, and then the jump-over from shoulder blade to shoulder blade like a spark leaping a gap. His hands were ravenous. And his eyes were beginning to feel hunger, as if they must look at something, anything, everything.

His wife said, "What *are* you doing?"

He balanced in space with the book in his sweating cold fingers.

A minute later she said, "Well, just don't stand there in the middle of the floor."

He made a small sound.

"What?" she asked.

He made more soft sounds. He stumbled toward the bed and shoved the book clumsily under the cold pillow. He fell into bed and his wife cried out, startled. He lay far across the room from her, on a winter island separated by an empty sea. She talked to him for what seemed a long while and she talked about this and she talked about that and it was only words, like the words he had heard once in a nursery at a friend's house, a two-year-old child building word patterns, talking jargon, making pretty sounds in the air. But Montag said nothing and after a long while when he only made the small sounds, he felt her move in the room and come to his bed and stand over him and put her hand down to feel his cheek. He knew that when she pulled her hand away from his face it was wet.

Late in the night he looked over at Mildred. She was awake. There was a tiny dance of melody in the air, her Seashell was tamped in her ear again and she was listening to far people in far places, her eyes wide and staring at the fathoms of blackness above her in the ceiling.

Wasn't there an old joke about the wife who talked so much on the telephone that her desperate husband ran out to the nearest store and telephoned her to ask what was for dinner? Well, then, why didn't he buy himself an audio-Seashell broadcasting station and talk to his wife late at night, murmur, whisper, shout, scream, yell. But what would he whisper, what would he yell? What could he say?

And suddenly she was so strange he couldn't believe he knew her at all. He was in someone else's house, like those other jokes people told of the gentleman, drunk, coming home late late at night, unlocking the wrong door, entering a wrong room, and bedding with a stranger and getting up early and going to work and neither of them the wiser.

"Millie . . . ?" he whispered.

"What?"

"I didn't mean to startle you. What I want to know is . . ."

"Well?"

"When did we meet? And *where?*"

"When did we meet for *what?*" she asked.

"I mean—originally."

He knew she must be frowning in the dark.

He clarified it. "The first time we ever met, where was it, and when?"

"Why, it was at—"

She stopped.

"I don't know," she said.

He was cold. "Can't you remember?"

"It's been so long."

"Only ten years, that's all, only ten!"

"Don't get excited, I'm trying to think." She laughed an odd little laugh that went up and up. "Funny, how funny, not to re-member where or when you met your husband or wife."

He lay massaging his eyes, his brow, and the back of his neck, slowly. He held both hands over his eyes and applied a steady pressure there as if to crush memory into place. It was suddenly more important than any other thing in a lifetime that he know where he had met Mildred.

"It doesn't matter." She was up, in the bathroom now, and he heard the water running, and the swallowing sound she made.

"No, I guess not," he said.

He tried to count how many times she swallowed and he thought of the visit from the two zinc-oxide-faced men with the cigarettes in their straight-lined mouths and the Electronic-Eyed Snake winding down into the layer upon layer of night and stone and stagnant spring water, and he wanted to call out to her, how many have you taken *tonight!* the capsules! how many will you take later and not know? and so on, every hour! or maybe not tonight, tomorrow night! And me not sleeping tonight or tomorrow night or any night for a long while, now that this has started. And he thought of her lying on the bed with the two technicians standing straight over her, not bent with concern, but only standing straight, arms folded. And he remembered thinking then that if she died, he was certain he wouldn't cry. For it would be the dying of an unknown, a street face, a newspaper image, and it was suddenly so very wrong that he had begun to cry, not at death but at the thought of *not crying* at death, a silly empty man near a silly empty woman, while the hungry snake made her still more empty.

How do you get so empty? he wondered. Who takes it out of you? And that awful flower the other day, the dandelion! It had summed up everything, hadn't it? "What a shame! You're not in love with anyone!" And why not?

Well, wasn't there a wall between him and Mildred, when you came down to it? Literally not just one wall but, so far, three! And expensive, too! And the uncles, the aunts, the cousins, the nieces, the nephews, that lived in those walls, the gibbering pack of tree-apes that said nothing, nothing, nothing and said it loud, loud, loud. He had taken to calling them relatives from the very first. "How's Uncle Louis today?" "Who?" "And Aunt Maude?" The most significant memory he had of Mildred, really, was of a little girl in a forest without trees (how odd!) or rather a little girl lost on a plateau where there used to be trees (you could feel the memory of their shapes all about) sitting in the center of the "living room." The living room; what a good job of labeling that was now. No matter when he came in, the walls were always talking to Mildred.

"Something must be done!"

"Yes, something must be *done!*"

"Well, let's not stand and talk!"

"Let's *do* it!"

"I'm so mad I could *spit!*"

What was it all about? Mildred couldn't say. Who was mad at whom? Mildred didn't quite know. What were they going to do? Well, said Mildred, wait around and see.

He had waited around to see.

A great thunderstorm of sound gushed from the walls. Music bombarded him at such an immense volume that his bones were almost shaken from their tendons; he felt his jaw vibrate, his eyes wobble in his head. He was a victim of concussion. When it was all over he felt like a man who had been thrown from a cliff, whirled in a centrifuge and spat out over a waterfall that fell and fell into emptiness and emptiness and never—quite—touched—bottom—never—never—quite—no not quite—touched—bottom . . . and you fell so fast you didn't touch the sides either . . . never . . . quite . . . touched . . . anything.

The thunder faded. The music died.

"There," said Mildred.

And it was indeed remarkable. Something had happened. Even though the people in the walls of the room had barely moved, and nothing had really been settled, you had the impression that someone had turned on a washing machine or sucked you up in a gigantic vacuum. You drowned in music and pure cacophony. He came out of the room sweating and on the point of collapse. Behind him, Mildred sat in her chair and the voices went on again:

"Well, everything will be all right now," said an "aunt."

"Oh, don't be too sure," said a "cousin."

"Now, don't get angry!"

"Who's angry?"

"*You* are!"

"*I* am?"

"You're mad!"

"Why would I be mad!"

"Because!"

"That's all very well," cried Montag, "but what are they mad about? Who *are* these people? Who's that man and who's that woman? Are they husband and wife, are they divorced, engaged, what? Good God, *nothing's* connected up."

"They—" said Mildred—"well, they—they had this fight, you see. They certainly fight a lot. You should listen. I think they're married. Yes, they're married. Why?"

And if it was not the three walls soon to be four walls and the dream complete, then it was the open car and Mildred driving a hundred miles an hour across town, he shouting at her and she shouting back and both trying to hear what was said, but hearing only the scream of the car. "At least keep it down to the minimum!" he yelled. "What?" she cried. "Keep it down to fifty-five, the minimum!" he shouted. "The what?" she shrieked. "Speed!" he shouted. And she pushed it up to one hundred and five miles an hour and tore the breath from his mouth.

When they stepped out of the car, she had the Seashells stuffed in her ears.

Silence. Only the wind blowing softly.

"Mildred." He stirred in bed.

He reached over and pulled the tiny musical insect out of her ear. "Mildred. Mildred?"

"Yes." Her voice was faint.

He felt he was one of the creatures electronically inserted between the slots of the phono-color walls, speaking, but the speech not piercing the crystal barrier. He could only pantomime, hoping she would turn his way and see him. They could not touch through the glass.

"Mildred, do you know that girl I was telling you about?"

"What girl?" She was almost asleep.

"The girl next door."

"What girl next door?"

"You know, the high-school girl. Clarisse, her name is."

"Oh, yes," said his wife.

"I haven't seen her for a few days—four days to be exact. Have you seen her?"

"No."

"I've meant to talk to you about her. Strange."

"Oh, I know the one you mean."

"I thought you would."

"Her," said Mildred in the dark room.

"What about her?" asked Montag.

"I meant to tell you. Forgot. Forgot."

"Tell me now. What is it?"

"I think she's gone."

"Gone?"

"Whole family moved out somewhere. But she's gone for good. I think she's dead."

"We couldn't be talking about the same girl."

"No. The same girl. McClellan. McClellan. Run over by a car. Four days ago. I'm not sure. But I think she's dead. The family moved out anyway. I don't know. But I think she's dead."

"You're not sure of it!"

"No, not sure. Pretty sure."

"Why didn't you tell me sooner?"

"Forgot."

"Four days ago!"

"I forgot all about it."

"Four days ago," he said, quietly, lying there.

They lay there in the dark room not moving, either of them. "Good night," she said.

He heard a faint rustle. Her hand moved. The electric thimble moved like a praying mantis on the pillow, touched by her hand. Now it was in her ear again, humming.

He listened and his wife was singing under her breath.

Outside the house, a shadow moved, an autumn wind rose up and faded away. But there was something else in the silence that he heard. It was like a breath exhaled upon the window. It was like a faint drift of greenish luminescent smoke, the motion of a single huge October leaf blowing across the lawn and away.

The Hound, he thought. It's out there tonight. It's out there now. If I opened the window . . .

He did not open the window.

He had chills and fever in the morning.

"You can't be sick," said Mildred.

He closed his eyes over the hotness. "Yes."

"But you were all right, last night."

"No, I wasn't all right." He heard the "relatives" shouting in the parlor.

Mildred stood over his bed, curiously. He felt her there, he saw her without opening his eyes, her hair burnt by chemicals to a brittle straw, her eyes with a kind of cataract unseen but suspect far behind the pupils, the reddened pouting lips, the body as thin as a praying mantis from dieting, and her flesh like white bacon. He could remember her no other way.

"Will you bring me aspirin and water?"

"You've got to get up," she said. "It's noon. You've slept five hours later than usual."

"Will you turn the parlor off?" he asked.

"That's my family."

"Will you turn it off for a sick man?"

"I'll turn it down."

She went out of the room and did nothing to the parlor and came back. "Is that better?"

"Thanks."

"That's my favorite program," she said.

"What about the aspirin?"

"You've never been sick before." She went away again.

"Well, I'm sick now. I'm not going to work tonight. Call Beatty for me."

"You acted funny lasted night." She returned, humming.

"Where's the aspirin?" He glanced at the water glass she handed him.

"Oh." She walked to the bath again. "Did something happen?"

"A fire, is all."

"I had a nice evening," she said, in the bathroom.

"What doing?"

"The parlor."

"What was on?"

"Programs."

"What programs?"

"Some of the best ever."

"Who?"

"Oh, you know, the bunch."

"Yes, the bunch, the bunch, the bunch." He pressed at the pain in his eyes and suddenly the odor of kerosene made him vomit.

Mildred came in, humming. She was surprised. "Why'd you do that?"

He looked with dismay at the floor. "We burned an old woman with her books."

"It's a good thing the rug's washable." She fetched a mop and worked on it. "I went to Helen's last night."

"Couldn't you get the shows in your own parlor?"

"Sure, but it's nice visiting."

She went out into the parlor. He heard her singing.

"Mildred?" he called.

She returned, singing, snapping her fingers softly.

"Aren't you going to ask me about last night?" he said.

"What about it?"

"We burned a thousand books. We burned a woman."

"Well?"

The parlor was exploding with sound.

"We burned copies of Dante and Swift and Marcus Aurelius."

"Wasn't he a European?"

"Something like that."

"Wasn't he a radical?"

"I never read him."

"He was a radical." Mildred fiddled with the telephone. "You don't expect me to call Captain Beatty, do you?"

"You must!"

"Don't shout!"

"I wasn't shouting." He was up in bed, suddenly, enraged

and flushed, shaking. The parlor roared in the hot air. "I can't call him. I can't tell him I'm sick."

"Why?"

Because you're afraid, he thought. A child feigning illness, afraid to call because after a moment's discussion, the conversation would run so: "Yes, Captain, I feel better already. I'll be in at ten o'clock tonight."

"You're not sick," said Mildred.

Montag fell back in bed. He reached under his pillow. The hidden book was still there.

"Mildred, how would it be if, well, maybe I quit my job awhile?"

"You want to give up everything? After all these years of working, because, one night, some woman and her books—"

"You should have seen her, Millie!"

"She's nothing to me; she shouldn't have had books. It was her responsibility, she should've thought of that. I hate her. She's got you going and next thing you know we'll be out, no house, no job, nothing."

"You weren't there, you didn't *see*," he said. "There must be something in books, things we can't imagine, to make a woman stay in a burning house; there must be something there. You don't stay for nothing."

"She was simple-minded."

"She was a rational as you and I, more so perhaps, and we burned her."

"That's water under the bridge."

"No, not water; fire. You ever seen a burned house? It smolders for days. Well, this fire'll last me the rest of my life. God! I've been trying to put it out, in my mind, all night. I'm crazy with trying."

"You should've thought of that before becoming a fireman."

"Thought!" he said. "Was I given a choice? My grandfather and father were firemen. In my sleep, I ran after them."

The parlor was playing a dance tune.

"This is the day you go on the early shift," said Mildred. "You should've gone two hours ago. I just noticed."

"It's not just the woman that died," said Montag. "Last night I thought about all that kerosene I've used in the past ten years. And I thought about books. And for the first time I realized that a man was behind each one of the books. A man had to think them up. A man had to take a long time to put them down on paper. And I'd never even thought that thought before." He got out of bed.

"It took some man a lifetime maybe to put some of his thoughts down, looking around at the world and life and then I come along in two minutes and boom! it's all over."

"Let me alone," said Mildred. "I didn't do anything."

"Let you alone! That's all very well, but how can I leave myself alone? We need not to be let alone. We need to be really bothered once in a while. How long is it since you were *really* bothered? About something important, about something real?"

And then he shut up, for he remembered last week and the two white stones staring up at the ceiling and the pumpsnake with the probing eye and the two soap-faced men with the cigarettes moving in their mouths when they talked. But that was another Mildred, that was a Mildred so deep inside this one, and so bothered, really bothered, that the two women had never met. He turned away.

Mildred said, "Well, now you've done it. Out front of the house. Look who's here."

"I don't care."

"There's a Phoenix car just drove up and a man in a black shirt with an orange snake stitched on his arm coming up the front walk."

"Captain Beatty?" he said.

"Captain Beatty."

Montag did not move, but stood looking into the cold whiteness of the wall immediately before him.

"Go let him in, will you? Tell him I'm sick."

"Tell him yourself!" She ran a few steps this way, a few steps that, and stopped, eyes wide, when the front door speaker called her name, softly, softly, Mrs. Montag, Mrs. Montag, someone here, someone here, Mrs. Montag, Mrs. Montag, someone's here. Fading.

Montag made sure the book was well hidden behind the pillow, climbed slowly back into bed, arranged the covers over his knees and across his chest, half-sitting, and after a while Mildred moved and went out of the room and Captain Beatty strolled in, his hands in his pockets.

"Shut the 'relatives' up," said Beatty, looking around at everything except Montag and his wife.

This time, Mildred ran. The yammering voices stopped yelling in the parlor.

Captain Beatty sat down in the most comfortable chair with a peaceful look on his ruddy face. He took time to prepare and light his brass pipe and puff out a great smoke cloud. "Just thought I'd come by and see how the sick man is."

"How'd you guess?"

Beatty smiled his smile which showed the candy pinkness of his gums and the tiny candy whiteness of his teeth. "I've seen it all. You were going to call for a night off."

Montag sat in bed.

"Well," said Beatty, "*take* the night off!" He examined his eternal matchbox, the lid of which said GUARANTEED: ONE MILLION LIGHTS IN THIS IGNITER, and began to strike the chemical match abstractedly, blow out, strike, blow out strike, speak a few words, blow out. He looked at the flame. He blew, he looked at the smoke. "When will you be well?"

"Tomorrow. The next day maybe. First of the week."

Beatty puffed his pipe. "Every fireman, sooner or later, hits this. They only need understanding, to know how the wheels run. Need to know the history of our profession. They don't feed it to rookies like they used to. Damn shame." Puff. "Only fire chiefs remember it now." Puff. "I'll let you in on it."

Mildred fidgeted.

Beatty took a full minute to settle himself in and think back for what he wanted to say.

"When did it all start, you ask, this job of ours, how did it come about, where, when? Well, I'd say it really got started around about a thing called the Civil War. Even though our rule book claims it was founded earlier. The fact is we didn't get along well until photography came into its own. Then—motion pictures in the early twentieth century. Radio. Television. Things began to have *mass.*"

Montag sat in bed, not moving.

"And because they had mass, they became simpler," said Beatty. "Once, books appealed to a few people, here, there, everywhere. They could afford to be different. The world was roomy. But then the world got full of eyes and elbows and mouths. Double, triple, quadruple population. Films and radios, magazines, books leveled down to a sort of paste pudding norm, do you follow me?"

"I think so."

Beatty peered at the smoke pattern he had put out on the air. "Picture it. Nineteenth-century man with his horses, dogs, carts, slow motion. Then, in the twentieth century, speed up your camera. Books cut shorter. Condensations. Digests, Tabloids. Everything boils down to the gag, the snap ending."

"Snap ending." Mildred nodded.

"Classics cut to fit fifteen-minute radio shows, then cut again to fill a two-minute book column, winding up at last as a ten- or twelve-line dictionary resume. I exaggerate, of course. The dictionaries were for reference. But many were those whose sole knowledge of *Hamlet* (you know the title certainly, Montag; it is probably only a faint rumor of a title to you, Mrs. Montag), whose sole knowledge, as I say, of *Hamlet* was a one-page digest in a book that claimed: *now at last you can read all the classics; keep up with your neighbors.* Do you see? Out of the nursery into the college and back to the nursery; there's your intellectual pattern for the past five centuries or more."

Mildred arose and began to move around the room, picking things up and putting them down. Beatty ignored her and continued:

"Speed up the film, Montag, quick. *Click, Pic, Look, Eye, Now, Flick, Here, There, Swift, Pace, Up, Down, In, Out, Why, How, Who, What, Where, Eh? Uh! Bang! Smack! Wallop, Bing, Bong, Boom!* Digest-digests, digest-digest-digests. Politics? One column, two sentences, a headline! Then, in mid-air, all vanishes! Whirl man's mind around about so fast under the pumping hands of publishers, exploiters, broadcasters that the centrifuge flings off all unnecessary, time-wasting thought!"

Mildred smoothed the bedclothes. Montag felt his heart jump and jump again as she patted his pillow. Right now she was pulling at his shoulder to try to get him to move so she could take the pillow out and fix it nicely and put it back. And perhaps cry out and stare or simply reach down her hand and say, "What's this?" and hold up the hidden book with touching innocence.

"School is shortened, discipline relaxed, philosophies, histories, languages dropped, English and spelling gradually gradually neglected, finally almost completely ignored. Life is immediate, the job counts, pleasure lies all about after work. Why learn anything save pressing buttons, pulling switches, fitting nuts and bolts?"

"Let me fix your pillow," said Mildred.

"No!" whispered Montag.

"The zipper displaces the button and a man lacks just that much time to think while dressing at dawn, a philosophical hour, and thus a melancholy hour."

Mildred said, "Here."

"Get away," said Montag.

"Life becomes one big pratfall, Montag; everything bang, boff, and wow!"

"Wow," said Mildred, yanking at the pillow.

"For God's sake, let me be!" cried Montag passionately.

Beatty opened his eyes wide.

Mildred's hand had frozen behind the pillow. Her fingers were tracing the book's outline and as the shape became familiar her face looked surprised and then stunned. Her mouth opened to ask a question. . . .

"Empty the theaters save for clowns and furnish the rooms with glass walls and pretty colors running up and down the walls like confetti or blood or sherry or sauterne. You like baseball, don't you, Montag?"

"Baseball's a fine game."

Now Beatty was almost invisible, a voice somewhere behind a screen of smoke.

"What's this?" asked Mildred, almost with delight. Montag heaved back against her arms. "What's this here?"

"Sit down!" Montag shouted. She jumped away, her hands empty. "We're talking!"

Beatty went on as if nothing had happened. "You like bowling, don't you, Montag?"

"Bowling, yes."

"And golf?"

"Golf is a fine game."

"Basketball?"

"A fine game."

"Billiards, pool? Football?"

"Fine games, all of them."

"More sports for everyone, group spirit, fun, and you don't have to think, eh? Organize and organize and super organize super-super sports. More cartoons in books. More pictures. The mind drinks less and less. Impatience. Highways full of crowds going somewhere, somewhere, somewhere, nowhere. The gasoline refugee. Towns turn into motels, people in nomadic surges from place to place, following the moon tides, living tonight in the room where you slept this noon and I the night before."

Mildred went out of the room and slammed the door. The parlor "aunts" began to laugh at the parlor "uncles."

"Now let's take up the minorities in our civilization, shall we? Bigger the population, the more minorities. Don't step on the toes of the dog-lovers, the cat-lovers, doctors, lawyers, merchants, chiefs, Mormons, Baptists, Unitarians, second-generation Chinese, Swedes, Italians, Germans, Texans, Brooklynites, Irishmen, people from Oregon or Mexico. The people in this book, this play, this TV serial are not meant to represent any actual painters, cartographers, mechanics anywhere. The bigger your market, Montag, the less you handle controversy, remember that! All the minor minor minorities with their navels to be kept clean. Authors, full of evil thoughts, lock up your typewriters. They *did*. Magazines became a nice blend of vanilla tapioca. Books, so the damned snobbish critics said, were dishwater. No *wonder* books stopped selling, the critics said. But the public, knowing what it wanted, spinning happily, let the comic books survive. And the three-dimensional sex magazines, of course. There you have it, Montag. It didn't come from the Government down. There was no dictum, no declaration, no censorship, to start with, no! Technology, mass exploitation, and minority pressure carried the trick, thank God. Today, thanks to them, you can stay happy all the time, you are allowed to read comics, the good old confessions, or trade journals."

"Yes, but what about the firemen, then?" asked Montag.

"Ah." Beatty leaned forward in the faint mist of smoke from his pipe. "What more easily explained and natural? With school turning out more runners, jumpers, racers, tinkerers, grabbers, snatchers, fliers, and swimmers instead of examiners, critics, knowers, and imaginative creators, the word 'intellectual,' of course, became the swear word it deserved to be. You always dread the unfamiliar. Surely you remember the boy in your own school class who was exceptionally 'bright,' did most of the reciting and answering while the others sat like so many leaden idols, hating him. And wasn't it this bright boy you selected for beatings and tortures after hours? Of course it was. We must all be alike. Not everyone born free and equal, as the Constitution says, but everyone *made* equal. Each man the image of every other; then all are happy, for there are no mountains to make them cower, to judge themselves against. So! A book is a loaded gun in the house next door. Burn it. Take the shot from the weapon. Breach man's mind. Who knows who might be the target of the well-read man? Me? I won't stomach them for a minute. And so when houses were finally fireproofed completely, all over the world (you were correct in your assumption the other night) there was no longer need of firemen for the old purposes. They were given the new job, as custodians of our peace of mind, the focus of our understandable and rightful dread of being inferior; official censors, judges, and executors. That's you, Montag, and that's me."

The door to the parlor opened and Mildred stood there looking in at them, looking at Beatty and then at Montag. Behind her the walls of the room were flooded with green and yellow and orange fireworks sizzling and bursting to some music composed almost completely of trap drums, tom-toms, and cymbals. Her mouth moved and she was saying something but the sound covered it.

Beatty knocked his pipe into the palm of his pink hand, studied the ashes as if they were a symbol to be diagnosed and searched for meaning.

"You must understand that our civilization is so vast that we can't have our minorities upset and stirred. Ask yourself, What do we want in this country, above all? People want to be happy, isn't that right? Haven't you heard it all your life? I want to be happy, people say. Well, aren't they? Don't we keep them moving, don't we give them fun? That's all we live for, isn't it? For pleasure, for titillation? And you must admit our culture provides plenty of these."

"Yes."

Montag could lip-read what Mildred was saying in the

doorway. He tried not to look at her mouth, because then Beatty might turn and read what was there, too.

"Colored people don't like *Little Black Sambo*. Burn it. White people don't feel good about *Uncle Tom's Cabin*. Burn it. Someone's written a book on tobacco and cancer of the lungs? The cigarette people are weeping? Burn the book. Serenity, Montag. Peace, Montag. Take your fight outside. Better yet, into the incinerator. Funerals are unhappy and pagan? Eliminate them, too. Five minutes after a person is dead he's on his way to the Big Flue, the Incinerators serviced by helicopters all over the country. Ten minutes after death a man's a speck of black dust. Let's not quibble over individuals with memoriams. Forget them. Burn all, burn everything. Fire is bright and fire is clean."

The fireworks died in the parlor behind Mildred. She had stopped talking at the same time; a miraculous coincidence. Montag held his breath.

"There was a girl next door," he said, slowly. "She's gone now, I think, dead. I can't even remember her face. But she was different. How—how did she *happen*?"

Beatty smiled. "Here or there, that's bound to occur. Clarisse McClellan? We've a record on her family. We've watched them carefully. Heredity and environment are funny things. You can't rid yourselves of all the odd ducks in just a few years. The home environment can undo a lot you try to do at school. That's why we've lowered the kindergarten age year after year until now we're almost snatching them from the cradle. We had some false alarms on the McClellans, when they lived in Chicago. Never found a book. Uncle had a mixed record; antisocial. The girl? She was a time bomb. The family had been feeding her subconscious, I'm sure, from what I saw of her school record. She didn't want to know *how* a thing was done, but *why*. That can be embarrassing. You ask Why to a lot of things and you wind up very unhappy indeed, if you keep at it. The poor girl's better off dead."

"Yes, dead."

"Luckily, queer ones like her don't happen often. We know how to nip most of them in the bud, early. You can't build a house without nails and wood. If you don't want a house built, hide the nails and wood. If you don't want a man unhappy politically, don't give him two sides to a question to worry him; give him one. Better yet, give him none. Let him forget there is such a thing as war. If the government is inefficient, top-heavy, and tax-mad, better it be all those than that people worry over it. Peace, Montag. Give the people contests they win by remembering the words to more popular songs or the names of state capitals or how much corn Iowa grew last year. Cram them full of non-combustible data, chock them so damned full of 'facts' they feel stuffed, but absolutely 'brilliant' with information. Then they'll feel they're thinking, they'll get a *sense* of motion without moving. And they'll be happy, because facts of that sort don't change. Don't give them any slippery stuff like philosophy or sociology to tie things up with. That way lies melancholy. Any man who can take a TV wall apart and put it back together again, and most men can, nowadays, is happier than any man who tries to slide rule, measure, and equate the universe, which just won't be measured or equated without making man feel bestial and lonely. I know, I've tried it; to hell with it. So bring on your clubs and parties, your acrobats and magicians, your daredevils, jet cars, motorcycle helicopters, your sex and heroin, more of everything to do with automatic reflex. If the drama is bad, if the film says nothing, if the play is hollow, sting me with the Theremin, loudly. I'll think I'm responding to the play, when it's only a tactile reaction to vibration. But I don't care. I just like solid entertainment."

Beatty got up. "I must be going. Lecture's over. I hope I've clarified things. The important thing for you to remember, Montag, is we're the Happiness Boys, the Dixie Duo, you and I and the others. We stand against the small tide of those who want to make everyone unhappy with conflicting theory and thought. We have our fingers in the dike. Hold steady. Don't let the torrent of melancholy and drear philosophy drown our world. We depend on you. I don't think you realize how important *you* are, *we* are, to our happy world as it stands now."

Beatty shook Montag's limp hand. Montag still sat, as if the house were collapsing about him and he could not move, in the bed. Mildred had vanished from the door.

"One last thing," said Beatty. "At least once in his career, every fireman gets an itch. What do the books *say*, he wonders. Oh, to *scratch* that itch, eh? Well, Montag, take my word for it, I've had to read a few in my time, to know what I was about, and the books say *nothing!* Nothing you can teach or believe. They're about nonexistent people, figments of imagination, if they're fiction. And if they're nonfiction, it's worse, one professor calling another an idiot, one philosopher screaming down another's gullet. All of them running about, putting out the stars and extinguishing the sun. You come away lost."

"Well, then, what if a fireman accidentally, really not intending anything, takes a book home with him?"

Montag twitched. The open door looked at him with its great vacant eye.

"A natural error. Curiosity alone," said Beatty. "We don't get overanxious or mad. We let the fireman keep the book twenty-four hours. If he hasn't burned it by then, we simply come burn it for him."

"Of course." Montag's mouth was dry.

"Well, Montag. Will you take another, later shift, today? Will we see you tonight perhaps?"

"I don't know," said Montag.

"What?" Beatty looked faintly surprised.

Montag shut his eyes. "I'll be in later. Maybe."

"We'd certainly miss you if you didn't show," said Beatty, putting his pipe in his pocket thoughtfully.

I'll never come in again, thought Montag.

"Get well and keep well," said Beatty.

He turned and went out through the open door.

Montag watched through the window as Beatty drove away in his gleaming yellow-flame-colored beetle with the black, char-colored tires.

Across the street and down the way the other houses stood with their flat fronts. What was it Clarisse had said one afternoon? "No front porches. My uncle says there used to be front porches. And people sat there sometimes at night, talking when they wanted to talk, rocking, and not talking when they didn't want to talk. Sometimes they just sat there and thought about things, turned things over. My uncle says the architects got rid of the front porches because they didn't look well. But my uncle says that was merely rationalizing it; the real reason, hidden underneath, might be they didn't want people sitting like that, doing nothing, rocking, talking; that was the wrong *kind* of social life. People talked too much. And they had time to think. So they ran off with the porches. And the gardens, too. Not many gardens anymore to sit around in. And look at the furniture. No rocking chairs anymore. They're too comfortable. Get people up and running around. My uncle says . . . and . . . my uncle . . . and . . . my uncle . . ." Her voice faded.

° ° °

Montag turned and looked at his wife, who sat in the middle of the parlor talking to an announcer, who in turn was talking to her. "Mrs. Montag," he was saying. This, that, and the other. "Mrs. Montag—" Something else and still another. The converter attachment, which had cost them one hundred dollars, automatically supplied her name whenever the announcer addressed his anonymous audience, leaving a blank where the proper syllables could be filled in. A special spot-wavex-scrambler also caused his televised image, in the area immediately about his lips, to mouth the vowels and consonants beautifully. He was a friend, no doubt of it, a good friend. "Mrs. Montag—now look right here."

Her head turned. Though she quite obviously was not listening.

Montag said, "It's only a step from not going to work today to not working tomorrow, to not working at the firehouse ever again."

"You are going to work tonight, though, aren't you?" said Mildred.

"I haven't decided. Right now I've got an awful feeling I want to smash things and kill things."

"Go take the beetle."

"No, thanks."

"The keys to the beetle are on the night table. I always like to drive fast when I feel that way. You get it up around ninety-five and you feel wonderful. Sometimes I drive all night and come back and you don't know it. It's fun out in the country. You hit rabbits, sometimes you hit dogs. Go take the beetle."

"No, I don't want to, this time. I want to hold onto this funny thing. God, it's gotten big on me. I don't know what it is. I'm so damned unhappy, I'm so mad, and I don't know why. I feel like I'm putting on weight. I feel fat. I feel like I've been saving up a lot of things, and don't know what. I might even start reading books."

"They'd put you in jail, wouldn't they?" She looked at him as if he were behind the glass wall.

He began to put on his clothes, moving restlessly about the bedroom. "Yes, and it might be a good idea. Before I hurt someone. Did you hear Beatty? Did you listen to him? He knows all the answers. He's right. Happiness is important. Fun is everything. And yet I kept sitting there saying to myself, I'm not happy, I'm not happy."

"*I* am." Mildred's mouth beamed. "And proud of it."

"I'm going to do something," said Montag. "I don't even know what yet, but I'm going to do something big."

"I'm tired of listening to this junk," said Mildred, turning from him to the announcer again.

Montag touched the volume control in the wall and the announcer was speechless.

"Millie?" He paused. "This is your house as well as mine. I feel it's only fair that I tell you something now. I should have told you before, but I wasn't even admitting it to myself. I have something I want you to see, something I've put away and hid during the past year, now and again, once in a while, I didn't know why, but I did it and I never told you."

He took hold of a straight-backed chair and moved it slowly and steadily into the hall near the front door and climbed up on it and stood for a moment like a statue on a pedestal, his wife standing under him, waiting. Then he reached up and pulled back the grill of the air-conditioning system and reached far back inside to the right and moved still another sliding sheet of metal and took out a book. Without looking at it he dropped it to the floor. He put his hand back up and took out two books and moved his hand down and dropped the two books to the floor. He kept moving his hand and dropping books, small ones, fairly large ones, yellow, red, green ones. When he was done he looked down upon some twenty books lying at his wife's feet.

"I'm sorry," he said. "I didn't really think. But now it looks as if we're in this together."

Mildred backed away as if she were suddenly confronted by a pack of mice that had come up out of the floor. He could hear her breathing rapidly and her face was paled out and her eyes were fastened wide. She said his name over, twice, three times. Then, moaning, she ran forward, seized a book and ran toward the kitchen incinerator.

He caught her, shrieking. He held her and she tried to fight away from him, scratching.

"No, Millie, no! Wait! Stop it, will you? You don't know . . . stop it!" He slapped her face, he grabbed her again and shook her.

She said his name and began to cry.

"Millie!" he said. "Listen. Give me a second, will you? We can't do anything. We can't burn these. I want to look at them, at least look at them once. Then if what the Captain says is true, we'll burn them together, believe me, we'll burn them together. You must help me." He looked down into her face and took hold of her chin and held her firmly. He was looking not only at her, but for himself and what he must do, in her face. "Whether we like this or not, we're in it. I've never asked for much from you in all these years, but I ask it now, I plead for it. We've got to start somewhere here, figuring out why we're in such a mess, you and the medicine nights, and the car, and me and my work. We're heading right for the cliff, Millie. God, I don't want to go over. This isn't going to be easy. We haven't anything to go on, but maybe we can piece it out and figure it and help each other. I need you so much right now, I can't tell you. If you love me at all you'll put up with this, twenty-four, forty-eight hours, that's all I ask, then it'll be over, I promise, I swear! And if there is something here, just one little thing out of a whole mess of things, maybe we can pass it on to someone else."

She wasn't fighting any more, so he let her go. She sagged away from him and slid down the wall, and sat on the floor looking at the books. Her foot touched one and she saw this and pulled her foot away.

"That woman, the other night, Millie, you weren't there. You didn't see her face. And Clarisse. You never talked to her. I talked to her. And men like Beatty are afraid of her. I can't understand it. Why should they be so afraid of someone like her? But I kept putting her alongside the firemen in the House last night, and I suddenly realized I didn't like them at all, and I didn't like myself at all any more. And I thought maybe it would be best if the firemen themselves were burnt."

"Guy!"

The front door voice called softly:

"Mrs. Montag, Mrs. Montag, someone here, someone here, Mrs. Montag, Mrs. Montag, someone here."

Softly.

They turned to the stare at the door and the books toppled everywhere, everywhere in heaps.

"Beatty!" said Mildred.

"It can't be him."

"He's come back!" she whispered.

The front door voiced called again softly. "Someone here. . . ."

"We won't answer." Montag lay back against the wall and

then slowly sank to a crouching position and began to nudge the books, bewilderedly, with his thumb, his forefinger. He was shivering and he wanted above all to shove the books up through the ventilator again, but he knew he could not face Beatty again. He crouched and then he sat and the voice of the front door spoke again, more insistently. Montag picked a single small volume from the floor. "Where do we begin?" He opened the book halfway and peered at it. "We begin by beginning, I guess."

"He'll come in," said Mildred, "and burn us and the books!"

The front door voice faded at last. There was a silence. Montag felt the presence of someone beyond the door, waiting, listening. Then the footsteps going away down the walk and over the lawn.

"Let's see what this is," said Montag.

He spoke the words haltingly and with a terrible self-consciousness. He read a dozen pages here or there and came at last to this:

"'It is computed, that eleven thousand persons have at several times suffered death rather than submit to break their eggs at the smaller end.'"

Mildred sat across the hall from him. "What does it mean? It doesn't mean *anything!* The Captain was right!"

"Here now," said Montag. "We'll start over again, at the beginning."

two
The Sieve
and the Sand

They read the long afternoon through, while the cold November rain fell from the sky upon the quiet house. They sat in the hall because the parlor was so empty and gray-looking without its wall lit with orange and yellow confetti and skyrockets and women in gold-mesh dresses and men in black velvet pulling one-hundred-pound rabbits from silver hats. The parlor was dead and Mildred kept peering in at it with a blank expression as Montag paced the floor and came back and squatted down and read a page as many as ten times, aloud.

"'We cannot tell the precise moment when friendship is formed. As in filling a vessel drop by drop, there is at last a drop which makes it run over; so in a series of kindnesses there is at least one which makes the heart run over.'"

Montag sat listening to the rain.

"Is that what it was in the girl next door? I've tried so hard to figure."

"She's dead. Let's talk about someone alive, for goodness' sake."

Montag did not look back at his wife as he went trembling along the hall to the kitchen, where he stood a long time watching the rain hit the windows before he came back down the hall in the gray light, waiting for the tremble to subside.

He opened another book.

"'That favorite subject, Myself.'"

He squinted at the wall. "'That favorite subject, Myself.'"

"I understand *that* one," said Mildred.

"But Clarisse's favorite subject wasn't herself. It was everyone else, and me. She was the first person in a good many years I've really liked. She was the first person I can remember who looked straight at me as if I counted." He lifted the two books. "These men have been dead a long time, but I know their words point, one way or another, to Clarisse."

Outside the front door, in the rain, a faint scratching.

Montag froze. He saw Mildred thrust herself back to the wall and gasp.

"Someone—the door—why doesn't the door-voice tell us—"

"I shut it off."

Under the doorsill, a slow, probing sniff, an exhalation of electric steam.

Mildred laughed. "It's only a dog, that's what! You want me to shoo him away?"

"Stay where you are!"

Silence. The cold rain falling. And the smell of blue electricity blowing under the locked door.

"Let's get back to work," said Montag quietly.

Mildred kicked at a book. "Books aren't people. You read and I look all around, but there isn't *anybody*!"

He stared at the parlor that was dead and gray as the waters of an ocean that might teem with life if they switched on the electronic sun.

"Now," said Mildred, "my 'family' is people. They tell me things; *I* laugh, *they* laugh! And the colors!"

"Yes, I know."

"And besides, if Captain Beatty knew about those books—" She thought about it. Her face grew amazed and then horrified. "He might come and burn the house and the 'family.' That's awful! Think of our investment. Why should I read? What *for*?"

"What for! Why!" said Montag. "I saw the damnedest snake in the world the other night. It was dead but it was alive. It could see but it couldn't see. You want to *see* that snake? It's at Emergency Hospital where they filed a report on all the junk the snake got out of you! Would you like to go and check their file? Maybe you'd look under Guy Montag or maybe under Fear or War. Would you like to go to that house that burnt last night? And rake ashes for the bones of the woman who set fire to her own house! What about Clarisse McClellan, where do we look for her? The morgue! Listen!"

The bombers crossed the sky and crossed the sky over the house, gasping, murmuring, whistling like an immense, invisible fan, circling in emptiness.

"Jesus God," said Montag. "Every hour so many damn things in the sky! How in hell did those bombers get up there every single second of our lives! Why doesn't someone want to talk about it! We've started and won two atomic wars since 2022! Is it because we're having so much fun at home we've forgotten the world? Is it because we're so rich and the rest of the world's so poor and we just don't care if they are? I've heard rumors; the world is starving, but we're well fed. Is it true, the world works hard and we play? Is that why we're hated so much? I've heard the rumors about hate, too, once in a long while, over the years. Do *you* know why? *I* don't, that's *sure!* Maybe the books can get us half out of the cave. They just *might* stop us from making the same damn insane mistakes! I don't hear those idiot bastards in your parlor talking about it. God, Millie, don't you *see?* An hour a day, two hours, with these books, and maybe . . ."

The telephone rang. Mildred snatched the phone.

"Ann!" She laughed. "Yes, the White Clown's on tonight!"

Montag walked to the kitchen and threw the book down. "Montag," he said, "you're really stupid. Where do we go from here? Do we turn the books in, forget it?" He opened the book to read over Mildred's laughter.

Poor Millie, he thought. Poor Montag, it's mud to you, too. But where do you get help, where do you find a teacher this late?

Hold on. He shut his eyes. Yes, of course. Again he found himself thinking of the green park a year ago. The thought had been with him many times recently but now he remembered how it was that day in the city park when he had seen that old man in the black suit hide something, quickly, in his coat.

. . . The old man leapt up as if to run. And Montag said, "Wait!"

"I haven't done anything!" cried the old man, trembling.

"No one said you did."

They had sat in the green soft light without saying a word for a moment and then Montag talked about the weather and then the old man responded with a pale voice. It was a strange quiet meeting. The old man admitted to being a retired English professor who had been thrown out upon the world forty years ago when the last liberal arts college shut for lack of students and patronage. His name was Faber, and when he finally lost his fear of Montag, he talked in a cadenced voice, looking at the sky and the trees and the green park, and when an hour had passed he said something to Montag and Montag sensed it was a rhymeless poem. Then the old man grew even more courageous and said something else and that was a poem, too. Faber held his hand over his left coat pocket and spoke these words gently, and Montag knew if he reached out, he might pull a book of poetry from the man's coat. But he did not reach out. His hands stayed on his knees, numbed and useless. "I don't talk *things*, sir," said Faber. "I talk the *meaning* of things. I sit here and *know* I'm alive."

That was all there was to it, really. An hour of monologue, a poem, a comment, and then without either acknowledging the fact that Montag was a fireman, Faber, with a certain trembling, wrote his address on a slip of paper. "For your file," he said, "in case you decide to be angry with me."

"I'm not angry," Montag said, surprised.

Mildred shrieked with laughter in the hall.

Montag went to his bedroom closet and flipped through his file-wallet to the heading: FUTURE INVESTIGATIONS (?). Faber's name was there. He hadn't turned it in and he hadn't erased it.

He dialed the call on a secondary phone. The phone on the far end of the line called Faber's name a dozen times before the professor answered in a faint voice. Montag identified himself and was met with a lengthy silence. "Yes, Mr. Montag?"

"Professor Faber, I have a rather odd question to ask. How many copies of the Bible are left in this country?"

"I don't know what you're talking about!"

"I want to know if there are *any* copies left at all."

"This is some sort of trap! I can't talk to just *anyone* on the phone!"

"How many copies of Shakespeare and Plato?"

"None! You know as well as I do. None!"

Faber hung up.

Montag put down the phone. None. A thing he knew of course from the firehouse listings. But somehow he had wanted to hear it from Faber himself.

In the hall Mildred's face was suffused with excitement. "Well, the ladies are coming over!"

Montag showed her a book. "This is the Old and New Testament, and . . ."

"Don't start that again!"

"It might be the last copy in this part of the world."

"You've got to hand it back tonight, don't you? Captain Beatty *knows* you got it, doesn't he?"

"I don't think he knows *which* book I stole. But how do I choose a substitute? Do I turn in Mr. Jefferson? Mr. Thoreau? Which is least valuable? If I pick a substitute and Beatty does know which book I stole, he'll guess we've an entire library here!"

Mildred's mouth twitched. "See what you're *doing*? You'll ruin us! Who's more important, me or that Bible?" She was beginning to shriek now, sitting there like a wax doll melting in its own heat.

He could hear Beatty's voice. "Sit down, Montag. Watch. Delicately, like the petals of a flower. Light the first page, light the second page. Each becomes a black butterfly. Beautiful, eh? Light the third page, from the second and so on, chain-smoking, chapter by chapter, all the silly things the words mean, all the false promises, all the secondhand notions and time-worn philosophies." There sat Beatty, perspiring gently, the floor littered with swarms of black moths that had died in a single storm.

Mildred stopped screaming as quickly as she started. Montag was not listening. "There's only one thing to do," he said. "Some time before tonight when I give the book to Beatty, I've got to have a duplicate made."

"You'll be here for the White Clown tonight, and the ladies coming over?" cried Mildred.

Montag stopped at the door, with his back turned. "Millie?"

A silence. "What?"

"Millie? Does the White Clown love you?"

No answer.

"Millie, does"—he licked his lips—"does your 'family' love you, love you *very* much, love you with all their heart and soul, Millie?"

He felt her blinking slowly at the back of his neck. "Why'd you ask a silly question like that?"

He felt he wanted to cry, but nothing would happen to his eyes or his mouth.

"If you see that dog outside," said Mildred, "give him a kick for me."

He hesitated, listening at the door. He opened it and stepped out.

The rain had stopped and the sun was setting in the clear sky. The street and the lawn and the porch were empty. He let his breath go in a great sigh.

He slammed the door.

He was on the subway.

I'm numb, he thought. When did the numbness really begin in my face? In my body? The night I kicked the pill bottle in the dark, like kicking a buried mine.

The numbness will go away, he thought. It'll take time, but I'll do it, or Faber will do it for me. Someone somewhere will give me back the old face and the old hands the way they were. Even the smile, he thought, the old burnt-in smile, that's gone. I'm lost without it.

The subway fled past him, cream-tile, jet-black, cream-tile, jet-black, numerals and darkness, more darkness and the total adding itself.

Once as a child he had sat upon a yellow dune by the sea in the middle of the blue and hot summer day, trying to fill a sieve with sand, because some cruel cousin had said, "Fill this sieve and you'll get a dime!" And the faster he poured, the faster it sifted through with a hot whispering. His hands were tired, the sand was boiling, the sieve was empty. Seated there in the midst of July, without a sound, he felt the tears move down his cheeks.

Now as the vacuum-underground rushed him through the dead cellars of town, jolting him, he remembered the terrible logic of that sieve, and he looked down and saw that he was carrying the Bible open. There were people in the suction train but he held the book in his hands and the silly thought came to him, if you read fast and read all, maybe some of the sand will stay in the sieve. But he read and the worlds fell through, and he thought, in a few hours, there will be Beatty, and here will be me handing this over, so no phrase must escape me, each line must be memorized. I will myself to do it.

He clenched the book in his fists.

Trumpets blared.

"Denham's Dentifrice."

Shut up, thought Montag. Consider the lilies of the field.

"Denham's Dentifrice."

They toil not—

"Denham's—"

Consider the lilies of the field, shut up, shut up.

"Dentifrice!"

He ̄tore the book open and flicked the pages and felt of them as if he were blind, he picked at the shape of the individual letters, not blinking.

"Denham's. Spelled: D-E-N—"

They toil not, neither do they . . .

A fierce whisper of hot sand through empty sieve.

"Denham's does it!"

Consider the lilies, the lilies, the lilies . . .

"Denham's dental detergent."

"Shut up, shut up, shut up!" It was a plea, a cry so terrible that Montag found himself on his feet, the shocked inhabitants of the loud car staring, moving back from this man with the insane, gorged face, the gibbering, dry mouth, the flapping book in his fist. The people who had been sitting a moment before, tapping their feet to the rhythm of Denham's Dentifrice, Denham's Dandy Dental Detergent, Denham's Dentifrice Dentifrice Dentifrice, one two, one two three, one two, one two three. The people whose mouths had been faintly twitching the words Dentifrice Dentifrice Dentifrice. The train radio vomited upon Montag, in retaliation, a great tonload of music made of tin, copper, silver, chromium, and brass. The people were pounded into submission; they did not run, there was no place to run; the great air train fell down its shaft in the earth.

"Lilies of the field."

"Denham's."

"*Lilies,* I said!"

The people stared.

"Call the guard."

"The man's off—"

"Knoll View!"

The train hissed to its stop.

"Knoll View!" A cry.

"Denham's." A whisper.

Montag's mouth barely moved. "Lilies . . ."

The train door whistled open. Montag stood. The door gasped, started shut. Only then did he leap past the other passengers, screaming in his mind, plunge through the slicing door only in time. He ran on the white tiles up through the tunnels, ignoring the escalators, because he wanted to feel his feet move, arms swing, lungs clench, unclench, feel his throat go raw with air. A voice drifted after him, "Denham's Denham's Denham's," the train hissed like a snake. The train vanished in its hole.

"Who is it?"

"Montag out here."

"What do you want?"

"Let me in."

"I haven't done anything!"

"I'm alone, dammit!"

"You swear it?"

"I swear!"

The front door opened slowly. Faber peered out, looking very old in the light and very fragile and very much afraid. The old man looked as if he had not been out of the house in years. He and the white plaster walls inside were much the same. There was white in the flesh of his mouth and his cheeks and his hair was white and his eyes had faded, with white in the vague blueness there. Then his eyes touched on the book under Montag's arm and he did not look so old any more and not quite as fragile. Slowly, his fear went.

"I'm sorry. One has to be careful."

He looked at the book under Montag's arm and could not stop. "So it's true."

Montag stepped inside. The door shut.

"Sit down." Faber backed up, as if he feared the book might vanish if he took his eyes from it. Behind him, the door to a bedroom stood open, and in that room a litter of machinery and steel tools were strewn upon a desktop. Montag had only a glimpse, before Faber, seeing Montag's attention diverted, turned quickly and shut the bedroom door and stood holding the knob with a trembling hand. His gaze returned unsteadily to Montag, who was now seated with the book in his lap. "The book—where did you—?"

"I stole it."

Faber, for the first time, raised his eyes and looked directly into Montag's face. "You're brave."

"No," said Montag. "My wife's dying. A friend of mine's already dead. Someone who may have been a friend was burnt less than twenty-four hours ago. You're the only one I knew might help me. To see. To see . . ."

Faber's hands itched on his knees. "May I?"

"Sorry." Montag gave him the book.

"It's been a long time. I'm not a religious man. But it's been a long time." Faber turned the pages, stopping here and there to read. "It's as good as I remember. Lord, how they've changed it in our 'parlors' these days. Christ is one of the 'family' now. I often wonder if God recognizes His own son the way we've dressed him up, or is it dressed him down? He's a regular peppermint stick now, all sugar-crystal and saccharine when he isn't making veiled references to certain commercial products that every wor- shiper *absolutely* needs." Faber sniffed the book. "Do you know that books smell like nutmeg or some spice from a foreign land? I loved to smell them when I was a boy. Lord, there were a lot of lovely books once, before we let them go." Faber turned the pages. "Mr. Montag, you are looking at a coward. I saw the way things were going, a long time back. I said nothing. I'm one of the innocents who could have spoken up and out when no one would listen to the 'guilty,' but I did not speak and thus became guilty myself. And when finally they set the structure to burn the books, using the firemen, I grunted a few times and subsided, for there were no others grunting or yelling with me, by then. Now, it's too late." Faber closed the Bible. "Well—suppose you tell me why you came here?"

"Nobody listens any more. I can't talk to the walls because they're yelling at *me*. I can't talk to my wife; she listens to the *walls*. I just want someone to hear what I have to say. And maybe if I talk long enough, it'll make sense. And I want you to teach me to understand what I read."

Faber examined Montag's thin, blue-jowled face. "How did you get shaken up? What knocked the torch out of your hands?"

"I don't know. We have everything we need to be happy, but we aren't happy. Something's missing. I looked around. The only thing I positively *knew* was gone was the books I'd burned in ten or twelve years. So I thought books might help."

"You're a hopeless romantic," said Faber. "It would be funny if it were not serious. It's not books you need, it's some of the things that once were in books. The same things *could* be in the 'parlor families' today. The same infinite detail and awareness could be projected through the radios and televisors, but are not. No, no, it's not books at all you're looking for! Take it where you can find it, in old phonograph records, old motion pictures, and in old friends; look for it in nature and look for it in yourself. Books were only one type of receptacle where we stored a lot of things we were afraid we might forget. There is nothing magical in them, at all. The magic is only in what books say, how they stitched the patches of the universe together into one garment for us. Of course you couldn't know this, of course you still can't understand what I mean when I say all this. You are intuitively right, that's what counts. Three things are missing.

"Number one: Do you know why books such as this are so important? Because they have quality. And what does the word quality mean? To me it means texture. This book has *pores*. It has features. This book can go under the microscope. You'd find life under the glass, streaming past in infinite profusion. The more pores, the more truthfully recorded details of life per square inch you can get on a sheet of paper, the more 'literary' you are. That's *my* definition, anyway. *Telling detail. Fresh* detail. The good writers touch life often. The mediocre ones run a quick hand over her. The bad ones rape her and leave her for the flies.

"So now do you see why books are hated and feared? They show the pores in the face of life. The comfortable people want only wax moon faces, poreless, hairless, expressionless. We are living in a time when flowers are trying to live on flowers, instead of growing on good rain and black loam. Even fireworks, for all their prettiness, come from the chemistry of the earth. Yet somehow we think we can grow, feeding on flowers and fireworks, without completing the cycle back to reality. Do you know the legend of Hercules and Antaeus, the giant wrestler, whose strength was incredible so long as he stood firmly on the earth? But when he was held, rootless, in midair, by Hercules, he perished easily. If there isn't something in that legend for us today, in this city, in our time, then I am completely insane. Well, there we have the first thing I said we needed. Quality, texture of information."

"And the second?"

"Leisure."

"Oh, but we've plenty of off hours."

"Off hours, yes. But time to think? If you're not driving a hundred miles an hour, at a clip where you can't think of anything else but the danger, then you're playing some game or sitting in some room where you can't argue with the four-wall televisor. Why? The televisor is 'real.' It is immediate, it has dimension. It tells you what to think and blasts it in. It *must* be right. It *seems* so right. It rushes you on so quickly to its own conclusions your mind hasn't time to protest, 'What nonsense!'"

"Only the 'family' is 'people.'"

"I beg pardon?"

"My wife says books aren't 'real.'"

"Thank God for that. You can shut them, say, 'Hold on a moment.' You play God to it. But who has ever torn himself from the claw that encloses you when you drop a seed in a TV parlor? It grows you any shape it wishes! It is an environment as real as the world. It *becomes* and *is* the truth. Books can be beaten down with reason. But with all my knowledge and skepticism, I have never been able to argue with a one-hundred-piece symphony orchestra, full color, three dimensions, and being in and part of those incredible parlors. As you see, my parlor is nothing but four plaster walls. And here." He held out two small rubber plugs. "For my ears when I ride the subway jets."

"Denham's Dentifrice; they toil not, neither do they spin," said Montag, eyes shut. "Where do we go from here? Would books help us?"

"Only if the third necessary thing could be given us. Number one, as I said, quality of information. Number two: leisure to digest it. And number three: the right to carry out actions based on what we learn from the interaction of the first two. And I hardly think a very old man and a fireman turned sour could *do* much this late in the game. . . ."

"I can *get* books."

"You're running a risk."

"That's the good part of dying; when you've nothing to lose, you run any risk you want."

"There, you've said an interesting thing," laughed Faber, "without having read it!"

"Are things like *that* in books? But it came off the top of my mind!"

"All the better. You didn't fancy it up for me or anyone, even yourself."

Montag leaned forward. "This afternoon I thought that if it turned out that books *were* worthwhile, we might get a press and print some extra copies—"

"We?"

"You and I."

"Oh, no!" Faber sat up.

"But let me tell you my plan—"

"If you insist on telling me, I must ask you to leave."

"But aren't *you* interested?"

"Not if you start talking the sort of talk that might get me burnt for my trouble. The only way I could *possibly* listen to you would be if somehow the fireman structure itself could be burnt. Now if you suggest that we print extra books and arrange to have them hidden in firemen's houses all over the country, so that seeds of suspicion would be sown among these arsonists, bravo, I'd say!"

"Plant the books, turn in an alarm, and see the firemen's houses burn, is that what you mean?"

Faber raised his brows and looked at Montag as if he were seeing a new man. "I was joking."

"If you thought it would be a plan worth trying, I'd have to take your word it would help."

"You can't guarantee things like that! After all, when we *had* all the books we needed, we still insisted on finding the highest cliff to jump off. But we *do* need a breather. We *do* need knowledge. And perhaps in a thousand years we might pick smaller cliffs to jump off. The books are to remind us what asses and fools we are. They're Caesar's praetorian guard, whispering as the parade roars down the avenue, 'Remember, Caesar, thou art mortal.' Most of us can't rush around, talk to everyone, know all the cities of the world, we haven't time, money or that many friends. The things you're looking for, Montag, are in the world, but the only way the average chap will ever see ninety-nine percent of them is in a book. Don't ask for guarantees. And don't look to be saved in any *one* thing, person, machine, or library. Do your own bit of saving, and if you drown, at least die knowing you were headed for shore."

Faber got up and began to pace the room.

"Well?" asked Montag.

"You're absolutely serious?"

"Absolutely."

"It's an insidious plan, if I do say so myself." Faber glanced nervously at his bedroom door. "To see the firehouses burn across the land, destroyed as hotbeds of treason. The salamander devours his tail! Ho, God!"

"I've a list of firemen's residences everywhere. With some sort of underground—"

"Can't trust people, that's the dirty part. You and I and who else will set the fires?"

"Aren't there professors like yourself, former writers, historians, linguists . . . ?"

"Dead or ancient?"

"The older the better; they'll go unnoticed. You know dozens, admit it!"

"Oh, there are many actors alone who haven't acted Pirandello or Shaw or Shakespeare for years because their plays are too *aware* of the world. We could use their anger. And we could use the honest rage of those historians who haven't written a line for forty years. True, we might form classes in thinking and reading."

"Yes!"

"But that would just nibble the edges. The whole culture's shot through. The skeleton needs melting and reshaping. Good God, it isn't as simple as just picking up a book you laid down half a century ago. Remember, the firemen are rarely necessary. The public itself stopped reading of its own accord. You firemen provide a circus now and then at which buildings are set off and crowds gather for the pretty blaze, but it's a small sideshow indeed, and hardly necessary to keep things in line. So few want to be rebels anymore. And out of those few, most, like myself, scare easily. Can you dance faster than the White Clown, shout louder than 'Mr. Gimmick' and the parlor 'families'? If you can, you'll win your way, Montag. In any event, you're a fool. People are having *fun*."

"Committing suicide! Murdering!"

A bomber fight had been moving east all the time they talked, and only now did the two men stop and listen, feeling the great jet sound tremble inside themselves.

"Patience, Montag. Let the war turn off the 'families.' Our civilization is flinging itself to pieces. Stand back from the centrifuge."

"There has to be someone ready when it blows up."

"What? Men quoting Milton? Saying, I remember Sophocles? Reminding the survivors that man has his good side, too? They will only gather up their stones to hurl at each other. Montag, go home. Go to bed. Why waste your final hours racing about your cage denying you're a squirrel?"

"Then you don't care any more?"

"I care so much I'm sick."

"And you won't help me?"

"Good night, good night."

Montag's hands picked up the Bible. He saw what his hands had done and he looked surprised.

"Would you like to own this?"

Faber said, "I'd give my right arm."

Montag stood there and waited for the next thing to happen. His hands, by themselves, like two men working together, began to rip the pages from the book. The hands tore the flyleaf and then the first and then the second page.

"Idiot, what're you doing!" Faber sprang up, as if he had been struck. He fell against Montag. Montag warded him off and let his hands continue. Six more pages fell to the floor. He picked them up and wadded the paper under Faber's gaze.

"Don't, oh, don't!" said the old man.

"Who can stop me? I'm a fireman. I can burn you!"

The old man stood looking at him. "You wouldn't."

"I could!"

"The book. Don't tear it any more." Faber sank into a chair, his face very white, his mouth trembling. "Don't make me feel any more tired. What do you want?"

"I need you to teach me."

"All right, all right."

Montag put the book down. He began to unwad the crumpled paper and flatten it out as the old man watched tiredly.

Faber shook his head as if he were waking up.

"Montag, have you any money?"

"Some. Four, five hundred dollars. Why?"

"Bring it. I know a man who printed our college paper half a century ago. That was the year I came to class at the start of the new semester and found only one student to sign up for Drama from Aeschylus to O'Neill. You see? How like a beautiful statue of ice it was, melting in the sun. I remember the newspapers dying like huge moths. No one *wanted* them back. No one missed them. And then the Government, seeing how advantageous it was to have people reading only about passionate lips and the fist in the stomach, circled the situation with your fire-eaters. So, Montag, there's this unemployed printer. We might start a few books, and wait on the war to break the pattern and give us the push we need. A few bombs and the 'families' in the walls of all the houses, like harlequin rats, will shut up! In the silence, our stage whisper might carry."

They both stood looking at the book on the table.

"I've tried to remember," said Montag. "But, hell, it's gone when I turn my head. God, how I want something to say to the Captain. He's read enough so he has all the answers, or seems to have. His voice is like butter. I'm afraid he'll talk me back the way I was. Only a week ago, pumping a kerosene hose, I thought: God, what fun!"

The old man nodded. "Those who don't build must burn. It's as old as history and juvenile delinquents."

"So that's what I am."

"There's some of it in all of us."

Montag moved toward the front door. "Can you help me in any way tonight, with the Fire Captain? I need an umbrella to keep off the rain. I'm so damned afraid I'll drown if he gets me again."

The old man said nothing, but glanced once more, nervously, at his bedroom. Montag caught the glance. "Well?"

The old man took a deep breath, held it, and let it out. He took another, eyes closed, his mouth tight, and at last exhaled. "Montag. . . ."

The old man turned at last and said, "Come along. I would actually have let you walk right out of my house. I *am* a cowardly old fool."

Faber opened the bedroom door and led Montag into a small chamber where stood a table upon which a number of metal tools lay among a welter of microscopic wire hairs, tiny coils, bobbins and crystals.

"What's this?" asked Montag.

"Proof of my terrible cowardice. I've lived alone so many years, throwing images on walls with my imagination. Fiddling with electronics, radio transmission, has been my hobby. My cowardice is of such a passion, complementing the revolutionary spirit that lives in its shadow, I was forced to design *this*."

He picked up a small green metal object no larger than a .22 bullet.

"I paid for all this—how? Playing the stock market, of course, the last refuge in the world for the dangerous intellectual out of a job. Well, I played the market and built all this and I've waited. I've waited, trembling, half a lifetime for someone to speak to me. I dared speak to no one. That day in the park when we sat together, I knew that some day you might drop by, with fire or friendship, it was hard to guess. I've had this little item ready for months. But I almost let you go, I'm *that* afraid!"

"It looks like a Seashell Radio."

"And something more! It *listens!* If you put it in your ear, Montag, I can sit comfortably home, warming my frightened bones, and hear and analyze the firemen's world, find its weaknesses, without danger. I'm the Queen Bee, safe in the hive. You will be the drone, the traveling ear. Eventually, I could put out ears into all parts of the city, with various men, listening and evaluating. If the drones die, I'm still safe at home, tending my fright with a maximum of comfort and a minimum of chance. See how safe I play it, how contemptible I am?"

Montag placed the green bullet in his ear. The old man inserted a similar object in his own ear and moved his lips.

"Montag!"

The voice was in Montag's head.

"I *hear* you!"

The old man laughed. "You're coming over fine, too!" Faber whispered, but the voice in Montag's head was clear. "Go to the firehouse when it's time. I'll be with you. Let's listen to this Captain Beatty together. He could be one of us. God knows. I'll give you things to say. We'll give him a good show. Do you hate me for this electronic cowardice of mine? Here I am sending you out into the night, while I stay behind the lines with my damned ears listening for you to get your head chopped off."

"We all do what we do," said Montag. He put the Bible in the old man's hands. "Here. I'll chance turning in a substitute. Tomorrow—"

"I'll see the unemployed printer, yes; *that* much I can do."

"Good night, Professor."

"Not good night. I'll be with you the rest of the night, a vinegar gnat tickling your ear when you need me. But good night and good luck, anyway."

The door opened and shut. Montag was in the dark street again, looking at the world.

You could feel the war getting ready in the sky that night. The way the clouds moved aside and came back, and the way the stars looked, a million of them swimming between the clouds, like the enemy disks, and the feeling that the sky might fall upon the city and turn it to chalk dust, and the moon go up in red fire; that was how the night felt.

Montag walked from the subway with the money in his pocket (he had visited the bank which was open all night every night with robot tellers in attendance) and as he walked he was listening to the Seashell Radio in one ear. . . . "We have mobilized a million men. Quick victory is ours if the war comes. . . ." Music flooded over the voice quickly and it was gone.

"Ten million men mobilized," Faber's voice whispered in his other ear. "But *say* one million. It's happier."

"Faber?"

"Yes?"

"I'm not thinking. I'm just doing like I'm told, like always. You said get the money and I got it. I didn't really think of it myself. When do I start working things out on my own?"

"You've started already, by saying what you just said. You'll have to take me on faith."

"I took the others on faith!"

"Yes, and look where we're headed. You'll have to travel blind for awhile. Here's my arm to hold onto."

"I don't want to change sides and just be *told* what to do. There's no reason to change if I do that."

"You're wise already!"

Montag felt his feet moving him on the sidewalk toward his house. "Keep talking."

"Would you like me to read? I'll read so you can remember. I go to bed only five hours a night. Nothing to do. So if you like, I'll read you to sleep nights. They say you retain knowledge even when you're sleeping, if someone whispers it in your ear."

"Yes."

"Here." Far away across town in the night, the faintest whisper of a turned page. "The Book of Job."

The moon rose in the sky as Montag walked, his lips moving just a trifle.

He was eating a light supper at nine in the evening when the front door cried out in the hall and Mildred ran from the parlor like a native fleeing an eruption of Vesuvius. Mrs. Phelps and Mrs. Bowles came through the front door and vanished into the volcano's mouth with martinis in their hands. Montag stopped eating. They were like a monstrous crystal chandelier tinkling in a thousand chimes, he saw their Cheshire cat smiles burning through the walls of the house, and now they were screaming at each other above the din.

Montag found himself at the parlor door with his food still in his mouth.

"Doesn't everyone look nice!"

"Nice."

"You look fine, Millie!"

"Fine."

"Everyone looks swell."

"Swell!"

Montag stood watching them.

"Patience," whispered Faber.

"I shouldn't be here," whispered Montag, almost to himself. "I should be on my way back to you with the money!"

"Tomorrow's time enough. Careful!"

"Isn't this show *wonderful?*" cried Mildred.

"Wonderful!"

On one wall a woman smiled and drank orange juice simultaneously. How does she do both at once, thought Montag, insanely. In the other walls an X ray of the same woman revealed the contracting journey of the refreshing beverage on its way to her delighted stomach! Abruptly the room took off on a rocket flight into the clouds; it plunged into a lime-green sea where blue fish ate red and yellow fish. A minute later, three White Cartoon Clowns chopped off each other's limbs to the accompaniment of immense incoming tides of laughter. Two minutes more and the room whipped out of town to the jet cars wildly circling an arena, bashing and backing up and bashing each other again. Montag saw a number of bodies fly in the air.

"Millie, did you *see* that?"

"I saw it, I *saw* it!"

Montag reached inside the parlor wall and pulled the main switch. The images drained away, as if the water had been let from a gigantic crystal bowl of hysterical fish.

The three women turned slowly and looked with unconcealed irritation and then dislike at Montag.

"When do you suppose the war will start?" he said. "I notice your husbands aren't here tonight."

"Oh, they come and go, come and go," said Mrs. Phelps. "In again out again Finnegan, the Army called Pete yesterday. He'll be back next week. The Army said so. Quick war. Forty-eight hours they said, and everyone home. That's what the Army said.

Quick war. Pete was called yesterday and they said he'd be back next week. Quick. . . ."

The three women fidgeted and looked nervously at the empty mud-colored walls.

"I'm not worried," said Mrs. Phelps. "I'll let Pete do all the worrying." She giggled. "I'll let old Pete do all the worrying. Not me. I'm not worried."

"It's always someone else's husband dies, they say."

"I've heard that, too. I've never known any dead man killed in a war. Killed jumping off buildings, yes, like Gloria's husband last week, but from wars? No."

"Not from wars," said Mrs. Phelps. "Anyway, Pete and I always said, no tears, nothing like that. It's our third marriage each and we're independent. Be independent, we always said. He said, if I get killed off, you just go right ahead and don't cry, but get married again, and don't think of me."

"That reminds me," said Mildred. "Did you see that Clara Dove five-minute romance last night in your wall? Well, it was all about this woman who—"

Montag said nothing but stood looking at the women's faces as he had once looked at the face of saints in a strange church he had entered when he was a child. The faces of those enameled creatures meant nothing to him, though he talked to them and stood in that church for a long time, trying to be of that religion, trying to know what that religion was, trying to get enough of the raw incense and special dust of the place into his lungs and thus into his blood to feel touched and concerned by the meaning of the colorful men and women with the porcelain eyes and the blood-ruby lips. But there was nothing, nothing; it was a stroll through another store, and his currency strange and unusable there, and his passion cold, even when he touched the wood and plaster and clay. So it was now, in his own parlor, with these women twisting in their chairs under his gaze, lighting cigarettes, blowing smoke, touching their sun-fired hair and examining their blazing fingernails as if they had caught fire from his look. Their faces grew haunted with silence. They leaned forward at the sound of Montag's swallowing his final bite of food. They listened to his feverish breathing. The three empty walls of the room were like the pale brows of sleeping giants now, empty of dreams. Montag felt that if you touched these three staring brows, you would feel a fine salt sweat on your fingertips. The perspiration gathered with the silence and the subaudible trembling around and about and in the women who were burning with tension. Any moment they might hiss a long sputtering hiss and explode.

Montag moved his lips.

"Let's talk."

The women jerked and stared.

"How're your children, Mrs. Phelps?" he asked.

"You know I haven't any! No one in his right mind, the Good Lord knows, would have children!" said Mrs. Phelps, not quite sure why she was angry with this man.

"I wouldn't say that," said Mrs. Bowles. "I've had *two* children by Caesarean section. No use going through all that agony for a baby. The world must reproduce, you know, the race must go on. Besides, they sometimes look just like you, and that's nice. Two Caesareans turned the trick, yes, sir. Oh, my doctor said, Caesareans aren't necessary; you've got the hips for it, everything's normal, but I *insisted*."

"Caesareans or not, children are ruinous; you're out of your mind," said Mrs. Phelps.

"I plunk the children in school nine days out of ten. I put up with them when they come home three days a month; it's not bad at all. You heave them into the 'parlor' and turn the switch. It's like washing clothes; stuff laundry in and slam the lid." Mrs. Bowles tittered. "They'd just as soon kick as kiss me. Thank God, I can kick back!"

The women showed their tongues, laughing.

Mildred sat a moment and then, seeing that Montag was still in the doorway, clapped her hands. "Let's talk politics, to please Guy!"

"Sounds fine," said Mrs. Bowles. "I voted last election, same as everyone, and I laid it on the line for President Noble. I think he's one of the nicest looking men ever became president."

"Oh, but the man they ran against him!"

"He wasn't much, was he? Kind of small and homely and he didn't shave too close or comb his hair very well."

"What possessed the 'Outs' to run him? You just don't go running a little short man like that against a tall man. Besides— he mumbled. Half the time I couldn't hear a word he said. And the words I *did* hear I didn't understand!"

"Fat, too, and didn't dress to hide it. No wonder the land-slide was for Winston Noble. Even their names helped. Compare Winston Noble to Hubert Hoag for ten seconds and you can almost figure the results."

"Damn it!" cried Montag. "What do you know about Hoag and Noble!"

"Why, they were right in that parlor wall, not six months ago. One was always picking his nose; it drove me wild."

"Well, Mr. Montag," said Mrs. Phelps, "do you want us to vote for a man like that?"

Mildred beamed. "You just run away from the door, Guy, and don't make us nervous."

But Montag was gone and back in a moment with a book in his hand.

"Guy!"

"Damn it all, damn it all, damn it!"

"What've you got there; isn't that a book? I thought that all special training these days was done by film." Mrs. Phelps blinked. "You reading up on fireman theory?"

"Theory, hell," said Montag. "It's poetry."

"Montag." A whisper.

"Leave me alone!" Montag felt himself turning in a great circling roar and buzz and hum.

"Montag, hold on, don't . . ."

"Did you *hear* them, did you hear these monsters talking about monsters? Oh God, the way they jabber about people and their own children and themselves and the way they talk about their husbands and the way they talk about war, dammit, I stand here and I can't believe it!"

"I didn't say a single word about *any* war, I'll have you know," said Mrs. Phelps.

"As for poetry, I hate it," said Mrs. Bowles.

"Have you ever heard any?"

"Montag," Faber's voice scraped away at him. "You'll ruin everything. Shut up, you fool!"

All three women were on their feet.

"Sit down!"

They sat.

"I'm going home," quavered Mrs. Bowles.

"Montag, Montag, please, in the name of God, what're you up to?" pleaded Faber.

"Why don't you just read us one of those poems from your little book." Mrs. Phelps nodded. "I think that'd be very interesting."

"That's not right," wailed Mrs. Bowles. "We can't do that!"

"Well, look at Mr. Montag, he wants to, I know he does. And if we listen nice, Mr. Montag will be happy and then maybe we can go on and do something else." She glanced nervously at the long emptiness of the walls enclosing them.

"Montag, go through with this and I'll cut off, I'll leave." The beetle jabbed his ear. "What good is this, what'll you prove!"

"Scare hell out of them, that's what, scare the living daylights out!"

Mildred looked at the empty air. "Now, Guy, just *who* are you talking to?"

A silver needle pierced his brain. "Montag, listen, only one way out, play it as a joke, cover up, pretend you aren't mad at all. Then—walk to your wall incinerator, and throw the book in!"

Mildred had already anticipated this in a quavery voice. "Ladies, once a year, every fireman's allowed to bring one book home, from the old days, to show his family how silly it all was, how nervous that sort of thing can make you, how crazy. Guy's surprise tonight is to read you one sample to show how mixed up things were, so none of us will ever have to bother our little old heads about that junk again, isn't that *right*, darling?"

He crushed the book in his fists.

"Say 'yes'."

His mouth moved like Faber's:

"Yes."

Mildred snatched the book with a laugh. "Here! Read this one. No, I take it back. Here's that real funny one you read out loud today. Ladies, you won't understand a word. It goes umpty-tumpty-ump. Go ahead, Guy, that page, dear."

He looked at the opened page.

A fly stirred its wings softly in his ear. "Read."

"What's the title, dear?"

"*Dover Beach.*" His mouth was numb.

"Now read in a nice clear voice and go *slow.*"

The room was blazing hot, he was all fire, he was all coldness; they sat in the middle of an empty desert with three chairs and him standing, swaying, and him waiting for Mrs. Phelps to stop straightening her dress hem and Mrs. Bowles to take her fingers away from her hair. Then he began to read in a low, stumbling voice that grew firmer as he progressed from line to line, and his voice went out across the desert, into the whiteness, and around the three sitting women there in the great hot emptiness.

The Sea of Faith

Was once, too, at the full, and round earth's shore
Lay like the folds of a bright girdle furled.
But now I only hear
Its melancholy, long, withdrawing roar,
Retreating, to the breath
Of the night-wind, down the vast edges drear
And naked shingles of the world.

The chairs creaked under the three women.

Montag finished it out:

Ah, love, let us be true
To one another! for the world, which seems
To lie before us like a land of dreams,
So various, so beautiful, so new,
Hath really neither joy, nor love, nor light,

Nor certitude, nor peace, nor help for pain;
And we are here as on a darkling plain
Swept with confused alarms of struggle and flight,
Where ignorant armies clash by night.

Mrs. Phelps was crying.

The others in the middle of the desert watched her crying grow very loud as her face squeezed itself out of shape. They sat, not touching her, bewildered with her display. She sobbed uncontrollably. Montag himself was stunned and shaken.

"Sh, sh," said Mildred. "You're all right, Clara, now, Clara, snap out of it! Clara, what's *wrong?*"

"I—I," sobbed Mrs. Phelps, "don't know, don't know, I just don't know, oh, oh. . . ."

Mrs. Bowles stood up and glared at Montag. "You see? I knew it, that's what I wanted to prove! I knew it would happen! I've always said, poetry and tears, poetry and suicide and crying and awful feelings, poetry and sickness; *all* that mush! Now I've had it proved to me. You're nasty, Mr. Montag, you're *nasty!*"

Faber said, "Now . . ."

Montag felt himself turn and walk to the wall slot and drop the book in through the brass notch to the waiting flames.

"Silly words, silly words, silly awful hurting words," said Mrs. Bowles. "Why *do* people want to hurt people? Not enough hurt in the world, you got to tease people with stuff like that!"

"Clara, now, Clara," begged Mildred, pulling her arm. "Come on, let's be cheery, you turn the 'family' on, now. Go ahead. Let's laugh and be happy, now, stop crying, we'll have a party!"

"No," said Mrs. Bowles. "I'm trotting right straight home. You want to visit my house and my 'family,' well and good. But I won't come in this fireman's crazy house again in my lifetime!"

"Go home." Montag fixed his eyes upon her, quietly. "Go home and think of your first husband divorced and your second husband killed in a jet and your third husband blowing his brains out, go home and think of the dozen abortions you've had, go home and think of that and your damn Caesarean sections, too, and your children who hate your guts! Go home and think how it all happened and what did you ever do to stop it? Go home, go home!" he yelled. "Before I knock you down and kick you out the door!"

Doors slammed and the house was empty. Montag stood alone in the winter weather, with the parlor walls the color of dirty snow.

In the bathroom, water ran. He heard Mildred shake the sleeping tablets into her hand.

"Fool, Montag, fool, fool, oh God you silly fool. . . ."

"Shut up!" He pulled the green bullet from his ear and jammed it into his pocket.

It sizzled faintly, ". . . fool . . . fool. . . ."

He searched the house and found the books where Mildred had stacked them behind the refrigerator. Some were missing and he knew that she had started on her own slow process of dispersing the dynamite in her house, stick by stick. But he was not angry now, only exhausted and bewildered with himself. He carried the books into the backyard and hid them in the bushes near the alley fence. For tonight only, he thought, in case she decides to do any more burning.

He went back through the house. "Mildred?" He called at the door of the darkened bedroom. There was no sound.

Outside, crossing the lawn, on his way to work, he tried not to see how completely dark and deserted Clarisse McClellan's house was. . . .

On the way downtown he was so completely alone with his terrible error that he felt the necessity for the strange warmness and goodness that came from a familiar and gentle voice speaking in the night. Already, in a few short hours, it seemed that he had known Faber for a lifetime. Now, he knew that he was two people, that he was, above all, Montag who knew nothing, who did not even know himself a fool, but only suspected it. And he knew that he was also the old man who talked to him and talked to him as the train was sucked from one end of the night city to the other on one long sickening gasp of motion. In the days to follow, and in the nights when there was no moon and in the nights when there was a very bright moon shining on the earth, the old man would go on with this talking and this talking, drop by drop, stone by stone, flake by flake. His mind would well over at last and he would not be Montag any more, this the old man told him, assured him, promised him. He would be Montag-plus-Faber, fire plus water, and then, one day, after everything had mixed and simmered and worked away in silence, there would be neither fire nor water, but wine. Out of two separate and opposite things, a third. And one day he would look back upon the fool and know the fool. Even now he could feel the start of the long journey, the leave taking, the going away from the self he had been.

It was good listening to the beetle hum, the sleepy mosquito buzz and delicate filigree murmur of the old man's voice at first scolding him and then consoling him in the late hour of night as he emerged from the steaming subway toward the firehouse world.

"Pity, Montag, pity. Don't haggle and nag them; you were so recently *of* them yourself. They are so confident that they will run on forever. But they won't run on. They don't know that this is all one huge big blazing meteor that makes a pretty fire in space, but that some day it'll have to *hit*. They see only the blaze, the pretty fire, as you saw it.

"Montag, old men who stay at home, afraid, tending their peanut-brittle bones, have no right to criticize. Yet you almost killed things at the start. Watch it! I'm with you, remember that. I understand how it happened. I must admit that your blind raging invigorated me. God, how young I felt! But now—I want you to feel old, I want a little of my cowardice to be distilled in you tonight. The next few hours, when you see Captain Beatty, tiptoe 'round him, let *me* hear him for you, let *me* feel the situation out. Survival is our ticket. Forget the poor, silly women...."

"I made them unhappier than they have been in years, I think," said Montag. "It shocked me to see Mrs. Phelps cry. Maybe they're right, maybe it's best not to face things, to run, have fun. I don't know. I feel guilty—"

"No, you mustn't! If there were no war, if there was peace in the world, I'd say fine, *have* fun! But, Montag, you mustn't go back to being just a fireman. All *isn't* well with the world."

Montag perspired.

"Montag, you listening?"

"My feet," said Montag. "I can't move them. I feel so damn silly. My feet won't move!"

"Listen. Easy now," said the old man gently. "I know, I know. You're afraid of making mistakes. *Don't* be. Mistakes can be profited by. Man, when I was younger I *shoved* my ignorance in people's faces. They beat me with sticks. By the time I was forty my blunt instrument had been honed to a fine cutting point for me. If you hide your ignorance, no one will hit you and you'll never learn. Now, pick up your feet, into the firehouse with you! We're twins, we're not alone any more, we're not separated out in different parlors, with no contact between. If you need help when Beatty pries at you, I'll be sitting right here in your eardrum making notes!"

Montag felt his right foot, then his left foot, move.

"Old man," he said, "stay *with* me."

The Mechanical Hound was gone. Its kennel was empty and the firehouse stood all about in plaster silence and the orange Salamander slept with its kerosene in its belly and the fire throwers crossed upon its flanks and Montag came in through the silence and touched the brass pole and slid up in the dark air, looking back at the deserted kennel, his heart beating, pausing, beating. Faber was a gray moth asleep in his ear, for the moment.

Beatty stood near the drop hole waiting, but with his back turned as if he were not waiting.

"Well," he said to the men playing cards, "here comes a very strange beast which in all tongues is called a fool."

He put his hand to one side, palm up, for a gift. Montag put the book in it. Without even glancing at the title, Beatty tossed the book in the trash basket and lit a cigarette. " 'Who are a little wise, the best fools be.' Welcome back, Montag. I hope you'll be staying with us, now that your fever is done and your sickness over. Sit in for a hand of poker?"

They sat and the cards were dealt. In Beatty's sight, Montag felt the guilt of his hands. His fingers were like ferrets that had done some evil and now never rested, always stirred and picked and hid in pockets, moving from under Beatty's alcohol-flame stare. If Beatty so much as breathed on them, Montag felt that his hands might wither, turn over on their sides, and never be shocked to life again; they would be buried the rest of his life in his coat sleeves, forgotten. For these were the hands that had acted on their own, no part of him, here was where the conscience first manifested itself to snatch books, dart off with Job and Ruth and Willie Shakespeare, and now, in the firehouse, these hands seemed gloved with blood.

Twice in half an hour, Montag had to rise from the game to go to the latrine to wash his hands. When he came back he hid his hands under the table.

Beatty laughed. "Let's have your hands in sight, Montag. Not that we don't trust you, understand, but—"

They all laughed.

"Well," said Beatty, "the crisis is past and all is well, the sheep returns to the fold. We're all sheep who have strayed at times. Truth is truth, to the end of reckoning, we've cried. They are never alone that are accompanied with noble thoughts, we've shouted to ourselves. 'Sweet food of sweetly uttered knowledge,' Sir Philip Sidney said. But on the other hand: 'Words are like leaves and where they most abound, Much fruit of sense beneath is rarely found.' Alexander Pope. What do you think of that, Montag?"

"I don't know."

"Careful," whispered Faber, living in another world, far away.

"Or this? 'A little learning is a dangerous thing. Drink deep, or taste not the Pierian spring; There shallow draughts intoxicate the brain, and drinking largely sobers us again.' Pope. Same essay. Where does that put you?"

Montag bit his lip.

"I'll tell you," said Beatty, smiling at his cards. "That made you for a little while a drunkard. Read a few lines and off you go over the cliff. Bang, you're ready to blow up the world, chop off heads, knock down women and children, destroy authority. I know, I've been through it all."

"I'm all right," said Montag, nervously.

"Stop blushing. I'm not needling, really I'm not. Do you know, I had a dream an hour ago. I lay down for a catnap and in this dream you and I, Montag, got into a furious debate on books. You towered with rage, yelled quotes at me. I calmly parried every thrust. 'Power,' I said. And you, quoting Dr. Johnson, said 'Knowledge is more than equivalent to force!' And I said, 'Well, Dr. Johnson also said, dear boy, that "He is no wise man that will quit a certainty for an uncertainty."' Stick with the firemen, Montag. All else is dreary chaos!"

"Don't listen," whispered Faber. "He's trying to confuse. He's slippery. Watch out!"

Beatty chuckled. "And you said, quoting, 'Truth will come to light, murder will not be hid long!' And I cried in good humor, 'Oh God, he speaks only of his horse!' And 'The Devil can cite Scripture for his purpose.' And you yelled, 'This age thinks better of a gilded fool, than of a threadbare saint in wisdom's school!' And I whispered gently, 'The dignity of truth is lost with much protesting.' And you screamed, 'Carcasses bleed at the sight of the murderer!' And I said, patting your hand, 'What, do I give you trench mouth?' And you shrieked, 'Knowledge is power!' and 'A dwarf on a giant's shoulders sees the furthest of the two!' and I summed my side up with rare serenity in, 'The folly of mistaking a metaphor for a proof, a torrent of verbiage for a spring of capital truths, and oneself as an oracle, is inborn in us, Mr. Valery once said.'"

Montag's head whirled sickeningly. He felt beaten unmercifully on brow, eyes, nose, lips, chin, on shoulders, on upflailing arms. He wanted to yell, "No! shut up, you're confusing things, stop it!" Beatty's graceful fingers thrust out to seize his wrist.

"God, what a pulse! I've got you going, have I, Montag? Jesus God, your pulse sounds like the day after the war. Everything but sirens and bells! Shall I talk some more? I like your look of panic. Swahili, Indian, English Lit., I speak them all. A kind of excellent dumb discourse, Willie!"

"Montag, hold on!" The moth brushed Montag's ear. "He's muddying the waters!"

"Oh, you were scared silly," said Beatty, "for I was doing a terrible thing in using the very books you clung to, to rebut you on every hand, on every point! What traitors books can be! you think they're backing you up, and they turn on you. Others can use them, too, and there you are, lost in the middle of the moor, in a great welter of nouns and verbs and adjectives. And at the very end of my dream, along I came with the Salamander and said, "Going my way?" And you got in and we drove back to the firehouse in beatific silence, all dwindled away to peace." Beatty let Montag's wrist go, let the hand slump limply on the table. "All's well that is well in the end."

Silence. Montag sat like a carved white stone. The echo of the final hammer on his skull died slowly away into the black cavern where Faber waited for the echoes to subside. And then when the startled dust had settled down about Montag's mind, Faber began, softly, "All right, he's had his say. You must take it in. I'll say my say, too, in the next few hours. And you'll take it in. And you'll try to judge them and make your decision as to which way to jump, or fall. But I want it to be your decision, not mine, and not the Captain's. But remember that the Captain belongs to the most dangerous enemy to truth and freedom, the solid unmoving cattle of the majority. Oh, God, the terrible tyranny of the majority. We all have our harps to play. And it's up to you now to know with which ear you'll listen."

Montag opened his mouth to answer Faber and was saved this error in the presence of others when the station bell rang.

The alarm voice in the ceiling chanted. There was a tacking-tacking sound as the alarm report telephone-typed out the address across the room. Captain Beatty, his poker cards in one pink hand, walked with exaggerated slowness to the phone and ripped out the address when the report was finished. He glanced perfunctorily at it, and shoved it in his pocket. He came back and sat down. The others looked at him.

"It can wait exactly forty seconds while I take all the money away from you," said Beatty, happily.

Montag put his cards down.

"Tired, Montag? Going out of this game?"

"Yes."

"Hold on. Well, come to think of it, we can finish this hand later. Just leave your cards face down and hustle the equipment. On the double now." And Beatty rose up again. "Montag, you don't look well? I'd hate to think you were coming down with another fever . . ."

"I'll be all right."

"You'll be fine. This is a special case. Come on, jump for it!"

They leaped into the air and clutched the brass pole as if it were the last vantage point above a tidal wave passing below, and then the brass pole, to their dismay, slid them down into darkness, into the blast and cough and suction of the gaseous dragon roaring to life!

"Hey!"

They rounded a corner in thunder and siren, with concussion of tires, with scream of rubber, with a shift of kerosene bulk in the glittery brass tank, like the food in the stomach of a giant, with Montag's fingers jolting off the silver rail, swinging into cold space, with the wind tearing his hair back from his head, with the wind whistling in his teeth, and him all the while thinking of the women, the chaff women in his parlor tonight, with the kernels blown out from under them by a neon wind, and his silly damned reading of a book to them. How like trying to put out fires with water pistols, how senseless and insane. One rage turned in for another. One anger displacing another. When would he stop being entirely mad and be quiet, be very quiet indeed?

"Here we go!"

Montag looked up. Beatty never drove, but he was driving tonight, slamming the Salamander around corners, leaning forward high on the driver's throne, his massive black slicker flapping out behind so that he seemed a great black bat flying above the engine, over the brass numbers, taking the full wind.

"Here we go to keep the world happy, Montag!"

Beatty's pink, phosphorescent cheeks glimmered in the high darkness, and he was smiling furiously.

"Here we are!"

The Salamander boomed to a halt, throwing men off in slips and clumsy hops. Montag stood fixing his raw eyes to the cold bright rail under his clenched fingers.

I can't do it, he thought. How can I go at this new assignment, how can I go on burning things? I can't go in this place.

Beatty, smelling of the wind through which he had rushed, was at Montag's elbow. "All right, Montag."

The men ran like cripples in their clumsy boots, as quietly as spiders.

At last Montag raised his eyes and turned.

Beatty was watching his face.

"Something the matter, Montag?"

"Why," said Montag slowly, "we've stopped in front of *my* house."

three
Burning Bright

Lights flicked on and house doors opened all down the street, to watch the carnival set up. Montag and Beatty stared, one with dry satisfaction, the other with disbelief, at the house before them, this main ring in which torches would be juggled and fire eaten.

"Well," said Beatty, "Now you *did* it. Old Montag wanted to fly near the sun and now that he's burnt his damn wings, he wonders why. Didn't I hint enough when I sent the Hound around your place?"

Montag's face was entirely numb and featureless; he felt his head turn like a stone carving to the dark place next door, set in its bright border of flowers.

Beatty snorted. "Oh, no! You weren't fooled by that little idiot's routine, now, were you? Flowers, butterflies, leaves, sunsets, oh, hell! It's all in her file. I'll be damned. I've hit the bull's-eye. Look at the sick look on your face. A few grass blades and the quarters of the moon. What trash. What good did she ever *do* with all that?"

Montag sat on the cold fender of the Dragon, moving his head half an inch to the left, half an inch to the right, left, right, left, right, left. . . .

"She saw everything. She didn't do anything to anyone. She just let them alone."

"Alone, hell! She chewed around you, didn't she? One of those damn do-gooders with their shocked, holier-than-thou silences, their one talent making others feel guilty. God damn, they rise like the midnight sun to sweat you in your bed!"

The front door opened; Mildred came down the steps, running, one suitcase held with a dreamlike clenching rigidity in her fist, as a beetle-taxi hissed to the curb.

"Mildred!"

She ran past with her body stiff, her face floured with powder, her mouth gone, without lipstick.

"Mildred, you *didn't* put in the alarm!"

She shoved the valise in the waiting beetle, climbed in, and sat mumbling, "Poor family, poor family, oh everything gone, everything, everything gone now. . . ."

Beatty grabbed Montag's shoulder as the beetle blasted away and hit seventy miles an hour, far down the street, gone.

There was a crash like the falling parts of a dream fashioned out of warped glass, mirrors, and crystal prisms. Montag drifted about as if still another incomprehensible storm had turned him, to see Stoneman and Black wielding axes, shattering windowpanes to provide cross ventilation.

The brush of a death's-head moth against a cold black screen. "Montag, this is Faber. Do you hear me? What's happening?'

"This is happening to *me*," said Montag.

"What a dreadful surprise," said Beatty. "For everyone nowadays knows, absolutely is *certain*, that nothing will ever happen to *me*. Others die, *I* go on. There are no consequences and no responsibilities. Except that there *are*. But let's not talk about them, eh? By the time the consequences catch up with you, it's too late, isn't it, Montag?"

"Montag, can you get away, run?" asked Faber.

Montag walked but did not feel his feet touch the cement and then the night grasses. Beatty flicked his igniter nearby and the small orange flame drew his fascinated gaze.

"What is there about fire that's so lovely? No matter what age we are, what draws us to it?" Beatty blew out the flame and lit it again. "It's perpetual motion; the thing man wanted to invent but never did. Or almost perpetual motion. If you let it go on, it'd burn our lifetimes out. What is fire? It's a mystery. Scientists give us gobbledegook about friction and molecules. But they don't really know. Its real beauty is that it destroys responsibility and consequences. A problem gets too burdensome, then into the furnace with it. Now, Montag, you're a burden. And fire will lift you off my shoulders, clean, quick, sure; nothing to rot later. Antibiotic, aesthetic, practical."

Montag stood looking in now at this queer house, made strange by the hour of the night, by murmuring neighbor voices, by littered glass, and there on the floor, their covers torn off and spilled out like swan feathers, the incredible books that looked so silly and really not worth bothering with, for these were nothing but black type and yellowed paper and raveled binding.

Mildred, of course. She must have watched him hide the books in the garden and brought them back in. Mildred. Mildred.

"I want you to do this job all by your lonesome, Montag. Not with kerosene and a match, but piecework, with a flame thrower. Your house, your clean-up."

"Montag, can't you run, get away!"

"No!" cried Montag helplessly. "The Hound! Because of the Hound!"

Faber heard and Beatty, thinking it was meant for him, heard. "Yes, the Hound's somewhere about the neighborhood, so don't try anything. Ready?"

"Ready." Montag snapped the safety catch on the flame thrower.

"Fire!"

A great nuzzling gout of fire leapt out to lap at the books and knock them against the wall. He stepped into the bedroom and fired twice and the twin beds went up in a great simmering whisper, with more heat and passion and light than he would have supposed them to contain. He burnt the bedroom walls and the cosmetics chest because he wanted to change everything, the chairs, the tables, and in the dining room the silverware and plastic dishes, everything that showed that he had lived here in this empty house with a strange woman who would forget him tomorrow, who had gone and quite forgotten him already, listening to her Seashell Radio pour in on her and in on her as she rode across town, alone. And as before, it was good to burn, he felt himself gush out in the fire, snatch, rend, rip in half with flame, and put away the senseless problem. If there was no solution, well then now there was no problem, either. Fire was best for everything.

"The books, Montag!"

The books leapt and danced like roasted birds, their wings ablaze with red and yellow feathers.

And then he came to the parlor where the great idiot monsters lay asleep with their white thoughts and their snowy dreams. And he shot a bolt at each of the three blank walls and the vacuum hissed out at him. The emptiness made an even emptier whistle, a senseless scream. He tried to think about the vacuum upon which the nothingnesses had performed, but he could not. He held his breath so the vacuum could not get into his lungs. He cut off its terrible emptiness, drew back, and gave the entire room a gift of one huge bright yellow flower of burning. The fireproof plastic sheath on everything was cut wide and the house began to shudder with flame.

"When you're quite finished," said Beatty behind him. "You're under arrest."

The house fell in red coals and black ash. It bedded itself down in sleepy pink-gray cinders and a smoke plume blew over it, rising and waving slowly back and forth in the sky. It was three-thirty in the morning. The crowd drew back into the houses; the great tents of the circus had slumped into charcoal and rubble and the show was well over.

Montag stood with the flame thrower in his limp hands, great islands of perspiration drenching his armpits, his face smeared with soot. The other firemen waited behind him, in the darkness, their faces illumined faintly by the smoldering foundation.

Montag started to speak twice and then finally managed to put his thought together.

"Was it my wife turned in the alarm?"

Beatty nodded. "But her friends turned in an alarm earlier, that I let ride. One way or the other, you'd have got it. It was pretty silly, quoting poetry around free and easy like that. It was the act of a silly damn snob. Give a man a few lines of verse and he thinks he's the Lord of all Creation. You think you can walk on water with your books. Well, the world can get by just fine without them. Look where they got you, in slime up to your lip. If I stir the slime with my little finger, you'll drown!"

Montag could not move. A great earthquake had come with fire and leveled the house and Mildred was under there somewhere and his entire life under there and he could not move. The earthquake was still shaking and falling and shivering inside him and he stood there, his knees half bent under the great load of tiredness and bewilderment and outrage, letting Beatty hit him without raising a hand.

"Montag, you idiot, Montag, you damn fool; why did you *really* do it?"

Montag did not hear, he was far away, he was running with his mind, he was gone, leaving this dead soot-covered body to sway in front of another raving fool.

"Montag, get out of there!" said Faber.

Montag listened.

Beatty struck him a blow on the head that sent him reeling back. The green bullet in which Faber's voice whispered and cried fell to the sidewalk. Beatty snatched it up, grinning. He held it half in, half out of his ear.

Montag heard the distant voice calling, "Montag, you all right?"

Beatty switched the green bullet off and thrust it in his pocket. "Well—so there's more here than I thought. I saw you tilt your head, listening. First I thought you had a Seashell. But when you turned clever later, I wondered. We'll trace this and drop in on your friend."

"No!" said Montag.

He twitched the safety catch on the flame thrower. Beatty glanced instantly at Montag's fingers and his eyes widened the faintest bit. Montag saw the surprise there and himself glanced to his hands to see what new thing they had done. Thinking back later he could never decide whether the hands or Beatty's reaction to the hands gave him the final push toward murder. The last rolling thunder of the avalanche stoned down about his ears, not touching him.

Beatty grinned his most charming grin. "Well, that's one way to get an audience. Hold a gun on a man and force him to listen to your speech. Speech away. What'll it be this time? Why don't you belch Shakespeare at me, you fumbling snob? 'There is no terror, Cassius, in your threats, for I am arm'd so strong in honesty that they pass by me as an idle wind, which I respect not!' How's that? Go ahead now, you second-hand literateur, pull the trigger." He took one step toward Montag.

Montag only said, "We never burned *right. . . .* "

"Hand it over, Guy," said Beatty with a fixed smile.

And then he was a shrieking blaze, a jumping, sprawling gibbering manikin, no longer human or known, all writhing flame on the lawn as Montag shot one continuous pulse of liquid fire on him. There was a hiss like a great mouthful of spittle banging a red-hot stove, a bubbling and frothing as if salt had been poured over a monstrous black snail to cause a terrible liquefaction and a boiling over of yellow foam. Montag shut his eyes, shouted, shouted, and fought to get his hands at his ears to clamp and to cut away the sound. Beatty flopped over and over and over, and at last twisted in on himself like a charred wax doll and lay silent.

The other two firemen did not move.

Montag kept his sickness down long enough to aim the flame thrower. "Turn around!"

They turned, their faces like blanched meat, streaming sweat; he beat their heads, knocking off their helmets and bringing them down on themselves. They fell and lay without moving.

The blowing of a single autumn leaf.

He turned and the Mechanical Hound was there.

It was half across the lawn, coming from the shadows, moving with such drifting ease that it was like a single solid cloud of black-gray smoke blown at him in silence.

It made a single last leap into the air coming down at Montag from a good three feet over his head, its spidered legs reaching, the procaine needle snapping out its single angry tooth. Montag caught it with a bloom of fire, a single wondrous blossom that curled in petals of yellow and blue and orange about the metal dog, clad it in a new covering as it slammed into Montag and threw him ten feet back against the bole of a tree, taking the flame gun with him. He felt it scrabble and seize his leg and stab the needle in for a moment before the fire snapped the Hound up in the air, burst its metal bones at the joints, and blew out its interior in a single flushing of red color like a skyrocket fastened to the street. Montag lay watching the dead-alive thing fiddle the air and die. Even now it seemed to want to get back at him and finish the injection which was now working through the flesh of his leg. He felt all of the mingled relief and horror at having pulled back only in time to have just his knee slammed by the fender of a car hurtling by at ninety miles an hour. He was afraid to get up, afraid he might not be able to gain his feet at all, with an anesthetized leg. A numbness in a numbness hollowed into a numbness. . . .

And now . . . ?

The street empty, the house burnt like an ancient bit of stage scenery, the other homes dark, the Hound here, Beatty there, the three other firemen another place, and the Salamander . . . ? He gazed at the immense engine. That would have to go, too.

Well, he thought, let's see how badly off you are. On your feet now. Easy, easy . . . *there*.

He stood and he had only one leg. The other was like a chunk of burnt pine log he was carrying along as a penance for some obscure sin. When he put his weight on it, a shower of silver needles gushed up the length of the calf and went off in the knee. He wept. Come on! Come on, you, you can't stay here!

A few house lights were going on again down the street, whether from the incidents just passed, or because of the abnormal silence following the fight, Montag did not know. He hobbled around the ruins, seizing at his bad leg when it lagged, talking and whimpering and shouting directions at it and cursing it and pleading with it to work for him now when it was vital. He heard a number of people crying out in the darkness and shouting. He reached the back yard and the alley. Beatty, he thought, you're not a problem now. You always said, don't face a problem, burn it. Well, now I've done both. Goodbye, Captain.

And he stumbled along the alley in the dark.

A shotgun blast went off in his leg every time he put it down and he thought, you're a fool, a damn fool, an awful fool, an idiot, an awful idiot, a damn idiot, and a fool, a damn fool; look at the mess and where's the mop, look at the mess, and what do you do? Pride, damn it, and temper, and you've junked it all, at the very start you vomit on everyone and on yourself. But everything at once, but everything one on top of another, Beatty, the women, Mildred, Clarisse, everything. No excuse, though, no excuse. A fool, a damn fool, go give yourself up!

No, we'll save what we can, we'll do what there is left to do. If we have to burn, let's take a few more with us. Here!

He remembered the books and turned back. Just on the off chance.

He found a few books where he had left them, near the

garden fence. Mildred, God bless her, had missed a few. Four books still lay hidden where he had put them. Voices were wailing in the night and flashbeams swirled about. Other Salamanders were roaring, their engines far away, and police sirens were cutting their way across town with their sirens.

Montag took the four remaining books and hopped, jolted, hopped his way down the alley and suddenly fell as if his head had been cut off and only his body lay there. Something inside had jerked him to a halt and flopped him down. He lay where he had fallen and sobbed, his legs folded, his face pressed blindly to the gravel.

Beatty wanted to die.

In the middle of the crying Montag knew it for the truth. Beatty had wanted to die. He had just stood there, not really trying to save himself, just stood there, joking, needling, thought Montag, and the thought was enough to stifle his sobbing and let him pause for air. How strange, strange, to want to die so much that you let a man walk around armed and then instead of shutting up and staying alive, you go on yelling at people and making fun of them until you get them mad, and then . . .

At a distance, running feet.

Montag sat up. Let's get out of here. Come on, get up, get up, you just can't sit! But he was still crying and that had to be finished. It was going away now. He hadn't wanted to kill anyone, not even Beatty. His flesh gripped him and shrank as if it had been plunged in acid. He gagged. He saw Beatty, a torch, not moving, fluttering out on the grass. He bit at his knuckles. I'm sorry, I'm sorry, oh God, sorry. . . .

He tried to piece it all together, to go back to the normal pattern of life a few short days ago before the sieve and the sand, Denham's Dentifrice, moth voices, fireflies, the alarms and excursions, too much for a few short days, too much, indeed, for a lifetime.

Feet ran in the far end of the alley.

"Get up!" he told himself. "Damn it, get up!" he said to the leg, and stood. The pains were spikes driven in the kneecap and then only darning needles and then only common ordinary safety pins, and after he had shagged along fifty more hops and jumps, filling his hand with slivers from the board fence, the prickling was like someone blowing a spray of scalding water on that leg. And the leg was at last his own leg again. He had been afraid that running might break the loose ankle. Now, sucking all the night into his open mouth and blowing it out pale, with all the blackness left heavily inside himself, he set out in a steady jogging pace. He carried the books in his hands.

He thought of Faber.

Faber was back there in the steaming lump of tar that had no name or identity now. He had burnt Faber, too. He felt so suddenly shocked by this that he felt Faber was really dead, baked like a roach in that small green capsule shoved and lost in the pocket of a man who was now nothing but a frame skeleton strung with asphalt tendons.

You must remember, burn them or they'll burn you, he thought. Right now it's as simple as that.

He searched his pockets, the money was there, and in his other pocket he found the usual Seashell upon which the city was talking to itself in the cold black morning.

"Police Alert. Wanted: Fugitive in city. Has committed murder and crimes against the State. Name: Guy Montag. Occupation: Fireman. Last seen . . ."

He ran steadily for six blocks in the alley and then the alley opened out onto a wide empty thoroughfare ten lanes wide. It seemed like a boatless river frozen there in the raw light of the high white arc lamps; you could drown trying to cross it, he felt; it was too wide, it was too open. It was a vast stage without scenery, inviting him to run across, easily seen in the blazing il-lumination, easily caught, easily shot down.

The Seashell hummed in his ear.

". . . watch for a man running . . . watch for the running man . . . watch for a man alone, on foot . . . watch . . ."

Montag pulled back in the shadows. Directly ahead lay a gas station, a great chunk of porcelain snow shining there, and two silver beetles pulling in to fill up. Now he must be clean and presentable if he wished to walk, not run, stroll calmly across that wide boulevard. It would give him an extra margin of safety if he washed up and combed his hair before he went on his way to get *where* . . . ?

Yes, he thought, where *am* I running?

Nowhere. There was nowhere to go, no friend to turn to, really. Except Faber. And then he realized that he was, indeed, running toward Faber's house, instinctively. But Faber couldn't hide him; it would be suicide even to try. But he knew that he would go to see Faber anyway, for a few short minutes. Faber's would be the place where he might refuel his fast draining belief in his own ability to survive. He just wanted to know that there was a man like Faber in the world. He wanted to see the man alive and not burned back there like a body shelled in another body. And some of the money must be left with Faber, of course, to be spent after Montag ran on his way. Perhaps he could make the open country and live on or near the rivers and near the highways, in the fields and hills.

A great whirling whisper made him look to the sky.

The police helicopters were rising so far away that it seemed someone had blown the gray head off a dry dandelion flower. Two dozen of them flurried, wavering, indecisive, three miles off, like butterflies puzzled by autumn, and then they were plummeting down to land, one by one, here, there, softly kneading the streets where, turned back to beetles, they shrieked along the boulevards or, as suddenly, leapt back into the air, continuing their search.

And here was the gas station, its attendants busy now with customers. Approaching from the rear, Montag entered the men's washroom. Through the aluminum wall he heard a radio voice saying, "War has been declared." The gas was being pumped outside. The men in the beetles were talking and the attendants were talking about the engines, the gas, the money owed. Montag stood trying to make himself feel the shock of the quiet statement from the radio, but nothing would happen. The war would have to wait for him to come to it in his personal file, an hour, two hours from now.

He washed his hands and face and toweled himself dry, making little sound. He came out of the washroom and shut the door carefully and walked into the darkness and at last stood again on the edge of the empty boulevard.

There it lay, a game for him to win, a vast bowling alley in the cool morning. The boulevard was as clean as the surface of an arena two minutes before the appearance of certain unnamed victims and certain unknown killers. The air over and above the vast concrete river trembled with the warmth of Montag's body alone; it was incredible how he felt his temperature could cause the whole immediate world to vibrate. He was a phosphorescent target; he knew it, he felt it. And now he must begin his little walk.

Three blocks away a few headlights glared. Montag drew a deep breath. His lungs were like burning brooms in his chest. His mouth was sucked dry from running. His throat tasted of bloody iron and there was rusted steel in his feet.

What about those lights there? Once you started walking you'd have to gauge how fast those beetles could make it down here. Well, how far was it to the other curb? It seemed like a hundred yards. Probably not a hundred, but figure for that anyway, figure that with him going very slowly, at a nice stroll, it might take as much as thirty seconds, forty seconds to walk all that way. The beetles? Once started, they could leave three blocks behind them in about fifteen seconds. So, even if halfway across he started to run . . . ?

He put his right foot out and then his left foot and then his right. He walked on the empty avenue.

Even if the street were entirely empty, of course, you couldn't be sure of a safe crossing, for a car could appear suddenly over the rise four blocks further on and be on and past you before you had taken a dozen breaths.

He decided not to count his steps. He looked neither to left nor right. The light from the overhead lamps seemed as bright and revealing as the midday sun and just as hot.

He listened to the sound of the car picking up speed two blocks away on his right. Its movable headlights jerked back and forth suddenly, and caught at Montag.

Keep going.

Montag faltered, got a grip on the books, and forced himself not to freeze. Instinctively he took a few quick running steps then talked out loud to himself and pulled up to stroll again. He was now half across the street, but the roar from the beetle's engines whined higher as it put on speed.

The police, of course. They see me. But slow now slow, quiet, don't turn, don't look, don't seem concerned. Walk, that's it, walk, walk.

The beetle was rushing. The beetle was roaring. The beetle raised its speed. The beetle was whining. The beetle was in high thunder. The beetle came skimming. The beetle came in a single whistling trajectory, fired from an invisible rifle. It was up to 120 mph. It was up to 130 at least. Montag clamped his jaws. The heat of the racing headlights burnt his cheeks, it seemed, and jittered his eyelids and flushed the sour sweat out all over his body.

He began to shuffle idiotically and talk to himself and then he broke and just ran. He put out his legs as far as they would go and down and then far out again and down and back and out and down and back. God! God! He dropped a book, broke pace, almost turned, changed his mind, plunged on, yelling in concrete emptiness, the beetle scuttling after its running food, two hundred, one hundred feet away, ninety, eighty, seventy, Montag gasping, flailing his hands, legs up down out, up down out, closer, closer, hooting, calling, his eyes burnt white now as his head jerked about to confront the flashing glare, now the beetle was swallowed in its own light, now it was nothing but a torch hurtling upon him; all sound, all blare. Now—almost on top of him!

He stumbled and fell.

I'm done! It's over.

But the falling made a difference. An instant before reaching him the wild beetle cut and swerved out. It was gone. Montag lay flat, his head down. Wisps of laughter trailed back to him with the blue exhaust from the beetle.

His right hand was extended above him, flat. Across the extreme tip of his middle finger, he saw now as he lifted that hand, a faint sixteenth of an inch of black tread where the tire had touched in passing. He looked at that black line with disbelief, getting to his feet.

That wasn't the police, he thought.

He looked down the boulevard. It was clear now. A carful of children, all ages, God knew, from twelve to sixteen, out whistling, yelling, hurrahing, had seen a man, a very extraordinary sight, a man strolling, a rarity, and simply said, "Let's get him," not knowing he was the fugitive Mr. Montag, simply a number of children out for a long night of roaring five or six hundred miles in a few moonlit hours, their faces icy with wind, and coming home or not coming at dawn, alive or not alive, that made the adventure.

They would have killed me, thought Montag, swaying, the air still torn and stirring about him in dust, touching his bruised cheek. For no reason at all in the world they would have killed me.

He walked toward the far curb telling each foot to go and keep going. Somehow he had picked up the spilled books; he didn't remember bending or touching them. He kept moving them from hand to hand as if they were a poker hand he could not figure.

I wonder if they were the ones who killed Clarisse?

He stopped and his mind said it again, very loud.

I wonder if they were the ones who killed Clarisse!

He wanted to run after them yelling.

His eyes watered.

The thing that had saved him was falling flat. The driver of that car, seeing Montag down, instinctively considered the probability that running over a body at such a high speed might turn the car upside down and spill them out. If Montag had remained an *upright* target . . . ?

Montag gasped.

Far down the boulevard, four blocks way, the beetle had slowed, spun about on two wheels, and was now racing back, slanting over on the wrong side of the street, picking up speed.

But Montag was gone, hidden in the safety of the dark alley for which he had set out on a long journey, an hour, or was it a minute, ago? He stood shivering in the night, looking back out as the beetle ran by and skidded back to the center of the avenue, whirling laughter in the air all about it, gone.

Further on, as Montag moved in darkness, he could see the helicopters falling falling like the first flakes of snow in the long winter to come. . . .

The house was silent.

Montag approached from the rear, creeping through a thick night-moistened scent of daffodils and roses and wet grass. He touched the screen door in back, found it open, slipped in, moved across the porch, listening.

Mrs. Black, are you asleep in there? he thought. This isn't good, but your husband did it to others and never asked and never wondered and never worried. And now since you're a fireman's wife, its your house and your turn, for all the houses your husband burned and the people he hurt without thinking.

The house did not reply.

He hid the books in the kitchen and moved from the house again to the alley and looked back and the house was still dark and quiet, sleeping.

On his way across town, with the helicopters fluttering like torn bits of paper in the sky, he phoned the alarm at a lonely phone booth outside a store that was closed for the night. Then he stood in the cold night air, waiting, and at a distance he heard the fire sirens start up and run, and the Salamanders coming, coming to burn Mr. Black's house while he was away at work, to make his wife stand shivering in the morning air while the roof let go and dropped in upon the fire, But now, she was still asleep.

Good night, Mrs. Black, he thought.

"Faber!"

Another rap, a whisper, and a long waiting. Then, after a minute, a small light flickered inside Faber's small house. After another pause, the back door opened.

They stood looking at each other in the half-light, Faber and Montag, as if each did not believe in the other's existence. Then Faber moved and put out his hand and grabbed Montag and moved him in and sat him down and went back and stood in the door, listening. The sirens were wailing off in the morning distance. He came in and shut the door.

Montag said, "I've been a fool all down the line. I can't stay long. I'm on my way God knows where."

"At least you were a fool about the right things," said Faber. "I thought you were dead. The audio-capsule I gave you—"

"Burnt."

"I heard the captain talking to you and suddenly there was nothing. I almost came out looking for you."

"The captain's dead. He found the audio-capsule, he heard your voice, he was going to trace it. I killed him with the flame thrower."

Faber sat down and did not speak for a time.

"My God, how did this happen?" said Montag. "It was only the other night everything was fine and the next thing I know I'm drowning. How many times can a man go down and still be alive? I can't breathe. There's Beatty dead, and he was my friend once, and there's Millie gone, I thought she was my wife, but now I don't know. And the house all burnt. And my job gone and myself on the run, and I planted a book in a fireman's house on the way. Good Christ, the things I've done in a single week!"

"You did what you had to do. It was coming on for a long time."

"Yes, I believe that, if there's nothing else I believe. It saved itself up to happen. I could feel it for a long time, I was saving something up, I went around doing one thing and feeling another. God, it was all there. It's a wonder it didn't show on me, like fat. And now here I am, messing up your life, too. They might follow me here."

"I feel alive for the first time in years," said Faber. "I feel I'm doing what I should've done a lifetime ago. For a little while I'm not afraid. Maybe it's because I'm doing the right thing at last. Maybe it's because I've done a rash thing and don't want to look the coward to you. I suppose I'll have to do even more violent things, exposing myself so I won't fall down on the job and turn scared again. What are your plans?"

"To keep running."

"You know the war's on?"

"I heard."

"God, isn't it funny?" said the old man. "It seems so remote because we have our own troubles."

"I haven't had time to think." Montag drew out a hundred dollars. "I want this to stay with you, use it any way that'll help when I'm gone."

"But—"

"I might be dead by noon; use this."

Faber nodded. "You'd better head for the river if you can, follow along it, and if you can hit the old railroad lines going out into the country, follow them. Even though practically everything's air-borne these days and most of the tracks are abandoned, the rails are still there, rusting. I've heard there are still hobo camps all across the country, here and there; walking camps they call them, and if you keep walking far enough and keep an eye peeled, they say there's lots of old Harvard degrees on the tracks between here and Los Angeles. Most of them are wanted and hunted in the cities. They survive, I guess. There aren't many of them, and I guess the government's never considered them a great enough danger to go in and track them down. You might hole up with them for a time and get in touch with me in St. Louis. I'm leaving on the five A.M. bus this morning, to see a retired printer there, I'm getting out in the open myself, at last. This money will be put to good use. Thanks and God bless you. Do you want to sleep a few minutes?"

"I'd better run."

"Let's check."

He took Montag quickly into the bedroom and lifted a picture frame aside revealing a television screen the size of a postal card. "I always wanted something very small, something I could walk to, something I could blot out with the palm of my hand, if necessary, nothing that could shout me down, nothing monstrous big. So, you see." He snapped it on.

"Montag," the TV set said, and lit up. "M-O-N-T-A-G." The name was spelled out by a voice. "Guy Montag. Still running. Police helicopters are up. A new Mechanical Hound has been brought from another district—"

Montag and Faber looked at each other.

"—Mechanical Hound *never* fails. Never since its first use in tracking quarry has this incredible invention made a mistake. Tonight, this network is proud to have the opportunity to follow the Hound by camera helicopter as it starts on its way to the target—"

Faber poured two glasses of whiskey. "We'll need these."

They drank.

"—nose so sensitive the Mechanical Hound can remember and identify ten thousand odor indexes on ten thousand men without resetting!"

Faber trembled the least bit and looked about at his house, at the walls, the door, the doorknob, and the chair where Montag now sat. Montag saw the look. They both looked quickly about the house and Montag felt his nostrils dilate and he knew that he was trying to track himself and his nose was suddenly good enough to sense the path he had made in the air of the room and the sweat of his hand hung from the doorknob, invisible but as numerous as the jewels of a small chandelier, he was everywhere, in and on and about everything, he was a luminous cloud, a ghost that made breathing once more impossible. He saw Faber stop up his own breath for fear of drawing that ghost into his own body, perhaps, being contaminated with the phantom exhalations and odors of a running man.

"The Mechanical Hound is now landing by helicopter at the site of the Burning!"

And there on the small screen was the burnt house, and the crowd and something with a sheet over it and out of the sky, fluttering, came the helicopter like a grotesque flower.

So they must have their game out, thought Montag. The circus must go on, even with war beginning within the hour. . . .

He watched the scene, fascinated, not wanting to move. It seemed so remote and no part of him; it was a play apart and separate, wondrous to watch, not without its strange pleasure. That's all for me, you thought, that's all taking place just for *me*, by God.

If he wished, he could linger here, in comfort, and follow the entire hunt on through its swift phases, down alleys, across streets, over empty running avenues, crossing lots and play-grounds, with pauses here or there for the necessary commercials, up other alleys to the burning house of Mr. and Mrs. Black, and so on finally to this house with Faber and himself seated, drinking while the Electric Hound snuffed down the last trail, silent as a drift of death itself, skidding to a halt outside that window there. Then, if he wished, Montag might rise, walk to the window, keep one eye on the TV screen, open the window, lean out, look back, and see himself dramatized, described, made over, standing there, limned in the bright small television screen from outside, a drama to be watched objectively, knowing that in other parlors he was large as life, in full color, dimensionally perfect! and if he kept his eye peeled quickly he would see himself, an instant before oblivion, being punctured for the benefit of how many civilian parlor-sitters who had been wakened from sleep a few minutes ago by the frantic sirening of their living room walls to come watch the big game, the hunt, the one-man carnival.

Would he have time for a speech? As the Hound seized him, in view of ten or twenty or thirty million people, mightn't he sum up his entire life in the last week in one single phrase or a word that would stay with them long after the Hound had turned, clenching him in its metal-plier jaws, and trotted off in darkness, while the camera remained stationary, watching the creature dwindle in the distance, a splendid fade-out! What could he say in a single word, a few words, that would sear all their faces and wake them up?

"There," whispered Faber.

Out of a helicopter glided something that was not machine,

not animal, not dead, not alive, glowing with a pale-green luminosity. It stood near the smoking ruins of Montag's house and the men brought his discarded flame thrower to it and put it down under the muzzle of the Hound. There was a whirring, clicking, humming.

Montag shook his head and got up and drank the rest of his drink. "It's time. I'm sorry about this."

"About what? Me? My house? I deserve everything. Run, for God's sake. Perhaps I can delay them here—"

"Wait. There's no use you being discovered. When I leave, burn the spread of this bed that I touched. Burn the chair in the living room, in your wall incinerator. Wipe down the furniture with alcohol, wipe the doorknobs. Burn the throw-rug in the parlor. Turn the air conditioning on full in all the rooms and spray with moth spray if you have it. Then, turn on your lawn sprinklers as high as they'll go and hose off the sidewalks. With any luck at all, we can kill the trail *in* here, anyway."

Faber shook his hand. "I'll tend to it. Good luck. If we're both in good health, next week, the week after, get in touch, General Delivery, St. Louis. I'm sorry there's no way I can go with you this time, by earphone. That was good for both of us. But my equipment was limited. You see, I never thought I would use it. What a silly old man. No thought there. Stupid, stupid. So I haven't another green bullet, the right kind, to put in your head. Go now!"

"One last thing. Quick. A suitcase, get it, fill it with your dirtiest clothes, an old suit, the dirtier the better, a shirt, some old sneakers and socks. . . ."

Faber was gone and back in a minute. They sealed the cardboard valise with clear tape. "To keep the ancient odor of Mr. Faber in, of course," said Faber, sweating at the job.

Montag doused the exterior of the valise with whiskey. "I don't want that Hound picking up two odors at once. May I take this whiskey? I'll need it later. Christ, I hope this works!"

They shook hands again and going out the door glanced at the TV. The Hound was on its way, followed by hovering helicopter cameras, silently, silently, sniffing the great night wind. It was running down the first alley.

"Goodbye!"

And Montag was out the back door lightly, running with the half-empty valise. Behind him he heard the lawn-sprinkling system jump up, filing the dark air with rain that fell gently and then with a steady pour all about, washing on the sidewalks and draining into the alley. He carried a few drops of this rain with him on his face. He thought he heard the old man call goodbye, but he wasn't certain.

He ran very fast away from the house, down toward the river.

Montag ran.

He could feel the Hound, like autumn, come cold and dry and swift, like a wind that didn't stir grass, that didn't jar windows or disturb leaf shadows on the white sidewalks as it passed. The Hound did not touch the world. It carried its silence with it, so you could feel the silence building up a pressure behind you all across town. Montag felt the pressure rising, and ran.

He stopped for breath, on his way to the river, to peer through dimly lit windows of wakened houses, and saw the silhouettes of people inside watching their parlor walls and there on the walls the Mechanical Hound, a breath of neon vapor, spidered along, here and gone, here and gone! Now at Elm Terrace, Lincoln, Oak, Park, and up the alley toward Faber's house!

Go past, thought Montag, don't stop, go on, don't turn in!

On the parlor wall, Faber's house, with its sprinkler system pulsing in the night air.

The Hound paused, quivering.

No! Montag held to the windowsill. This way! *Here!*

The procaine needle flicked out and in, out and in. A single clear drop of the stuff of dreams fell from the needle as it vanished in the Hound's muzzle.

Montag held his breath, like a doubled fist, in his chest.

The Mechanical Hound turned and plunged away from Faber's house down the alley again.

Montag snapped his gaze to the sky. The helicopters were closer, a great blowing of insects to a single light source.

With an effort, Montag reminded himself again that this was no fictional episode to be watched on his run to the river; it was in actuality his own chess game he was witnessing, move by move.

He shouted to give himself the necessary push away from this last house window, and the fascinating séance going on in there! *Hell!* and he was away and gone! The alley, a street, the alley, a street, and the smell of the river. Leg out, leg down, leg out and down. Twenty million Montags running, soon, if the cameras caught him. Twenty million Montags running, running like an ancient flickery Keystone Comedy, cops, robbers, chasers and the chased, hunters and hunted, he had seen it a thousand times. Behind him now twenty million silently baying Hounds, ricocheted across parlors, three-cushion shooting from right wall to center wall to left wall, gone, right wall, center wall, left wall, gone!

Montag jammed his Seashell to his ear:

"Police suggest entire population in the Elm Terrace area do as follows: Everyone in every house in every street open a front or rear door or look from the windows. The fugitive cannot escape if everyone in the next minute looks from his house. Ready!"

Of course! Why hadn't they done it before! Why, in all the years, hadn't this game been tried! Everyone up, everyone out! He couldn't be missed! The only man running alone in the night city, the only man proving his legs!

"At the count of ten now! *One! Two!*"

He felt the city rise.

"Three!"

He felt the city turn to its thousands of doors.

"Four!"

The people sleepwalking in their hallways.

"Five!"

He felt their hands on the doorknobs!

The smell of the river was cool and like a solid rain. His throat was burnt rust and his eye were wept dry with running. He yelled as if this yell would jet him on, fling him the last hundred yards.

"Six, seven, eight!"

The doorknobs turned on five thousand doors.

"Nine!"

He ran out away from the last row of houses, on a slope leading down to a solid moving blackness.

"Ten!"

The doors opened.

He imagined thousands on thousands of faces peering into yards, into alleys, and into the sky, faces hid by curtains, pale, night-frightened faces, like gray animals peering from electric caves, faces with gray colorless eyes, gray tongues and gray thoughts looking out through the numb flesh of the face.

But he was at the river.

He touched it, just to be sure it was real. He waded in and stripped in darkness to the skin, splashed his body, arms, legs, and head with raw liquor; drank it and snuffed some up his nose. Then he dressed in Faber's old clothes and shoes. He tossed his own clothing into the river and watched it swept away. Then, holding the suitcase, he walked out in the river until there was no bottom and he was swept away in the dark.

He was three hundred yards downstream when the Hound reached the river. Overhead the great racketing fans of the helicopters hovered. A storm of light fell upon the river and Montag dived under the great illumination as if the sun had broken the clouds. He felt the river pull him further on its way, into darkness. Then the lights switched back to the land, the helicopters swerved over the city again, as if they had picked up another trail. They were gone. The Hound was gone. Now there was only the cold river and Montag floating in a sudden peacefulness, away from the city and the lights and the chase, away from everything.

He felt as if he had left a stage behind and many actors. He felt as if he had left the great séance and all the murmuring ghosts. He was moving from an unreality that was frightening into a reality that was unreal because it was new.

The black land slid by and he was going into the country among the hills. For the first time in a dozen years the stars were coming out above him, in great processions of wheeling fire. He saw a great juggernaut of stars form in the sky and threaten to roll over and crush him.

He floated on his back when the valise filled and sank; the river was mild and leisurely, going away from the people who ate shadows for breakfast and steam for lunch and vapors for supper. The river was very real; it held him comfortably and gave him the time at last, the leisure, to consider this month, this year, and a lifetime of years. He listened to his heart slow. His thoughts stopped rushing with his blood.

He saw the moon low in the sky now. The moon there, and the light of the moon caused by what? By the sun, of course. And what lights the sun? Its own fire. And the sun goes on, day after day, burning and burning. The sun and time. The sun and time and burning. Burning. The river bobbled him along gently. Burning. The sun and every clock on the earth. It all came together and became a single thing in his mind. After a long time of floating on the land and a short time of floating in the river he knew why he must never burn again in his life.

The sun burned every day. It burned Time. The world rushed in a circle and turned on its axis and time was busy burning the years and the people anyway, without any help from him. So if *he* burned things with the firemen and the sun burned Time, that meant that *everything* burned!

One of them had to stop burning. The sun wouldn't, certainly. So it looked as if it had to be Montag and the people he had worked with until a few short hours ago. Somewhere the saving and putting away had to begin again and someone had to do the saving and keeping, one way or another, in books, in records, in people's heads, any way at all so long as it was safe, free from moths, silverfish, rust and dry rot, and men with matches. The world was full of burning of all types and sizes. Now the guild of the asbestos-weaver must open shop very soon.

He felt his heel bump land, touch pebbles and rocks, scrape sand. The river had moved him toward shore.

He looked in at the great black creature without eyes or

light, without shape, with only a size that went a thousand miles, without wanting to stop, with its grass hills and forests that were waiting for him.

He hesitated to leave the comforting flow of the water. He expected the Hound there. Suddenly the trees might blow under a great wind of helicopters.

But there was only the normal autumn wind high up, going by like another river. Why wasn't the Hound running? Why had the search veered inland? Montag *listened.* Nothing. Nothing.

Millie, he thought. All this country here. Listen to it! Nothing and nothing. So much silence, Millie, I wonder how you'd take it? Would you shout Shut up, shut up! Millie, Millie. And he was sad.

Millie was not here and the Hound was not here, but the dry smell of hay blowing from some distant field put Montag on the land. He remembered a farm he had visited when he was very young, one of the rare few times he discovered that somewhere behind the seven veils of unreality, beyond the walls of parlors and beyond the tin moat of the city, cows chewed grass and pigs sat in warm ponds at noon and dogs barked after white sheep on a hill.

Now, the dry smell of hay, the motion of the waters, made him think of sleeping in fresh hay in a lonely barn away from the loud highways, behind a quiet farmhouse, and under an ancient windmill that whirred like the sound of the passing years overhead. He lay in the high barn loft all night, listening to distant animals and insects and trees, the little motions and stirrings.

During the night, he thought, below the loft, he would hear a sound like feet moving, perhaps. He would tense and sit up. The sound would move away. He would lie back and look out the loft window, very late in the night and see the lights go out in the farmhouse itself, until a very young and beautiful woman would sit in an unlit window, braiding her hair. It would be hard to see her, but her face would be like the face of the girl so long ago in his past now, so very long ago, the girl who had known the weather and never been burned by the fireflies, the girl who had known what dandelions meant rubbed off on your chin. Then, she would be gone from the warm window and appear again upstairs in her moon-whitened room. And then, to the sound of death, the sound of the jets cutting the sky in two black pieces beyond the horizon, he would lie in the loft, hidden and safe, watching those strange new stars over the rim of the earth, fleeing from the soft color of dawn.

In the morning he would not have needed sleep, for all the warm odors and sights of a complete country night would have rested and slept him while his eyes were wide and his mouth, when he thought to test it, was half a smile.

And there at the bottom of the hayloft stair waiting for him, would be the incredible thing. He would step carefully down, in the pink light of early morning, so fully aware of the world that he would be afraid, and stand over the small miracle and at last bend to touch it.

A cool glass of fresh milk, and a few apples and pears laid at the foot of the steps.

This was all he wanted now. Some sign that the immense world would accept him and give him the long time he needed to think all the things that must be thought.

A glass of milk, an apple, a pear.

He stepped from the river.

The land rushed at him, a tidal wave. He was crushed by darkness and the look of the country and the million odors on a wind that iced his body. He fell back under the breaking curve of darkness and sound and smell, his ears roaring. He whirled. The stars poured over his sight like flaming meteors. He wanted to plunge in the river again and let it idle him safely on down somewhere. This dark land rising was like that day in his childhood, swimming, when from nowhere the largest wave in the history of remembering slammed him down in salt mud and green darkness, water burning mouth and nose, retching his stomach, screaming! Too much water!

Too much land.

Out of the black wall before him, a whisper. A shape. In the shape, two eyes. The night looking at him. The forest, seeing him.

The Hound!

After all the running and rushing and sweating it out and half drowning, to come this far, work this hard, and think yourself safe and sigh with relief and come out on the land at last only to find . . .

The Hound!

Montag gave one last agonized shout as if this were too much for any man.

The shape exploded away. The eyes vanished. The leaf piles flew up in a dry shower.

Montag was alone in the wilderness.

A deer. He smelled the heavy musk like perfume mingled with blood and the gummed exhalation of the animal's breath, all cardamom and moss and ragweed odor in this huge night where the trees ran at him, pulled away, ran, pulled away, to the pulse of the heart behind his eyes.

There must have been a billion leaves on the land; he waded in them, a dry river smelling of hot cloves and warm dust. And the other smells! There was a smell like a cut potato from all the land, raw and cold and white from having the moon on it most of the night. There was a smell like pickles from a bottle and a smell like parsley on the table at home. There was a faint yellow odor like mustard from a jar. There was a smell like carnations from the yard next door. He put down his hand and felt a weed rise up like a child brushing him. His fingers smelled of licorice.

He stood breathing, and the more he breathed the land in, the more he was filled up with all the details of the land. He was not empty. There was more than enough here to fill him. There would always be more than enough.

He walked in the shallow tide of leaves, stumbling.

And in the middle of the strangeness, a familiarity.

His foot hit something that rang dully.

He moved his hand on the ground, a yard this way, a yard that.

The railroad track.

The track that came out of the city and rusted across the land, through forests and woods, deserted now, by the river.

Here was the path to wherever he was going. Here was the single familiar thing, the magic charm he might need a little while, to touch, to feel beneath his feet, as he moved on into the bramble bushes and the lakes of smelling and feeling and touching, among the whispers and the blowing down of leaves.

He walked on the track.

And he was surprised to learn how certain he suddenly was of a single fact he could not prove.

Once, long ago, Clarisse had walked here, where he was walking now.

Half an hour later, cold, and moving carefully on the tracks, fully aware of his entire body, his face, his mouth, his eyes stuffed with blackness, his ears stuffed with sound, his legs prickled with burrs and nettles, he saw the fire ahead.

The fire was gone, then back again, like a winking eye. He stopped, afraid he might blow the fire out with a single breath. But the fire was there and he approached warily, from a long way off. It took the better part of fifteen minutes before he drew very close indeed to it, and then he stood looking at it from cover. That small motion, the white and red color, a strange fire because it meant a different thing to him.

It was not burning, it was *warming*.

He saw many hands held to its warmth, hands without arms, hidden in darkness. Above the hands, motionless faces that were only moved and tossed and flickered with firelight. He hadn't known fire could look this way. He had never thought in his life that it could give as well as take. Even its smell was different.

How long he stood he did not know, but there was a foolish and yet delicious sense of knowing himself as an animal come from the forest, drawn by the fire. He was a thing of brush and liquid eye, of fur and muzzle and hoof, he was a thing of horn and blood that would smell like autumn if you bled it out on the ground. He stood a long long time, listening to the warm crackle of the flames.

There was a silence gathered all about that fire and the silence was in the men's faces, and time was there, time enough to sit by this rusting track under the trees, and look at the world and turn it over with the eyes, as if it were held to the center of the bonfire, a piece of steel these men were all shaping. It was not only the fire that was different. It was the silence. Montag moved toward this special silence that was concerned with all of the world.

And then the voices began and they were talking, and he could hear nothing of what the voices said, but the sound rose and fell quietly and the voices were turning the world over and looking at it; the voices knew the land and the trees and the city which lay down the track by the river. The voices talked of everything, there was nothing they could not talk about, he knew, from the very cadence and motion and continual stir of curiosity and wonder in them.

And then one of the men looked up and saw him, for the first or perhaps the seventh time, and a voice called to Montag:

"All right, you can come out now!"

Montag stepped back in the shadows.

"It's all right," the voice said. "You're welcome here."

Montag walked slowly toward the fire and the five old men sitting there dressed in dark blue denim pants and jackets and dark blue shirts. He did not know what to say to them.

"Sit down," said the man who seemed to be the leader of the small group. "Have some coffee?"

He watched the dark steaming mixture pour into a collapsible tin cup, which was handed him straight off. He sipped it gingerly and felt them looking at him with curiosity. His lips were scalded, but that was good. The faces around him were bearded, but the beards were clean, neat, and their hands were clean. They had stood up as if to welcome a guest, and now they sat down again. Montag sipped.

"Thanks," he said. "Thanks very much."

"You're welcome, Montag. My name's Granger." He held out a small bottle of colorless fluid. "Drink this, too. It'll change the chemical index of your perspiration. Half an hour from now you'll smell like two other people. With the Hound after you, the best thing is bottoms up."

Montag drank the bitter fluid.

"You'll stink like a bobcat, but that's all right," said Granger.

"You know my name," said Montag.

Granger nodded to a portable battery TV set by the fire. "We've watched the chase. Figured you'd wind up south along the river. When we heard you plunging around out in the forest like a drunken elk, we didn't hide as we usually do. We figured you were in the river, when the helicopter cameras swung back in over the city. Something funny there. The chase is still running. The other way, though."

"The other way?"

"Let's have a look."

Granger snapped the portable viewer on. The picture was a nightmare, condensed, easily passed from hand to hand, in the forest, all whirring color and flight. A voice cried:

"The chase continues north in the city! Police helicopters are converging on Avenue 87 and Elm Grove Park!"

Granger nodded. "They're faking. You threw them off at the river. They can't admit it. They know they can hold their audience only so long. The show's got to have a snap ending, quick! If they started searching the whole damn river it might take all night. So they're sniffing for a scapegoat to end things with a bang. Watch. They'll catch Montag in the next five minutes!"

"But how—"

"Watch."

The camera, hovering in the belly of a helicopter, now swung down at an empty street:

"See that?" whispered Granger. "It'll be you; right up at the end of that street is our victim. See how our camera in coming in? Building the scene. Suspense. Long shot. Right now, some poor fellow is out for a walk. A rarity. An odd one. Don't think the police don't know the habits of queer ducks like that, men who walk mornings for the hell of it, or for reasons of insomnia. Anyway, the police have had him charted for months, years. Never know when that sort of information might be handy. And today, it turns out, it's very usable indeed. It saves face. Oh, God, look there!"

The men at the fire bent forward.

On the screen, a man turned a corner. The Mechanical Hound rushed forward into the viewer, suddenly. The helicopter lights shot down a dozen brilliant pillars that built a cage all about the man.

A voice cried, "There's Montag! The search is *done!*"

The innocent man stood bewildered, a cigarette burning in his hand. He stared at the Hound, not knowing what it was. He probably never knew. He glanced up at the sky and the wailing sirens. The camera rushed down. The Hound leapt up into the air with a rhythm and a sense of timing that was incredibly beautiful. Its needle shot out. It was suspended for a moment in their gaze, as if to give the vast audience time to appreciate everything, the raw look of the victim's face, the empty street, the steel animal a bullet nosing the target.

"Montag, don't move!" said a voice from the sky.

The camera fell upon the victim, even as did the Hound. Both reached him simultaneously. The victim was seized by Hound and camera in a great spidering, clenching grip. He screamed. He screamed. He screamed!

Blackout.

Silence.

Darkness.

Montag cried out in the silence and turned away.

Silence.

And then, after a time of the men sitting around the fire, their faces expressionless, an announcer on the dark screen said, "The search is over, Montag is dead; a crime against society has been avenged."

Darkness.

"We now take you to the Sky Room of the Hotel Lux for a half hour of Just-Before-Dawn, a program of—"

Granger turned it off.

"They didn't show the man's face in focus. Did you notice? Even your best friends couldn't tell if it was you. They scrambled it just enough to let the imagination take over. Hell," he whispered. "Hell."

Montag said nothing but now, looking back, sat with his eyes fixed to the black screen, trembling.

Granger touched Montag's arm. "Welcome back from the dead." Montag nodded. Granger went on. "You might as well know all of us, now. This is Fred Clement, former occupant of the Thomas Hardy chair at Cambridge in the years before it became an Atomic Engineering School. This other is Dr. Simmons from U.C.L.A., a specialist in Ortega y Gasset; Professor West here did quite a bit for ethics, an ancient study now, for Columbia University quite some years ago. Reverend Padover here gave a few lectures thirty years ago and lost his flock between one Sunday and the next for his views. He's been bumming with us some time now. Myself: I wrote a book called *The Fingers in the Glove; the Proper Relationship between the Individual and Society*, and here I *am!* Welcome, Montag!"

"I don't belong with you," said Montag, at last, slowly. "I've been an idiot all the way."

"We're used to that. We all made the *right* kind of mistakes, or we wouldn't be here. When we were separate individuals, all we had was rage. I struck a fireman when he came to burn my library years ago. I've been running ever since. You want to join us, Montag?"

"Yes."

"What have you to offer?"

"Nothing. I thought I had part of the Book of Ecclesiastes and maybe a little of Revelation, but I haven't even that now."

"The Book of Ecclesiastes would be fine. Where was it?"

"Here." Montag touched his head.

"Ah." Granger smiled and nodded.

"What's wrong? Isn't that all right?" said Montag.

"Better than all right: perfect!" Granger turned to the Reverend. "Do we have a Book of Ecclesiastes?"

"One. A man named Harris in Youngstown."

"Montag." Granger took Montag's shoulder firmly. "Walk carefully. Guard your health. If anything should happen to Harris, *you* are the Book of Ecclesiastes. See how important you've become in the last minute!"

"But I've forgotten!"

"No, nothing's ever lost. We have ways to shake down your clinkers for you."

"But I've tried to remember!"

"Don't try. It'll come when we need it. All of us have photographic memories, but spend a lifetime learning how to block off the things that are really *in* there. Simmons here has worked on it for twenty years and now we've got the method down to where we can recall anything that's been read once. Would you like, some day, Montag, to read Plato's *Republic*?"

"Of course!"

"*I* am Plato's *Republic*. Like to read Marcus Aurelius? Mr. Simmons is Marcus."

"How do you do?" said Mr. Simmons.

"Hello," said Montag.

"I want you to meet Jonathan Swift, the author of that evil political book, *Gulliver's Travels*! And this other fellow is Charles

Darwin, and this one is Schopenhauer, and this one is Einstein, and this one here at my elbow is Mr. Albert Schweitzer, a very kind philosopher indeed. Here we all are, Montag. Aristophanes and Mahatma Gandhi and Gautama Buddha and Confucius and Thomas Love Peacock and Thomas Jefferson and Mr. Lincoln, if you please. We are also Matthew, Mark, Luke, and John."

Everyone laughed quietly.

"It can't *be*," said Montag.

"It *is*," replied Granger smiling. "*We're* book burners, too. We read the books and burnt them, afraid they'd be found. Microfilming didn't pay off; we were always traveling, we didn't want to bury the film and come back later. Always the chance of discovery. Better to keep it in the old heads, where no one can see it or suspect it. We are all bits and pieces of history and literature and international law, Byron, Tom Paine, Machiavelli or Christ, it's here. And the hour's late. And the war's begun. And we are out here, and the city is there, all wrapped up in its own coat of a thousand colors. What do you think, Montag?"

"I think I was blind trying to go at things my way, planting books in firemen's houses and sending in alarms."

"You did what you had to do. Carried out on a national scale, it might have worked beautifully. But our way is simpler and, we think, better. All we want to do is keep the knowledge we think we will need, intact and safe. We're not out to incite or anger anyone yet. For if we are destroyed, the knowledge is dead, perhaps for good. We are model citizens, in our own special way; we walk the old tracks, we lie in the hills at night, and the city people let us be. We're stopped and searched occasionally, but there's nothing on our persons to incriminate us. The organization is flexible, very loose, and fragmentary. Some of us have had plastic surgery on our faces and fingerprints. Right now we have a horrible job; we're waiting for the war to begin and, as quickly, end. It's not pleasant, but then we're not in control, we're the odd minority crying in the wilderness. When the war's over, perhaps we can be of some use in the world."

"Do you really think they'll listen then?"

"If not, we'll just have to wait. We'll pass the books on to our children, by word of mouth, and let our children wait, in turn, on the other people. A lot will be lost that way, of course. But you can't *make* people listen. They have to come round in their own time, wondering what happened and why the world blew up under them. It can't last."

"How many of you are there?"

"Thousands on the roads, the abandoned railtracks, tonight, bums on the outside, libraries inside. It wasn't planned, at first. Each man had a book he wanted to remember, and did. Then, over a period of twenty years or so, we met each other, traveling, and got the loose network together and set out a plan. The most important single thing we had to pound into ourselves is that we were not important, we mustn't be pedants; we were not to feel superior to anyone else in the world. We're nothing more than dust jackets for books, of no significance otherwise. Some of us live in small towns. Chapter One of Thoreau's *Walden* in Green River, Chapter Two in Willow Farm, Maine. Why, there's one town in Maryland, only twenty-seven people, no bomb'll ever touch that town, is the compete essays of a man named Bertrand Russell. Pick up that town, almost, and flip the pages, so many pages to a person. And when the war's over, some day, some year, the books can be written again, the people will be called in, one by one, to recite what they know and we'll set it up in type until another Dark Age, when we might have to do the whole damn thing over again. But that's the wonderful thing about man; he never gets so discouraged or disgusted that he gives up doing it all over again, because he knows very well it is important and *worth* the doing."

"What do we do tonight?" asked Montag.

"Wait," said Granger. "And move downstream a little ways, just in case."

He began throwing dust and dirt in the fire.

The other men helped, and Montag helped, and there, in the wilderness, the men all moved their hands, putting out the fire together.

They stood by the river in the starlight.

Montag saw the luminous dial of his waterproof. Five. Five o'clock in the morning. Another year ticked by in a single hour, and dawn waiting beyond the far bank of the river.

"Why do you trust me?" said Montag.

A man moved in the darkness.

"The look of you's enough. You haven't seen yourself in a mirror lately. Beyond that, the city has never cared so much about us to bother with an elaborate chase like this to find us. A few crackpots with verses in their heads can't touch them, and they know it and we know it; everyone knows it. So long as the vast population doesn't wander about quoting the Magna Carta and the Constitution, it's all right. The firemen were enough to check that, now and then. No, the cities don't bother us. And *you* look like hell."

They moved along the bank of the river, going south. Montag tried to see the men's faces, the old faces he remembered from the firelight, lined and tired. He was looking for a brightness, a resolve, a triumph over tomorrow that hardly seemed to be there. Perhaps he had expected their faces to burn and glitter with the knowledge they carried, to glow as lanterns glow, with the light in them. But all the light had come from the campfire, and these men had seemed no different than any others who had run a long race, searched a long search, seen good things destroyed, and now, very late, were gathered to wait for the end of the party and the blowing out of the lamps. They weren't at all certain that the things they carried in their heads might make every future dawn glow with a purer light, they were sure of nothing save that the books were on file behind their quiet eyes, the books were waiting, with their pages uncut, for the customers who might come by in later years, some with clean and some with dirty fingers.

Montag squinted from one face to another as they walked.

"Don't judge a book by its cover," someone said.

And they all laughed quietly, moving downstream.

There was a shriek and the jets from the city were gone overhead long before the men looked up. Montag stared back at the city, far down the river, only a faint glow now.

"My wife's back there."

"I'm sorry to hear that. The cities won't do well in the next few days," said Granger.

"It's strange, I don't miss her, it's strange I don't feel much of anything," said Montag. "Even if she dies, I realized a moment ago, I don't think I'll feel sad. It isn't right. Something must be wrong with me."

"Listen," said Granger, taking his arm, and walking with him, holding aside the bushes to let him pass. "When I was a boy my grandfather died, and he was a sculptor. He was also a very kind man who had a lot of love to give the world, and he helped clean up the slum in our town; and he made toys for us and he did a million things in his lifetime; he was always busy with his hands. And when he died, I suddenly realized I wasn't crying for him at all, but for all the things he did. I cried because he would never do them again, he would never carve another piece of wood or help us raise doves and pigeons in the back yard or play the violin the way he did, or tell us jokes the way he did. He was part of us and when he died, all the actions stopped dead and there was no one to do them just the way he did. He was individual. He was an important man. I've never gotten over his death. Often I think, what wonderful carvings never came to birth because he died. How many jokes are missing from the world, and how many homing pigeons untouched by his hands. He shaped the world. He *did* things to the world. The world was bankrupted of ten million fine actions the night he passed on."

Montag walked in silence. "Millie, Millie," he whispered. "Millie."

"What?"

"My wife, my wife. Poor Millie, poor, poor Millie. I can't remember anything. I think of her hands but I don't see them doing anything at all. They just hang there at her sides or they lie there on her lap or there's a cigarette in them, but that's all."

Montag turned and glanced back.

What did you give to the city, Montag?

Ashes.

What did the others give to each other?

Nothingness.

Granger stood looking back with Montag. "Everyone must leave something behind when he dies, my grandfather said. A child or a book or a painting or a house or a wall built or a pair of shoes made. Or a garden planted. Something your hand touched some way so your soul has somewhere to go when you die, and when people look at that tree or that flower you planted, you're there. It doesn't matter what you do, he said, so long as you change something from the way it was before you touched it into something that's like you after you take your hands away. The difference between the man who just cuts lawns and a real gardener is in the touching, he said. The lawn-cutter might just as well not have been there at all; the gardener will be there a lifetime."

Granger moved his hand. "My grandfather showed me some V-2 rocket films once, fifty years ago. Have you ever seen the atom bomb mushroom from two hundred miles up? It's a pinprick, it's nothing. With the wilderness all around it.

"My grandfather ran off the V-2 rocket film a dozen times and then hoped that some day our cities would open up more and let the green and the land and the wilderness in more, to remind people that we're allotted a little space on earth and that we survive in that wilderness that can take back what it has given, as easily as blowing its breath on us or sending the sea to tell us we are not so big. When we forget how close the wilderness is in the night, my grandpa said, some day it will come in and get us, for we will have forgotten how terrible and real it can be. You see?" Granger turned to Montag. "Grandfather's been dead for all these years, but if you lifted my skull, by God, in the convolutions of my brain you'd find the big ridges of his thumbprint. He touched me. As I said, earlier, he was a sculptor. 'I hate a Roman named Status Quo!' he said to me. 'Stuff your eyes with wonder,' he said, 'live as if you'd drop dead in ten seconds. See the world. It's more fantastic than any dream made or paid for in factories. Ask no guarantees, ask for no security, there never was such an animal. And if there were, it would be related to the great sloth which hangs upside down in a tree all day every day, sleeping its life away. To hell with that,' he said, 'shake the tree and knock the great sloth down on his ass.'"

"Look!" cried Montag.

And the war began and ended in that instant.

Later, the men around Montag could not say if they had really seen anything. Perhaps the merest flourish of light and motion in the sky. Perhaps the bombs were there, and the jets, ten miles, five miles, one mile up, for the merest instant, like grain thrown over the heavens by a great sowing hand, and the bombs drifting with dreadful swiftness, yet sudden slowness, down upon the morning city they had left behind. The bombardment was to all intents and purposes finished, once the jets had sighted their target, alerted their bombardier at five thousand miles an hour; as quick as the whisper of a scythe the war was finished. Once the bomb release was yanked, it was over. Now, a full three seconds, all of the time in history, before the bombs struck, the enemy ships themselves were gone half around the visible world, like bullets in which a savage islander might not believe because they were invisible; yet the heart is suddenly shattered, the body falls in separate motions and the blood is astonished to be freed on the air; the brain squanders its few precious memories and, puzzled, dies.

This was not to be believed. It was merely a gesture. Montag saw the flirt of a great metal fist over the far city and he knew the scream of the jets that would follow, would say, after the deed, *disintegrate, leave no stone on another, perish. Die.*

Montag held the bombs in the sky for a single moment, with his mind and his hands reaching helplessly up at them. "Run!" he cried to Faber. To Clarisse, "Run!" To Mildred, "Get out, get out of there!" But Clarisse, he remembered, was dead. And Faber *was* out; there in the deep valleys of the country somewhere the five A.M. bus was on its way from one desolation to another. Though the desolation had not yet arrived, was still in the air, it was certain as man could make it. Before the bus had run another fifty yards on the highway, its destination would be meaningless, and its point of departure changed from metropolis to junkyard.

And Mildred . . .

Get out, run!

He saw her in her hotel room somewhere now in the half second remaining with the bombs a yard, a foot, an inch from her building. He saw her leaning toward the great shimmering walls of color and motion where the family talked and talked and talked to her, where the family prattled and chatted and said her name and smiled at her and said nothing of the bomb that was an inch, now a half inch, now a quarter inch from the top of the hotel. Leaning into the wall as if all the hunger of looking would find the secret of her sleepless unease there. Mildred, leaning anxiously nervously, as if to plunge, drop, fall into that swarming immensity of color to drown in its bright happiness.

The first bomb struck.

"Mildred!"

Perhaps, who would ever know? perhaps the great broadcasting stations with their beams of color and light and talk and chatter went first into oblivion.

Montag, falling flat, going down, saw or felt, or imagined he saw or felt the walls go dark in Millie's face, heard her screaming, because in the millionth part of time left, she saw her own face reflected there, in a mirror instead of a crystal ball, and it was such a wildly empty face, all by itself in the room, touching nothing, starved and eating of itself, that at last she recognized it as her own and looked quickly up at the ceiling as it and the entire structure of the hotel blasted down upon her, carrying her with a million pounds of brick, metal, plaster, and wood, to meet other people in the hives below, all on their quick way down to the cellar where the explosion rid itself of them in its own unreasonable way.

I remember. Montag clung to the earth. I remember. Chicago. Chicago a long time ago. Millie and I. *That's* where we met! I remember now. Chicago. A long time ago.

The concussion knocked the air across and down the river, turned the men over like dominoes in a line, blew the water in lifting sprays, and blew the dust and made the trees above them mourn with a great wind passing away south. Montag crushed himself down, squeezing himself small, eyes tight. He blinked once. And in that instant saw the city, instead of the bombs, in the air. They had displaced each other. For another of those impossible instants the city stood, rebuilt and unrecognizable, taller than it had ever hoped or strived to be, taller than man had built it, erected at last in gouts of shattered concrete and sparkles of torn metal into a mural hung like a reversed avalanche, a million colors, a million oddities, a door where a window should be, a top for a bottom, a side for a back, and then the city rolled over and fell down dead.

The sound of its death came after.

Montag, lying there, eyes gritted shut with dust, a fine wet cement of dust in his now shut mouth, gasping and crying, now thought again, I remember, I remember, I remember something else. What is it? Yes, yes, part of Ecclesiastes. Part of Ecclesiastes and Revelation. Part of that book, part of it, quick now, quick before it gets away, before the shock wears off, before the wind dies. Book of Ecclesiastes. Here. He said it over to himself silently, lying flat to the trembling earth, he said the words of it many times and they were perfect without trying and there was no Denham's Dentifrice anywhere, it was just the Preacher by himself, standing there in his mind, looking at him. . . .

"There," said a voice.

The men lay gasping like fish laid out on the grass. They held to the earth as children hold to familiar things, no matter how cold or dead, no matter what has happened or will happen, their fingers were clawed into the dirt, and they were all shouting to keep their eardrums from bursting, to keep their sanity from bursting, mouths open, Montag shouting with them, a protest against the wind that ripped their faces and tore at their lips, making their noses bleed.

Montag watched the great dust settle and the great silence move down upon their world. And lying there it seemed that he saw every single grain of dust and every blade of grass and that he heard every cry and shout and whisper going up in the world now. Silence fell down in the sifting dust, and all the leisure they might need to look around, to gather the reality of this day into their senses.

Montag looked at the river. We'll go on the river. He looked at the old railroad tracks. Or we'll go that way. Or we'll walk on the highways now, and we'll have time to put things into ourselves. And some day, after it sets in us a long time, it'll come out our hands and our mouths. And a lot of it will be wrong, but just enough of it will be right. We'll just start walking today and see the world and the way the world walks around and talks, the way it really looks. I want to see everything now. And while none of it will be me when it goes in, after a while it'll all gather together inside and it'll be me. Look at the world out there, my God, my God, look at it out there, outside me, out there beyond my face and the only way to really touch it is to put it where it's finally me, where it's in the blood, where it pumps around a thousand times ten thousand a day. I'll get hold of it so it'll never run off. I'll hold onto the world tight some day. I've got one finger on it now; that's a beginning.

The wind died.

The other men lay awhile, on the dawn edge of sleep, not yet ready to rise up and begin the day's obligations, its fires and foods, its thousand details of putting foot after foot and hand after hand. They lay blinking their dusty eyelids. You could hear them breathing fast, then slower, then slow. . . .

Montag sat up.

He did not move any farther, however. The other men did likewise. The sun was touching the black horizon with a faint red tip. The air was cold and smelled of a coming rain.

Silently, Granger arose, felt of his arms and legs, swearing, swearing incessantly under his breath, tears dripping from his face. He shuffled down to the river to look upstream.

"It's flat," he said, a long time later. "City looks like a heap of baking powder. It's gone." And a long time after that. "I wonder how many knew it was coming? I wonder how many were surprised?"

And across the world, thought Montag, how many other cities dead? And here in our country, how many? A hundred, a thousand?

Someone struck a match and touched it to a piece of dry paper taken from their pocket, and shoved this under a bit of grass and leaves, and after a while added tiny twigs which were wet and sputtered but finally caught, and the fire grew larger in the early morning as the sun came up and the men slowly turned from looking up river and were drawn to the fire, awkwardly, with nothing to say, and the sun colored the back of their necks as they bent down.

Granger unfolded an oilskin with some bacon in it. "We'll have a bite. Then we'll turn around and walk upstream. They'll be needing us up that way."

Someone produced a small frying pan and the bacon went into it and the frying pan was set on the fire. After a moment the bacon began to flutter and dance in the pan and the sputter of it filled the morning air with its aroma. The men watched this ritual silently.

Granger looked into the fire. "Phoenix."

"What?"

"There was a silly damn bird called a Phoenix back before Christ, every few hundred years he built a pyre and burned himself up. He must have been first cousin to Man. But every time he burnt himself up he sprang out of the ashes, he got himself born all over again. And it looks like we're doing the same thing, over and over, but we've got one damn thing the Phoenix never had. We know the damn silly thing we just did. We know all the damn silly things we've done for a thousand years and as long as we know that and always have it around where we can see it, some day we'll stop making the goddam funeral pyres and jumping in the middle of them. We pick up a few more people that remember, every generation."

He took the pan off the fire and let the bacon cool and they ate it, slowly, thoughtfully.

"Now, let's get on upstream," said Granger. "And hold onto one thought: You're not important. You're not anything. Some day the load we're carrying with us may help someone. But even when we had the books on hand, a long time ago, we didn't use what we got out of them. We went right on insulting the dead.

We went right on spitting in the graves of all the poor ones who died before us. We're going to meet a lot of lonely people in the next week and the next month and the next year. And when they ask us what we're doing, you can say, We're remembering. That's where we'll win out in the long run. And some day we'll remember so much that we'll build the biggest goddam steamshovel in history and dig the biggest grave of all time and shove war in and cover it up. Come on now, we're going to go build a mirror factory first and put out nothing but mirrors for the next year and take a long look in them."

They finished eating and put out the fire. The day was brightening all about them as if a pink lamp had been given more wick. In the trees, the birds that had flown away quickly now came back and settled down.

Montag began walking and after a moment found that the others had fallen in behind him, going north. He was surprised, and moved aside to let Granger pass, but Granger looked at him and nodded him on. Montag went ahead. He looked at the river and the sky and the rusting track going back down to where the farms lay, where the barns stood full of hay, where a lot of people had walked by in the night on their way from the city. Later, in a month or six months, and certainly not more than a year, he would walk along here again, alone, and keep right on going until he caught up with the people.

But now there was a long morning's walk until noon, and if the men were silent it was because there was everything to think about and much to remember. Perhaps later in the morning, when the sun was up and had warmed them they would begin to talk, or just say the things they remembered, to be sure they were there, to be absolutely certain that things were safe in them. Montag felt the slow stir of words, the slow simmer. And when it came his turn, what could he say, what could he offer on a day like this, to make the trip a little easier? To everything there is a season. Yes. A time to break down, and a time to build up. Yes. A time to keep silence and a time to speak. Yes, all that. But what else. What else? Something, something. . . .

And on either side of the river was there a tree of life, which bare twelve manner of fruits, and yielded her fruit every month; And the leaves of the tree were for the healing of the nations.

Yes, thought Montag, that's the one I'll save for noon. For noon. . . .

When we reach the city.

HISTORY, CONTEXT, AND CRITICISM

Edited by Jonathan R. Eller

"'You can't ever have my books,' she said." Joseph Mugnaini's frontispiece appeared in the initial printings of the first American and British editions of *Fahrenheit 451*.

Contents

PART ONE

THE STORY OF *FAHRENHEIT 451*

*Books were only one type of receptacle where we stored a lot of
things we were afraid we might forget. There is nothing magical in
them, at all. The magic is only in what books say, how they stitched
the patches of the universe together into one garment for us.*
—Ray Bradbury, *Fahrenheit 451*

THE STORY OF *FAHRENHEIT 451*

Jonathan R. Eller

Ray Bradbury never really figured out how to learn in a lecture hall or a classroom environment. The printed word seemed far more real to him, and the pages of countless library books formed the core of his education. Bradbury would never attend college; after his 1938 graduation from Los Angeles High School, he spent four years selling evening newspapers at the corner of Norton and Olympic, earning one penny for every three-cent newspaper he sold. But he continued to read voraciously, absorbing a wide range of classics as well as the works of contemporary writers. Sometime in 1944 he read Arthur Koestler's *Darkness at Noon*, and from that point on, *Fahrenheit 451* was inevitable.

In revealing the underlying terror of Stalin's show trials, *Darkness at Noon* became the great cautionary tale for Bradbury. It fueled his subsequent confrontations with intolerant authority, and with those who denied the existence of intolerance. Bradbury's unpublished speaking notes of the mid-1950s contain his most forceful acknowledgment of this inspiration: "People have often asked me what effect Huxley and Orwell had on me, and whether either of them influenced the creation of *Fahrenheit 451*. The best response is Arthur Koestler. . . . [O]nly a few perceived the intellectual holocaust and the revolution by burial that Stalin achieved. . . . Only Koestler got the full range of desecration, execution, and forgetfulness on a mass and nameless graveyard scale. Koestler's *Darkness at Noon* was therefore . . . true father, mother, and lunatic brother to my *F. 451*."

The "intellectual holocaust" revealed by Koestler recharged Bradbury's own conviction that literature is every bit as precious as life itself. From a young age he was greatly affected by accounts of the burning of the ancient library at Alexandria and the loss of many classical works that we now know only by title or through fragments of surviving parchment. Bradbury virtually lived in the public libraries of his time, and came to see the shelves as populations of living authors: to burn the book is to burn the author, and to burn the author is to deny our own humanity. Koestler's cautionary tale soon inspired a series of writing experiments about books—and about those who would burn them. But nine years would pass before the reading public first learned the temperature at which book paper combusts.

Bradbury made notes for a story about book-burning firemen as early as February 1946, but he soon set this project aside. Initially, the path to *Fahrenheit 451* led through an unfinished and entirely different story line—*Where Ignorant Armies Clash by Night*, which survives only in fragmentary drafts of a few episodes written at intervals during 1946 and 1947. These all focus on a nightmare inversion of traditional values in a post-apocalyptic world where death provides the best way out of a ravaged landscape. The modernist lament for lost homelands and lost values weighed heavily on him during this time, and Bradbury briefly experimented with the darker possibilities of the rapidly emerging atomic age: "If you can't fight the meaninglessness with a religion, then slide along down the chute with it into oblivion. Make a religion of Meaninglessness." To this end, Bradbury imagined an elite class of public assassins who also performed ritualized burnings of the books and fine art that gave meaning to an earlier age, including the poem that would play a central role in *Fahrenheit 451*—Matthew Arnold's "Dover Beach."

In the fragmentary *Ignorant Armies*, which takes its title from the last line of Arnold's poem, a prominent assassin actually reads "Dover Beach" to a massed crowd "in order that you may know what we are destroying," and subsequently burns all of Arnold's works as a warm-up to the destruction of what is perhaps the last copy of Shakespeare's works. But the assassin finds that he cannot take the ultimate step of cultural annihilation by burning Shakespeare and becomes a fugitive from the mob. For *Fahrenheit*, Bradbury transformed this image into the scene where Fireman Montag reads "Dover Beach" to his wife and her friends. This reading would become the pivotal point of no return for Montag, who will be betrayed by his own wife for giving voice to the forbidden words.

Where Ignorant Armies Clash by Night ended up a creative dead end for Bradbury, but his metaphor-rich description of the burning of Matthew Arnold's book offers an early glimpse of the powerful prose he would bring to Montag's story:

> The book turned and fought, like some small white animal caught within the fire. It seemed to want very much to live, it writhed and sparkled and a small gust of gaseous vapor blew up from it. Leaf by leaf it burned in upon itself, as if hands of fire were turning each page, scanning and burning with the same fire. The pages cringed into black curls and the curls departed on puffs of illumination.

This unsettling image—the death of living words—emerges from a world without hope or meaning, but Bradbury soon realized that predicting this kind of dark future ran counter to his creative instincts. He was more effective at exploring the sources and celebrating the achievements of the human imagination, and gradually began to examine where present-day threats to creativity might lead. At first, these new stories focused on supernatural fiction, a field where he had found his first success as a writer during the early 1940s; his extended tale "Pillar of Fire" (1948) and his story "The Mad Wizards of Mars" (1949; better known as "The Exiles") warn that such labels as *horror, fantasy,* and *supernatural*—genres that were already coming under increased scrutiny in the late 1940s—could be extended to include many of Shakespeare's works as well as other classics of mainstream literature.

Bradbury's well-known "Carnival of Madness," given an even longer life as "Usher II" in *The Martian Chronicles*, extended the scope of his storytelling to include broader threats to canonical literature and other creative aspects of the cultural tapestry. His vengeful protagonist Stendahl, the millionaire who builds all of Poe's infamous death devices into a single, Usheresque mansion, uses these horrors to destroy the governing elite responsible for the burning of all art and literature. Stendahl's account of this future history is clearly a trying-out of the explanations that Professor Faber will convey to Montag in *Fahrenheit 451*: "They began by controlling books and, of course, films, one way or another, one group or another, political bias, religious prejudice, union pressures, there was always a minority afraid of something, and a great majority afraid of the dark, afraid of thefuture, afraid of the past, afraid of the present, afraid of themselves and shadows of themselves."

In revising "Usher II" for *The Martian Chronicles*, Bradbury

> The book turned and fought, like some small white animal caught within the fire. It seemed to want very much to live, it writhed and sparkled and a small gust of gaseous vapor blew up from it. Leaf by leaf it burned in upon itself, as if hands of fire were turning each page, scanning and burning with the same fire. The pages cringed into b lack curls and the curls departed on puffs of illumination. The Killer thrust his sword into the heart of the book and held it up so a shower of burning pages fell glittering down into the crowd. The pages were caught in eager hands and clenched and popped into mouths like sweetmeats.
>
> The book was now a dwindling torch. His face, turned up in the light, wore a fixed and ghastly smile. Within, he was cold and felt nothing. No elation, no emotion except a heavy weariness and a sickness that made each of his bones groan with the weight of a simple book. He picked out the evilest, jeering face in the crowd and hurled the now fire-emptied book Bull into that face.
>
> There remained only Shakespeare.

Bradbury's earliest sustained images of book burning survive in the fragmentary episodes of his unfinished 1946–47 novel, *Where Ignorant Armies Clash by Night.* In this postapocalyptic culture where all treasures of the old world are reviled, a volume of Matthew Arnold's poetry is burned in front of a frenzied crowd as a prelude to the burning of the world's last volume of Shakespeare's works. The metaphorical agonies of the burning book, and the secret misgivings of the book burner himself, anticipate the emotions that Bradbury would fully develop in "The Fireman" and *Fahrenheit 451.*

added "books of cartoons and then detective books" to the destruction list, an allusion to the earliest targets of local groups and national organizations intent on enforcing behavioral "norms" in the early postwar era. Given these activities and the emerging agenda of the House Un-American Activities Committee in Washington, it required a relatively small leap of the imagination for Bradbury to extend his storytelling into civil liberties. As Bradbury has often noted, "The Pedestrian" provided the final bridge into "The Fireman," the short novella that later bloomed into *Fahrenheit 451*. By 1950, he had come to view the pedestrian as a threshold or indicator species capable of foretelling things to come—if the rights of the pedestrian were threatened, it would be an early indicator that broader freedoms of thought and action were also at risk.

This conclusion was deeply rooted in personal experience. In 1941, while walking through Pershing Square late at night with friend and occasional coauthor Henry Hasse, Bradbury had his first relatively mild encounter with police. The specific incident that sparked "The Pedestrian" involved a similar late-night walk with a friend along Wilshire Boulevard near Western Avenue sometime in late 1949. Bradbury often wrote and spoke about being questioned that evening by a passing patrolman, and usually described as well his somewhat confrontational response ("What am I *doing*? Just putting one foot in front of the other . . ."). He wrote "The Pedestrian" while the emotions were still close at hand, and in March 1950 sent it on to his New York agent, Don Congdon. Although it didn't reach print in *The Reporter* until August 7, 1951, its composition in the early months of 1950 predates Bradbury's conception of "The Fireman."

Sometime in the spring of 1950, Bradbury suddenly envisioned his solitary pedestrian, considered a dangerous deviant in a culture where virtual-reality entertainments had replaced evening walks, in an entirely different role and gender. The pedestrian became young Clarisse McClellan, a reader of forbidden books, a questioner of authority, and a solitary late-night walker. She turns a corner and encounters Guy Montag, fireman, walking home from his station shift in a future where firemen set fires rather than prevent them. She smells the kerosene on his tunic and says, "I know what you do." Montag does not know her, but her fleeting companionship kindles a new joy in living and helps him understand why he has secretly hidden some of the books that he is sworn to destroy by fire. This time, Bradbury was able to avoid the nihilistic dead ends of *Ignorant Armies* and instead developed a protagonist who could survive, and, with other survivors, preserve the forbidden literatures that define what it means to be human.

During the summer of 1950, Bradbury composed the first draft of "The Fireman," at this point titled "Long After Midnight."[1] It was the result of nine days of self-enforced isolation in the UCLA Library's subterranean typing room, alternating half-hour stints at the dime-a-dance machines with inspirational walks through the literature collections on the upper levels. Bradbury soon sent a subsequent hand-revised typescript, now titled "The Fire Man," to Don Congdon. In early September 1950 Congdon had a clean copy prepared and began to circulate it. His initial impulse was to start with *Amazing Stories,* one of the oldest magazines in the pulp tradition of science fiction and fantasy, but he and Bradbury quickly decided to try mainstream magazines first, where Congdon had long-standing connections as both an agent and an editor. In quick succession, *Esquire*, the Canadian weekly *Maclean's, The Saturday Evening Post*, and *Cosmopolitan* all declined the novella, which now carried the slightly shortened title "The Fireman." Congdon then sent it on to *Town & Country,* planning to submit it to *Astounding* if it failed to find a home there.[2]

Mr. Leonard Montag had a dream.

He dreamt that he was an old man hidden with six million powdery books, his yellow hands trembling over yellower pages, and his face like a smashed mirror of wrinkles by candlelight.

And then, there was a bright eye at the keyhole!

Mr. Montag yanked the door wide. A boy fell in.

"Spying!"

"You got books!" cried the boy. "It's against the law; I'll tell my father!"

He seized hold of the boy who writhed and screamed, beating at him.

"Don't boy, don't," pleaded Mr. Montag. "Don't tell. I'll give you money, books, clothes, but don't tell!"

"I seen you reading!" The boy broke away, the door slammed and shook down dust from the ceilings, and Mr. Montag stood alone.

A crowd rushed up the street, health officials burst in, followed by an alarmed police, fierce with silver badges. And then himself, Leonard Montag, appeared in the door, as a young man, dressed in a charcoal-black Fire uniform, a torch in his hand. The room swarmed while the old Montag pleaded with his younger self, but the books crashed down and were stripped and torn, while the windows splashed in bright pieces on the floor, and the drapes plunged in sooty clouds.

Outside, watching, stood the little boy who had turned him in.

A variant opening page for "Long After Midnight," the first complete draft of the *Fahrenheit 451* concept. This page was probably composed around August 1950, close to the time that Bradbury produced the complete draft in the UCLA library typing room. The "Long After Midnight" stage of work opens with a vivid nightmare of discovery as Leonard (not yet Guy) Montag is turned in by a neighbor boy for hiding and reading forbidden books. This opening scene disappears from all subsequent versions of *Fahrenheit 451*.

But while "The Fireman" was under consideration at *Town & Country*, Horace Gold, publisher of the recently launched magazine *Galaxy Science Fiction*, expressed strong interest in the novella. In mid-October *Town & Country* declined, and Gold immediately purchased serial rights for *Galaxy*. Bradbury made some revisions to the first half of the novella during November 1950, but refused Gold's suggestion to corrupt the memories of Montag and the Book People. Gold's idea was to render Montag unable to recall his texts without massive, Joycean juxtapositions of commercial ads and unrelated literary fragments—corruptions that the other Book People would be unable to detect or repair. Bradbury was convinced that such a pessimistic turn would destroy the restorative, healing conclusion that he had worked so hard to kindle out of the ashes of *Ignorant Armies*, and he published "The Fireman" without substantive changes beginning in the February 1951 issue of *Galaxy Science Fiction*.[3]

The completion of "The Fireman" capped a miracle year of creativity for Bradbury. Between summer 1949 and summer 1950, he had also transformed and bridged many of his Martian stories into *The Martian Chronicles* and woven a looser but no less compelling tapestry of unrelated science fiction stories into *The Illustrated Man* collection, which was released in February 1951. His newest stories were now reaching the pages of *Collier's*, *The Saturday Evening Post*, and *Esquire* for the first time, extending his popularity in the mainstream magazine market. But even as he moved ahead with new stories, Bradbury began to consider refashioning "The Fireman." Once again, Arthur Koestler's *Darkness at Noon* provided the initial spark. After seeing Sidney Kingsley's award-winning Broadway dramatization of Koestler's novel during his June 1951 trip to New York, Bradbury was inspired to expand "The Fireman" in ways that spoke to the increasing tensions of the times.[4]

Bradbury and Congdon wanted to package "The Fireman" with "The Creatures That Time Forgot" (1946) and "Pillar of Fire" to form a single-volume trio of science fiction novellas that had been published but never collected in book form. This book concept found little interest among publishing houses until August 7, 1952, when Congdon had dinner with Stanley Kauffmann of the newly founded Ballantine Books. Congdon was immediately impressed with an unusual aspect of this venture: Ian Ballantine's goal was to provide both quality hardbound and mass-market paper printings from a single publishing house—the main advantage being that his authors would not have to share the paperback royalties with the original hardback publisher, as was then the prevailing practice. It was a complicated gamble for Ballantine, involving printing and distribution arrangements with other publishers, but for a few years it worked well enough to attract a number of mainstream and genre authors.

Bradbury signed a contract with Ballantine in mid-January 1953, but by this time the novella collection had taken on a very different focus. Of the three proposed works, only "The Fireman" remained; the collection was now to be filled out by eight of Bradbury's newer short stories, bound together under a title as yet to be determined. But Bradbury's planned expansion of "The Fireman" would form the core of the collection, and he wanted a title allusion to the self-ignition temperature for book paper—an allusion that would transcend the character-focused title of the original work.

His earliest known working title was *Fahrenheit 270*, but other variants were also in play; his good friend Joseph Mugnaini, an experienced illustrator, was already at work on the cover art, producing preliminaries titled *Fahrenheit 204* and *Fahrenheit 205*. On January 22, after a fruitless sequence of telephone calls by Bradbury to several university physics and chemistry departments, a single call to the Los Angeles Fire Department revealed the book-paper combustion point to be 451 degrees Fahrenheit.

Mugnaini developed a cover concept from two of his own paintings that Bradbury found particularly relevant: one an angular rendering of Don Quixote, the other an illustration of a newsprint-clad Diogenes. The resulting fireman, wearing

THE FIRE MAN   1.

            The four men sat playing Blackjack under a green drop-light
in the dark morning. They did not speak for a time. Only a voice
in the ceiling spoke on occasion; ~~it murmured~~. [WHISPERED]

            "It is now one thirty-five a.m., Thursday morning, October
4th, 2052, A.D." [IT IS NOW ONE FORTY-ONE A.M. . . . .]
~~They didn't hear the voice.~~ Their hands twitched. [MEANS]

            Mr. Montag sat among the other Fire Men in the Fire House,
and he heard the voice tell the time of morning, the hour, the day,
the year, and he shivered.

            "What's eating you, Montag?" The three other men looked
at him. "Play your cards."

            A radio played in the smoky ceiling overhead. "War may
be declared at any hour. This country stands ready to defend its
destiny. War may be. . ."

            The Fire House shook. Some night jet-planes were flying
over, filling the sky with a great scream and whistle.

            The men sat in their coal-black uniforms, trim men, with
the look of thirty years in their blue-shaved, sharp, pink faces, and
their receding, burnt-looking hair. In the corner, piled in neat,
gleaming rows, lay auxiliary helmets and thick overcoats. On the
walls, in precise sharpness, hung gold-plated hatchets, inscribed

As Bradbury revised "Long After Midnight" for publication as "The Fireman," he deleted Montag's opening nightmare and began the narrative with the next scene—a tense late-night shift in the firehouse, where Montag and his colleagues are playing cards. Bradbury's handwritten revisions carry into the February 1951 issue of *Galaxy* magazine, shown on the following page. Courtesy of the University Archives & Special Collections Unit, Pollack Library, California State University, Fullerton.

THE FIREMAN

By RAY BRADBURY

A master of science fiction presents his masterwork of frightening conviction... the world of the future WE are creating!

I

Fire, Fire, Burn Books

THE four men sat silently playing blackjack under a green drop-light in the dark morning. Only a voice whispered from the ceiling:

"One thirty-five a.m. Thursday morning, October 4th, 2052, A.D. . . . One forty a.m. . . . one fifty . . ."

Mr. Montag sat stiffly among the other firemen in the fire house, heard the voice-clock mourn out the cold hour and the cold year, and shivered.

The other three glanced up.

"What's wrong, Montag?"

A radio hummed somewhere.

". . . War may be declared any

GALAXY SCIENCE FICTION

Expansion of the novella proved surprisingly difficult. . . . Bradbury spent the spring and much of the summer of 1953 transforming "The Fireman" into *Fahrenheit 451*.

newsprint armor amid a pile of burning books, would become a popular and recurring design for many subsequent editions of *Fahrenheit 451* down through time. But expansion of the novella proved surprisingly difficult; many discarded pages, preserved in the Pollak Library at California State University, Fullerton, mark his painfully slow progress through the spring of 1953. Finally, during June 1953, he decided to return to the UCLA Library's typing room for what ended up being another nine-day stint, once again inserting a dime for every half hour of typewriter use.

Ballantine and Kauffmann were concerned when Bradbury's initial April deadline passed, but were greatly relieved when Congdon forwarded the first 126 pages of the final typescript. This bought more time for Bradbury to work through the expansions of the rest of the novel, and he sent periodic installments through July, when the final pages of the fifty-thousand-word novel reached New York. Now it was Ballantine's turn to act under pressure; he had scheduled an October 1953 release, and had arranged more publicity and review coverage than he had done for any of his earlier titles. Ballantine sent Kauffmann and the galley sheets to Los Angeles, where he worked with Bradbury from August 5 through 8 on final revisions and corrections. One crucial aspect of format also had to be settled: the full expansion of the "Fireman" novella into *Fahrenheit 451* necessitated all but two of the projected eight companion stories be left out of the collection. Bradbury decided to include "And the Rock Cried Out" and "The Playground" to comply with the story-collection concept of the volume; most subsequent editions, as well as reprints and reissues of the Ballantine first edition, deleted the companion stories entirely and presented the novel as a stand-alone title.[5]

Within weeks, Ian Ballantine sent several hundred hardbound copies to review editors; the hardbound print run was designed to reinforce the quality of the content in the minds of the major magazine and newspaper reviewers, as well as the established ABA bookstore chains that privileged hardbound trade titles. But Ballantine took the unprecedented step of distributing six thousand copies of the mass-market paperback to other reviewers, editors, authors, and distributors in an effort to get maximum exposure for the book prior to its October release. It was an unusual step for any publisher, let alone a new enterprise trying to carry the burden of both hardbound and paperbound book publishing. But Ballantine was an experienced publisher who had founded the highly successful Bantam Books nearly a decade earlier, and he knew what he was doing. He also knew that the troubled times demanded a book like *Fahrenheit 451*.

In fact, world events seemed to form a grim backdrop for Bradbury's revisions. His transformation of "The Fireman" into *Fahrenheit 451* extended through two of the most disturbing announcements the world had known since the dark days of World War II. In late October 1952, the United States proclaimed the successful test of a hydrogen bomb, a weapon far more destructive than the atomic bombs that had ended the war in the Pacific. Then in July 1953, the Soviet Union unexpectedly exploded its first hydrogen bomb, an ominous indicator that the West was no longer ahead of the Eastern Bloc superpower in terms of destructive potential. The Doomsday Clock, a chilling metaphor whose image appears on the cover of the *Bulletin of the Atomic Scientists*, reached two minutes before midnight. The hands would not come as close to midnight again for the rest of the twentieth century.

— KENYON-ECKHARDT DEAL. "TO THE FUTURE"
— VAN WOODWARD "MARS IS HEAVEN?"
✳ RAPUNZEL?
— TIGER, TIGER, BURNING BRIGHT.
❋ THE PUMPERNICKEL —
❋ — THE PEDESTRIAN? RITA?
— TO COLLIER'S AGAIN? —
AVON A:
BANTAM ANTHOLOGY !

— "THE FIREMAN" AS A BOOK?
— NO BOOK IN 1951 OUTSIDE
OF "THE ILL. MAN"

"THE SILVER LOCUSTS"
IN BRITAIN —

COPYRIGHTS — RECENTLY
PLANET?
WEIRD?
POPULAR? ETC,

"THE PLAY GROUND" — EL. STIERHAM?
"THE PIPE ORGAN" — ?

"'THE FIREMAN' AS A BOOK?" Framed in typical Bradbury doodles, his brainstorming list of projects for 1951–52 includes his earliest known intention to expand "The Fireman" into a novel-length work of fiction. As the list indicates, Bradbury was somewhat concerned that *The Illustrated Man,* published in February 1951, was his only new book that year. His June 1951 encounter with the Broadway adaptation of Arthur Koestler's *Darkness at Noon,* the novel that most directly inspired "The Fireman," finalized his intention to expand his novella. From the Albright Collection; reproduced courtesy of Donn Albright and Ray Bradbury.

Bradbury's revision and expansion doubled the size of the original work, but the result offered far more than a doubled word count; the heightened domestic and international tensions of the real world were reflected in the way Bradbury intensified Montag's quest to read and understand the books he had sworn to destroy. As he worked, Bradbury found that the best way to increase the thematic impact of this quest was to concentrate on expanding Montag's interactions with the other major characters—the young Clarisse McClellan, the secretive Professor Faber, and Fire Captain Leahy, the towering figure who represents Montag's potential future.

The only significant structural change involved the opening scenes, and Bradbury began his revisions there. "The Fireman" had opened in the firehouse, with Montag and the other firemen playing cards, ready to answer the first call to burn. Bradbury now realized that Clarisse was the key to the entire story, and as he expanded Montag's first meeting with her, he also moved the scene to the beginning of *Fahrenheit 451*. Even before his breakthrough in the UCLA Library, he described this new insight in a letter to his British publisher, Rupert Hart-Davis: "[T]he young girl who lives next door is really the pivotal character; without her and her influence . . . our Fire Man may not have changed when he did. The story, in order to achieve balance, should show The Fire Man enjoying his work, meeting the young neighbor, and changing, beginning to think what in hell he's been up to for a number of years. This way we get some sort of character growth in the tale."[6]

Bradbury also needed to expand Fire Captain Leahy's cultural commentaries. In his final form, Leahy (renamed Beatty) brings out a far richer description of the way the world became a mindless consumerist society incapable of saving itself from looming nuclear annihilation. And during the transformation of the text, Bradbury's "Seashell" radio earpieces provided a new plot element—Professor Faber's two-way communicating device—that kept Montag and his new mentor in contact during the crucial stages when Montag begins to think things out for himself. Beatty senses what he terms a new cleverness in Montag, and holds him in check by relating a "dream"—an imaginary debate masking a one-sided and very persuasive attack on the dangers of book-learned wisdom.

Through the secret earpiece, Faber's small-voice counterpoint urges Montag to stand up to this debate, which represents the greatest enemy of all: "But remember that the Captain belongs to the most dangerous enemy to truth and freedom, the solid unmoving cattle of the majority." As Faber observes, it's now up to Montag to decide for himself "which way to jump, or fall." This was all new text that greatly enhanced the drama of the story and allowed Bradbury to raise the intensity to match the rising political tensions of the times.

Bradbury was an ocean away when *Fahrenheit 451* was published in America. More than a month before the October 1953 release, Bradbury had accepted an offer from legendary Hollywood director John Huston to go to Ireland and London to write the screenplay for a new motion-picture adaptation of Herman Melville's cinematically challenging novel *Moby-Dick*. Bradbury would not return to the United States until the end of May 1954, when he would find that Senator McCarthy's speaking engagements were no longer filled to capacity. *Fahrenheit 451* had not become a best seller—nonconformist literature sells best when there is no fear in the land—but the reviews were generally very favorable. *New York Times* reviewer Orville Prescott, who had not read any of Bradbury's earlier books, b' came a lifelong fan. Other favorable voices included the eminent Columbia University scholar and radio reviewer Gilbert Highet and future British poet laureate John Betjeman.

Chicago novelist Nelson Algren, approaching the height of his popularity as a best-selling champion of harsh mid-century realism, found *Fahrenheit 451* extremely relevant and

```
            Of course I'm happy. What does she think?  I'm
not? he asked the quiet rooms.  He looked at a blank wall.
The girl's face was there, really quite beautiful in
memory; astonishing, in fact.  She had a very thin face
like the dial of a small clock seen faintly in a dark
room in the middle of a night when you waken to see the
time and see the clock telling you the hour and the minute
and the second, with a white silence and a glowing, all
certainty and knowing what it has to tell in the hours of
the night passing swiftly on toward further darknesses,
but moving also toward a new sun.
```

```
            Of course I'm happy. What does she think?  I'm not?
he asked the quiet rooms.  He stood looking up at the ventilator
grille in the hall and suddenly he remembered that there was
something hidden behind the grille, something that almost
seemed to peer down at him now, and he took his eyes away quickly.
                                                      kkknk
kkkkkkkkkkk
            What a strange meeting on a strange night.  He remembered
none like it save one afternoon not long ago when he had met an
old man in the park and they had talked.  kkkkkkkkkk
            Montag shook his head.  He looked at a blank wall.  The
girl's face was there, really quite beautiful in memory;
```

In its final form, *Fahrenheit 451* opens with Montag's solitary late-night walk home, and his first meeting with his young neighbor, Clarisse Mc-Clellan. In the final typescript (*top*), just above his description of Clarisse, Bradbury attached a last-minute insert (*bottom*) containing the very first reference to Montag's hidden books and the first mention of Montag's mentor, Professor Faber. From a carbon of the original submission in the Albright Collection; image courtesy of Donn Albright and Ray Bradbury.

attuned to the more disturbing political and social tendencies of the time. The book also advanced Bradbury's reputation in broader literary circles: Nobel laureate Bertrand Russell was greatly impressed by the implications of the novel, and in early April 1954 he hosted Bradbury for an evening at his home during Bradbury's stay in London. Upon his return to the United States, Bradbury received a literary prize for *Fahrenheit 451* at the annual ceremony of the American Academy of Arts and Letters.

In spite of these recognitions, the more subtle threats to the novel's longevity remained for decades. In one of the great ironies of literary history, *Fahrenheit 451* was itself silently modified in the 1960s to make the novel more likely to win school-board approval as a classroom text. A special "Bal-Hi" edition, first printed in 1967, retained the typesetting of the first edition, but the text was altered at nearly a hundred points to remove profanity and references to sexuality, drinking, drug use, and nudity.[7] This version was never intended to replace the mass-market paperback, but beginning in 1973 the censored text was accidentally transferred to successive printings of the commercial text. For the next six years no uncensored paperback copies were in print, and no one seemed to notice it. Students eventually noted the differences between their school texts and older mass-market printings and brought this mystery to Bradbury's attention. Since 1979 new typesettings of the restored text—and *only* the restored text—have reached print.

Fortunately, the censorship episode did not obscure the universal message that Bradbury had envisioned for *Fahrenheit 451* from the beginning. Bradbury was initially inspired by Arthur Koestler's riveting exposé of Stalin's political terrors and finally motivated to write by the emerging climate of fear during the early years of the

Cold War. His hatred of all totalitarian regimes came into sharp focus in his "Day After Tomorrow" essay, published in *The Nation* just as he was about to finish the final draft of *Fahrenheit 451*:

> Consider the similarity of two books—Koestler's "Darkness at Noon," laid in our recent past, and George Orwell's "1984," set in our immediate future. And here *we* are, poised between the two, between a dreadful reality and an unformed terror, trying to make such decisions as will avoid the tyranny of the very far right and the tyranny of the very far left, the two of which can often be seen coalescing into a tyranny pure and simple, with no qualifying adjective in front of it at all.[8]

As the McCarthy era's climate of fear slowly receded in America, it became clear that Bradbury had succeeded in dramatizing important ideas—fundamental ideas that define our humanity—with vitality, intensity, and emotional impact. Over time, *Fahrenheit 451* even surpassed the enduring popularity of *The Martian Chronicles*, *The Illustrated Man*, and his more nostalgic *Dandelion Wine*. Sixty years out, *Fahrenheit 451* has come to symbolize the importance of literacy and reading in an increasingly visual culture, offering hope that the wonders of technology and the raptures of multimedia entertainments will never obscure the vital importance of an examined life.

Jonathan R. Eller is Chancellor's Professor of English and Director of the Center for Ray Bradbury Studies at Indiana University–Purdue University, Indianapolis. His most recent book, *Becoming Ray Bradbury*, examines Bradbury's early life and career, culminating in the publication of *Fahrenheit 451*.

NOTES

1. In his "Afterword" to the more recent Ballantine trade and mass-market paperback editions of *Fahrenheit 451*, Bradbury states that this creative burst of typing occurred in the spring of 1950. He probably began work on this project during the spring, but his correspondence of the period strongly suggests that the UCLA typing sessions occurred during August 1950, just after Bradbury moved his family from Venice Beach to Clarkson Road in Los Angeles.

2. The preparation and shopping of the "Fireman" manuscript is documented in Don Congdon to Ray Bradbury, 13 and 21 September, 20 October, and 7 and 10 November 1950, Albright Collection.

3. Gold's comments on the text and on marketing "The Fireman" are preserved in Horace Gold to Ray Bradbury, 30 October, [ca. November], and 21 December 1950, Albright Collection. In the spring of 1954, during Bradbury's first visit with celebrated Renaissance art authority Bernard Berenson in Florence, Italy, Berenson suggested a similar scenario in which the Book People misremember the texts.

4. This was at first a subconscious impulse: "I left the theater, unknowingly, with child. Various short stories and the novel were inevitable."

5. At the time Bradbury was under contract with Doubleday for his next novel, and Ballantine was obligated to keep the expansion of "The Fireman" in the context of a story collection. Doubleday's subsequent publication of *Dandelion Wine* (1957) obviated the need for this distinction; of the many later trade editions of *Fahrenheit 451*, only Simon & Schuster's 1967 hardbound edition retained Ballantine's original companion stories.

6. Ray Bradbury to Rupert Hart-Davis, 26 February 1953, Hart-Davis Collection, University of Tulsa, Tulsa, Oklahoma.

7. The first and most comprehensive analysis of the Bal-Hi changes to Bradbury's text is George R. Guffey's "*Fahrenheit 451* and the 'Cubby-Hole Editors' of Ballantine Books," in George E. Slusser, Eric S. Rabkin, and Robert Scholes, eds., *Coordinates: Placing Science Fiction and Fantasy* (Carbondale, IL: Southern Illinois University Press, 1983), 99–106.

8. Ray Bradbury, "The Day After Tomorrow: Why Science Fiction?" *The Nation* (May 2, 1953): 364–67.

Bradbury's first extended expression of his purposes in writing science fiction appeared in the May 2, 1953, issue of *The Nation*. Editor Carey McWilliams had requested this article for an issue of *The Nation* that focused on literature and books; in response, Bradbury opened his article with a lengthy prologue describing how the radio earpieces he was creating during his revision of "The Fireman" were already appearing, quite independently of his work, among pedestrians he had recently encountered near his home. Bradbury's reflections on this phenomenon, excerpted here along with major points from his essay, were composed just as he was transforming "The Fireman" into *Fahrenheit 451*.

FROM "THE DAY AFTER TOMORROW: WHY SCIENCE FICTION?"

Ray Bradbury

Three years ago I wrote a short novel entitled "The Fire Man" which told the story of a municipal department in the year 1999 that came to your house to *start* fires, instead of to put them out. If your neighbors suspected you of reading a mildly subversive book, or any book at all for that matter, they simply turned in an alarm. The hose-bearing sensors then thundered up in their red engines and squirted kerosene on your books, your house, and sometimes on you. Then a match was struck. This short novel was intended as science fiction.

Elsewhere in the narrative I described my Fire Man arriving home after midnight to find his wife in bed afflicted with two varieties of stupor. She is in a trance, a condition so withdrawn as to resemble catatonia, compounded of equal parts liquor and a small Seashell thimble-radio tucked in her ear. The Seashell

croons and murmurs its music and commercials and private little melodramas for her alone. The room is silent. The husband
cannot even try to guess the communion between Seashell and
wife. Awakening her is not unlike applying shock to a cataleptic.

I thought I was writing a story of prediction, describing a
world that might evolve in four or five decades. But only a month
ago, in Beverly Hills one night, a husband and wife passed me,
walking their dog. I stood staring after them, absolutely stunned.
The woman held in one hand a small cigarette-package-sized
radio, its antenna quivering. From this sprang tiny copper wires
which ended in a dainty cone plugged into her right ear. There she
was, oblivious to man and dog, listening to far winds and whispers
and soap-opera cries, sleepwalking, helped up and down curbs by
a husband who might just as well not have been there. This was
not science fiction. This was a new fact in our changing society.

As you can see, I must start writing very fast indeed about
our future world in order to stand still. I thought I had raced
ahead of science, predicting the radio-induced semi-catatonic.
In the long haul, science pulled abreast, tipped its hat, and fed
me the dust. The woman with the radio-thimble crammed in her
ear the other night symbolized my failure to count on certain
psychological needs which demanded satisfaction earlier than
I supposed.

Whether or not my ideas on censorship via the fire depart-
ment will be old hat by this time next week, I dare not predict.
When the wind is right, a faint odor of kerosene is exhaled from
Senator McCarthy. . . .

So much depends, of course, on what the individual *hears*
when he gives himself over to the electronic tides breaking on
the shore of his Seashell. The voice of conscience and reason?
An echo of morality? A new thought? A fresh idea? A morsel

of philosophy? Or bias, hatred, fear, prejudice, nightmare, lies, half-truths, and suspicions? Or, perhaps even worse, the sound of one emptiness striking hollowly against yet another and another emptiness, broken at two-minute intervals by a jolly commercial, preferably in rhymed quatrains or couplets?

In writing a science-fiction story around such an idea, the author must consider many things. Is there, for instance, a delicate interplay where the society does not crush the individual but where the individual realizes that without his cooperation society would fly to pieces through the centrifugal force of anarchy? Is the programming on such an ear-button receiver of a caliber to enable a man to be a gyroscope, both taking from and giving to society, beautifully balanced? Does it tell him what to do *every* hour and *every* minute of *every* day? Or, fearing knowledge of any sort, tell him nothing, and spoonfeed him mush? The challenge and the fun come in handling all the above ideas and materials in such a way as to predict how perversely or how well man will use himself, and therefore his mechanical extensions, in the coming time of our lives. . . .

This, I think, should answer why I have more often than not written stories which, for a convenient label, are called science fiction. There are few literary fields, it seems to me, that deal so strikingly with themes that concern us all today; there are few more exciting genres; there are none fresher or so full of continually renewed and renewable concepts.

It is, after all, the fiction of ideas, the fiction where philosophy can be tinkered with, torn apart, and put back together again, it is the fiction of sociology and psychology and history compounded and squared by time. It is the fiction where you may set up and knock down your own political and religious and moral states. It can be a high form of Swiss watch-making. It *can* be poetry. It *has* resulted in some of the greatest writing in our past, from Plato and Lucian to Sir Thomas More and François Rabelais and on down through Jonathan Swift and Johannes Kepler to Poe and Edward Bellamy and George Orwell. . . .

I once strongly suspected that fun was the handmaiden, if not the progenitor, of the arts; now I *know* this for certain. And with a great sense of pleasure and personal well-being, I intend to continue in the field for a good many years along with those others who are interested in trying to find a bridge to cross that vast gulf of communication permanently for all of us. I do not know whether tomorrow's street will be full of human beings with Seashell thimble-radios whispering in their ears and all the world and its problems moved away and neglected. Or whether by some miracle we may all carry supersonic stethoscopes with us on our rounds, so that each may know the sound of every other human heart. I only know that it would be interesting to walk on that street and think about it and write about it, before that evening sun goes down.

". . . the great shadowing, motioned silence of the Hound leaping out like a moth in the raw light, finding, holding its victim, inserting the needle and going back to its kennel. . . ." Ray Bradbury's ink sketch of the Mechanical Hound composed in the fall of 2005. From the Albright Collection; reproduced courtesy of Donn Albright and Ray Bradbury.

Bradbury's fiction has always been a popular subject for audio recording, but it would take almost a quarter of a century to finally record the author's voice reading *Fahrenheit 451*. This transcript of Bradbury's commentary on the making of the novel derives from the Listening Library's 1976 two-LP recording of the author reading extensive passages from the novel. His commentary was presented extemporaneously, and reflects Bradbury's deep-seated memories of the highly emotional motivation, spontaneous creativity, and determined originality that resulted in a timeless cautionary tale.

FAHRENHEIT 451: AUDIO INTRODUCTION
Ray Bradbury

I think it's always fascinating (at least, it's always fascinating to me) to discuss the genesis of a short story or a poem or a novel. I look upon ideas as great big bulldogs that bite me, grab me, hold on, and won't let go, and when I get a good idea it simply seizes me and holds on very tightly. And maybe an hour later or ten hours later or two days later, it lets go and I'm finished with it. I'm not in control; I have no schedule for my life, these ideas just come up and beg to bite me, and I let them. . . .

I've learned, over the years, to go with this sort of thing. . . . I was walking with a friend, and a police car pulled up and asked us what we were doing, and I made the mistake of saying, "Putting one foot in front of the other," which was the wrong answer. The policeman interrogated us, thinking that we were up to some terrible criminal activity; the whole logic of the situation was beyond him. I became so enraged with the encounter, the fact that my innocence was doubted, that I ran home and wrote an angry short story called "The Pedestrian." Well, now, if it hadn't been for that encounter with that policeman, a lot of other wonderful things would never have happened. When I look back now, I realize how fortunate it was that policeman stopped me that particular night, because it set in order, and in a certain kind of emotional progression, a whole series of things rolling.

Not only did I finish the short story "The Pedestrian," but then, a number of months or perhaps a year later, I took that pedestrian out into the streets of the city of the future and I wandered that pedestrian around. And along the way, I changed the sex of that pedestrian from a man to a girl named Clarisse McClellan, and I had her out walking late at night, scuffing the leaves, looking at the stars, smelling the wind, waiting for rain. And she smells kerosene. Around the corner, from the other direction, comes a man smelling of kerosene, and she speaks to him, and says, "Oh, I know who you are. I know what you do. I can tell from the smell of the kerosene on your uniform. You are a fireman. You're one of those men who goes to places to start fires."

Well, my gosh, I didn't know she was going to be saying that, I didn't know Montag was going to be coming around that corner. I became very excited, and within seven, eight, nine days I finished the first draft of a short story that turned into a novel, that turned into a longer novel, called "The Fireman." And in order to finish the novel—I had no office, I looked around for a good place to write this fantastic story that was coming to birth, and I thought, "Well, what's a better place to write a novel about book burning in the future than a library?" And I discovered, in that time, that wonderful downstairs basement room in the UCLA library with a typewriter that you fed a dime into every half hour. So I sat there and fed dimes into this typewriter for eight or nine days, twenty cents an hour, and finished the short novel "The Fireman" on that typewriter in a room with ten or fifteen or twenty other students who didn't know what I was up to.

But what a wonderful place to write a novel about the future and about books and about libraries. Also, I wrote very quickly, because I wanted to be very honest—I wanted to be emotionally honest. I've always believed in quick writing, so that I could get things out before I had time to think about them. I wanted to be true to whatever inner logic there was in myself. I didn't want to be true to any one group of people in the world. I wanted to be true to my own anger. I've always been afraid of belonging to groups. I don't want to be a Democrat or a Republican or a Communist or a Fascist, or—just an all-American. I wanted to be, as far as I can be, myself, and find out what *I* think, and get it out in the open and *then* intellectualize about it. And see what I think.

So suddenly here I am, writing an angry short novel because I lived, that particular year, in 1950, at a time at the end of World War II when politics in the United States were going through a very difficult period, when we had Joseph McCarthy, the strange senator, on our hands, who was trying to browbeat us, and trying to scare us. So it was a combination of many things that went into my anger and caused me to write the novel. And when I finished it and published a short version of it, we were still in the midst of the scare period in our political history; even President Truman was running scared at that time. I decided I would like to do a longer version of it, and I sat down in a similar nine- or ten-day period, added another fifteen, twenty, twenty-five thousand words to it, again with the same sort of emotional resources. I wanted to be emotional so I could get all of my own truths out, so that I wouldn't be slanting toward any one particular group.

As a result of writing the novel in this way—it's a great adventure, that's the first thing it is. It has things to say politically, it has things to say aesthetically, it has things to say about literature. It has all sorts of intellectual things to say along the way. But they are enclosed in an emotional framework, which is very important. I believe in having fun first, and along the way, if you teach people, if you influence people, well and good. But I don't want to set out to influence people. I don't want to set out to change the world in any self-conscious way. That way leads to self-destruction; that way, you're pontificating, and that's dangerous and it's boring—you're going to put people right to sleep.

So instead of doing that—I've always loved adventure stories, I've always loved adventure films. I've loved murder mysteries and science fiction adventures. I took a framework, then, of a suspense—actually a pursuit and escape thing—and you then hang on all the things that you want to say, all the things that you want to do, about a particular time that you live in, about a time that you would like to prevent, because I'm a preventer of futures, I'm not a predictor of them. So Montag is myself running through the future, as afraid as I am at times. Brave only because he's angry (I'm not a brave person; I'm an angry person on occasion). And along the way, meeting other people who are really myself—a character like Faber, who pops up in the novel later on, and is Montag's conscience speaking to him in the night through his little Seashell radio. Well, that really is myself, hiding away—the writer who's afraid to come out in the open and has to get all of his kicks and do all of his influencing of the world by whispering in people's ears. And I suppose that's what I do. I'm like Faber, whispering in people's ears and telling them what to do, here and there, along the way. So Faber is a part of myself. Even the fire chief, I suppose, when you come right down to it, is a part of myself that could be destructive if I allowed that destructive self to come to the surface.

So here we have, then, Montag running through the future, pursued by book burners, trying to save knowledge. And all this goes back into my own background when I was a child. I'm a library-educated person; I've never made it to college. When I left high school, I began to go to the library every day of my life for five, ten, fifteen years. So the library was my nesting place, it was my birthing place, it was my growing place. And my books are full of libraries and librarians and book people, and booksellers. So my love of books is so intense that I finally have done— what? I have written a book about a man falling in love with books. How unusual that is—it's not a love story on any other level. And when the film finally came out, it wasn't a love story, *except* it was the love story of Montag and literature. I think that's quite unusual in the history of the world. I don't think there are very many writers around who have written that many books about books, about libraries, about knowledge, and how precious it is, and how we must keep it.

And finally, how did I title this? Well, I called it all sorts of things along the way. At one time it was called "Long After Midnight." It was called "The Fireman" for a while. But I didn't like any of those titles. And then I asked myself, "Well, what *is* the temperature that books catch fire at and burn?" And I called the UCLA physics department, and I called the chemistry department. I called several other universities. Nobody knew, and nobody seemed to be able to look it up for me. And finally a light went on in my head, and I called the fire department. And I said, "Put me through to the fire chief." I got hold of the fire chief here in Los Angeles, and I said, "At what temperature does book paper catch fire and burn?" He said, "Just a moment, be right back." He came back and said, "451 Fahrenheit." And I thought, "Oh, that's beautiful." That's absolutely beautiful. It's perfect. So I reversed it, and said Fahrenheit 451, and there you have the title. And if we start using Celsius in the next few years, I will be severely disappointed.

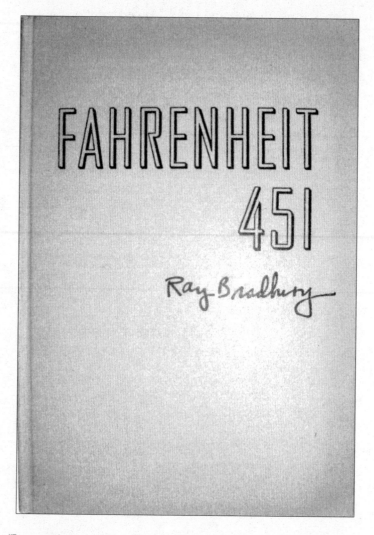

"It was a pleasure to burn." A limited issue of two hundred signed and numbered copies of *Fahrenheit 451* were bound in white asbestos boards and released (without dust jackets) along with the first-edition trade hardbound issue in October 1953. They are easily distinguished from the red cloth binding of the trade edition. Approximately fifty of the asbestos-bound copies were sold in the Los Angeles area with trade dust jackets.

From its initial publication in 1953 until 1967, editions of *Fahrenheit 451* carried no author's introduction at all. Bradbury composed his most extensive introduction in 1982 for the Limited Editions Club; in 1989 it was titled and reprinted for *Zen in the Art of Writing*, a collection of Bradbury's essays on creativity, and this version serves as the source of the present text. The essay eventually became the afterword to the 1996 Ballantine trade paperback edition of *Fahrenheit 451*, confirming Bradbury's abiding enthusiasm for the stage and film versions that emerged from the original novel.

INVESTING DIMES: *FAHRENHEIT 451*
Ray Bradbury

I didn't know it, but I was literally writing a dime novel. In the spring of 1950 it cost me nine dollars and eighty cents to write and finish the first draft of *The Fire Man*, which later became *Fahrenheit 451*.

In all the years from 1941 to that time, I had done most of my typing in the family garages, either in Venice, California (where we lived because we were poor, not because it was the "in" place to be), or behind the tract house where my wife, Marguerite, and I raised our family. I was driven out of my garage by my loving children, who insisted on coming around to the rear window and singing and tapping on the panes. Father had to choose between finishing a story or playing with the girls. I chose to play, of course, which endangered the family income. An office had to be found. We couldn't afford one.

Finally, I located just the place: the typing room in the basement of the library at the University of California at Los Angeles. There, in neat rows, were a score or more of old Remington or Underwood typewriters which rented out at a dime a half hour. You thrust your dime in, the clock ticked madly, and you typed wildly, to finish before the half hour was out. Thus I was twice driven; by children to leave home, and by a typewriter timing device to be a maniac at the keys. Time was indeed money. I finished the first draft in roughly nine days. At twenty-five thousand words, it was half the novel it eventually would become.

Between investing dimes and going insane when the typewriter jammed (for there went your precious time!) and whipping pages in and out of the device, I wandered upstairs. There I strolled, lost in love, down the corridors and through the stacks, touching books, pulling volumes out, turning pages, thrusting volumes back, drowning in all the good stuffs that are the essence of libraries. What a place, don't you agree, to write a novel about burning books in the future!

So much for pasts. What about *Fahrenheit 451* in this day and age? Have I changed my mind about much that it said to me, when I was a younger writer? Only if by change you mean has my love of libraries widened and deepened, to which the answer is a yes that ricochets off the stacks and dusts talcum off the librarian's cheek. Since writing this book, I have spun more stories, novels, essays, and poems about writers than any other writer in history that I can think of. I have written poems about Melville, Melville and Emily Dickinson, Emily Dickinson and Charles Dickens, Hawthorne, Poe, Edgar Rice Burroughs, and along the way I compared Jules Verne and his Mad Captain to Melville and his equally obsessed mariner. I have scribbled poems about librarians, taken night trains with my favorite authors across the continental wilderness, staying up all night gambling and drinking, drinking and chatting. I warned Melville, in one poem, to stay away from land (it never was his stuff!) and turned Bernard Shaw into a robot, so as to conveniently stow him aboard a rocket and wake him on the long journey to Alpha Centauri to hear his Prefaces piped off his tongue and into my delighted ear. I have written a Time Machine story in which I hum back to sit at the deathbeds of Wilde, Melville, and Poe to tell of my love and warm their bones in their last hours. . . . But enough. As you can see, I am madness—maddened when it comes to books, writers, and the great granary silos where their wits are stored.

Recently, with the Studio Theatre Playhouse in Los Angeles at hand, I called all my characters from *F. 451* out of the shadows. What's new, I said to Montag, Clarisse, Faber, Beatty, since last we met in 1953?

I asked. *They* answered.

They wrote new scenes, revealed odd parts of their as-yet undiscovered souls and dreams. The result was a two-act drama, staged with good results, and in the main, fine reviews.

Beatty came farthest out of the wings in answer to my question: How did it start? Why did you make the decision to become Fire Chief, a burner of books? Beatty's surprising answer came in a scene where he takes our hero, Guy Montag, home to his apartment. Entering, Montag is stunned to discover the thousands upon thousands of books lining the walls of the Fire Chief's hidden library! Montag turns and cries out to his superior:

"But you're the Chief Burner! You can't have books on your premises!"

To which the Chief, with a dry, light smile, replies:

"It's not *owning* books that's a crime, Montag, it's *reading* them! Yes, that's right. I own books, but don't *read* them!"

Montag, in shock, awaits Beatty's explanation.

"Don't you see the beauty, Montag? I never read them. Not one book, not one chapter, not one page, not one paragraph. I *do* play with ironies, don't I? To have thousands of books and never crack one, to turn your back on the lot and say: No. It's like having a house full of beautiful women and, smiling, not touching . . . one. So, you see, I'm not a criminal at all. If you ever catch me *reading* one, yes, then turn me in! But this place is as pure as a twelve-year-old virgin girl's cream-white summer night bedroom. These books die on the shelves. Why? Because I say so. I do not give them sustenance, no hope with hand or eye or tongue. They are no better than dust."

Montag protests: "I don't see how you can't be—"

"Tempted?" cries the Fire Chief. "Oh, *that* was long ago. The apple is eaten and gone. The snake has returned to its tree. The garden has grown to weed and rust."

"Once—" Montag hesitates, then continues, "Once you must have loved books very much."

"Touché!" the Fire Chief responds. "Below the belt. On the chin. Through the heart. Ripping the gut. Oh, look at me, Montag. The man who loved books, no, the boy who was wild for them, insane for them, who climbed the stacks like a chimpanzee gone mad for them.

"I ate them like salad, books were my sandwich for lunch, my tiffin and dinner and midnight munch. I tore out the pages, ate them with salt, doused them with relish, gnawed on the bindings, turned the chapters with my tongue! Books by the dozen, the score, and the billion. I carried so many home I was hunchbacked for years. Philosophy, art history, politics, social science, the poem, the essay, the grandiose play, you name 'em, I ate 'em. And then . . . and then . . ." The Fire Chief's voice fades.

Montag prompts: "And then?"

"Why, life happened to me." The Fire Chief shuts his eyes to remember. "Life. The usual. The same. The love that wasn't quite right, the dream that went sour, the sex that fell apart, the deaths that came swiftly to friends not deserving, the murder of someone or another, the insanity of someone close, the slow death of a mother, the abrupt suicide of a father—a stampede of elephants, an onslaught of disease. And nowhere, nowhere the right book for the right time to stuff in the crumbling wall of the breaking dam to hold back the deluge, give or take a metaphor, lose or find a simile. And by the far edge of thirty, and the near rim of thirty-one, I picked myself up, every bone broken, every centimeter of flesh abraded, bruised, or scarred. I looked in the mirror and found an old man lost behind the frightened face of a young man, saw a hatred there for everything and anything, you name it, I'd damn it, and opened the pages of my fine library books and found what, what, what?!"

Montag guesses. "The pages were empty?"

"Bull's eye! Blank! Oh, the words were there, all right, but they ran over my eyes like hot oil, signifying nothing. Offering no help, no solace, no peace, no harbor, no true love, no bed, no light."

Montag thinks back: "Thirty years ago . . . the final library burnings . . ."

"On target." Beatty nods. "And having no job, and being a failed Romantic or whatever in hell, I put in for Fireman First Class. First up the steps, first into the library, first in the burning furnace heart of his ever-blazing countrymen, douse me with kerosene, hand me my torch!

"End of lecture. There you go, Montag. Out the door!"

Montag leaves, with more curiosity than ever about books, well on his way to becoming an outcast, soon to be pursued and almost destroyed by the Mechanical Hound, my robot clone of A. Conan Doyle's great Baskerville beast.

In my play, old man Faber, the teacher-not-quite-in-residence, speaking to Montag through the long night (via the Seashell tamp-in ear radio) is victimized by the Fire Chief. How? Beatty suspects Montag is being instructed by such a secret device, knocks it out of his ear, and shouts at the far-removed teacher:

"We're coming to get you! We're at the door! We're up the stairs! Gotcha!"

Which so terrifies Faber, his heart destroys him.

All good stuff. Tempting, this late in time. I've had to fight not to stuff it into the novel.

Finally, many readers have written protesting Clarisse's disappearance, wondering what happened to her. François Truffaut felt the same curiosity, and, in his film version of my novel, rescued Clarisse from oblivion and located her with the Book People wandering in the forest, reciting their litany of books to themselves. I felt the same need to save her, for after all, she, verging on silly star-struck chatter, was in many ways responsible for Montag's beginning to wonder about books and what was in them. In my play, therefore, Clarisse emerges to welcome Montag and give a somewhat happier ending to what was, in essence, pretty grim stuff.

The novel, however, remains true to its former self. I don't believe in tampering with any young writer's material, especially when that young writer was once myself. Montag, Beatty, Mildred, Faber, Clarisse, all stand, move, enter, and exit as they did thirty-two years ago when I first wrote them down, at a dime a half-hour, in the basement of the UCLA Library. I have changed not one thought or word.

A last discovery. I write all of my novels and stories, as you have seen, in a great surge of delightful passion. Only recently, glancing at the novel, I realized that Montag is named after a paper manufacturing company. And Faber, of course, is a maker of pencils! What a sly thing my subconscious was, to name them thus.

And not tell *me*!

SCENE TWO:

Out of the darkness the faint outline of the city is seen
on the backdrop. As the stagelights brighten we find,
stage-left, a steep flight of rickety steps leading up to
part of an ancient porch. The rest of the old house cannot be seen.

Far away, the sound of the FIRE SIREN.

A WOMAN, dressed in black, with a dark shawl about her
shoulders, her face chalk-pale, comes out on the porch as
if drawn by the wail of the siren. As the siren draws
nearer she stiffens, then visibly forces herself to relax.
Slowly, she begins to walk down the porch steps. When she
is halfway down, thinking of each step she makes, holding
to the rickety porch rail, she is interrupted by:

The bursting out on the stage of the FIREMEN, at full tilt,
as if they had just been thrown running from the braked
Engine which we hear thundering and knocking to a halt just
beyond stage-right. MONTAG is in the lead, carrying a
silver torch in which a blue flame burns steadily. At sight
of the woman waiting, he freezes and lets the others collide
with themselves.

They stand thus for a moment, MONTAG and his three associates.
Behind them, from stage-right, BEATTY appears walking last,
slowly.

The WOMAN waits without speaking.

BEATTY looks at his men and moves slowly through them to
stop at the bottom of the stairs, looking up at the woman
in black.

                    IS THIS THE
              BEATTY (bleakly)
    Good Lord, who's that? The owner of the
    house? Where are the police? There's been
    a mixup. The authorities should have been
    here before us and taken her away. Now she'll
    give us trouble. (he steps forward)
    Mrs. John L. Hudson, 11 St. James Street?

              Mrs. HUDSON
    You must know who I am. Why are you
    here?

During the late summer and fall of 1954, Academy Award–winning actor
Charles Laughton and producer Paul Gregory backed Bradbury's first attempt at adapting *Fahrenheit 451* for the stage. This opening page of act 1,
scene ii, describes the woman who will ignite herself and her books rather
than yield to the incinerating flames of the Firemen. Bradbury's holograph
revisions quicken the action and condense the dialogue. Although this version was never produced, the experience provided important lessons for
Bradbury's subsequent successful stage adaptations of his works. Courtesy
of Donn Albright and Ray Bradbury.

Bradbury's hand-painted box lid for his spring 1979 *Fahrenheit 451* stage adaptation typescript; this script served as the basis for his first stage production during the summer and fall of 1979 in Los Angeles. The box now contains Bradbury's carbons of the original 1955 script, which served as the basis for the 1979 rewrite. From the Albright collection; reproduced courtesy of Donn Albright and Ray Bradbury.

In the fall of 1978, a Missouri high school English teacher and his students discovered that student copies of *Fahrenheit 451* differed from the teacher's personal copy—certain words or phrases deemed controversial or offensive had been eliminated from the special edition printed for school-age readers more than a decade earlier. This class may not have been the first group of readers to notice the differences, but they were the first to write to Ray Bradbury, who was unaware of the changes. A restored edition soon followed in 1979, completely reset and concluding with Bradbury's final word on the sanctity of texts.

CODA

Ray Bradbury

About two years ago, a letter arrived from a solemn young Vassar lady telling me how much she enjoyed reading my experiment in space mythology, *The Martian Chronicles*.

But, she added, wouldn't it be a good idea, this late in time, to rewrite the book inserting more women's characters and roles?

A few years before that I got a certain amount of mail concerning the same Martian book complaining that the blacks in the book were Uncle Toms, and why didn't I "do them over"?

Along about then came a note from a Southern white suggesting that I was prejudiced in favor of the blacks and the entire story should be dropped.

Two weeks ago my mountain of mail delivered forth a pipsqueak mouse of a letter from a well-known publishing house that wanted to reprint my story "The Fog Horn" in a high school reader.

In my story, I had described a lighthouse as having, late at night, an illumination coming from it that was a "God-Light." Looking up at it from the viewpoint of any sea-creature, one would have felt that one was in "the Presence."

The editors had deleted "God-Light" and "in the Presence."

Some five years back, the editors of yet another anthology for school readers put together a volume with some 400 (count 'em) short stories in it. How do you cram 400 short stories by Twain, Irving, Poe, Maupassant, and Bierce into one book?

Simplicity itself. Skin, debone, demarrow, scarify, melt, render down, and destroy. Every adjective that counted, every verb that moved, every metaphor that weighed more than a mosquito—out! Every simile that would have made a sub-moron's mouth twitch—gone! Any aside that explained the two-bit philosophy of a first-rate writer—lost.

Every story, slenderized, starved, bluepenciled, leeched, and bled white, resembled every other story. Twain read like Poe read like Shakespeare read like Dostoevsky read like—in the finale—Edgar Guest. Every word of more than three syllables had been razored. Every image that demanded so much as one instant's attention—shot dead.

Do you begin to get the damned and incredible picture?

How did I react to all of the above?

By "firing" the whole lot.

By sending rejection slips to each and every one.

By ticketing the assembly of idiots to the far reaches of hell.

The point is obvious. There is more than one way to burn a book. And the world is full of people running about with lit matches. Every minority, be it Baptist/Unitarian, Irish/Italian /Octogenarian/Zen Buddhist, Zionist/Seventh-day Adventist, Women's Lib/Republican, Mattachine/Four Square Gospel feels it has the will, the right, the duty to douse the kerosene, light the fuse. Every dimwit editor who sees himself as the source of all dreary blanc-mange plain-porridge unleavened literature licks his guillotine and eyes the neck of any author who dares to speak above a whisper or write above a nursery rhyme.

Fire Captain Beatty, in my novel *Fahrenheit 451*, described how the books were burned first by minorities, each ripping a page or a paragraph from this book, then that, until the day came when the books were empty and the minds shut and the libraries closed forever.

"Shut the door, they're coming through the window, shut the window, they're coming through the door," are the words to an old song. They fit my lifestyle with newly arriving butcher/censors every month. Only six weeks ago, I discovered that, over the years, some cubby-hole editors at Ballantine Books, fearful of contaminating the young, had, bit by bit, censored some seventy-five separate sections from the novel. Students reading the novel, which, after all, deals with censorship and book-burning in the future, wrote to tell me of this exquisite irony. Judy-Lynn del Rey, one of the new Ballantine editors, is having the entire book reset and republished this summer with all the damns and hells back in place.

A final test for old Job II here: I sent a play, *Leviathan 99*, off to a university theater a month ago. My play is based on the *Moby-Dick* mythology, dedicated to Melville, and concerns a rocket crew and a blind space captain who venture forth to encounter a Great White Comet and destroy the destroyer. My drama premiers as an opera in Paris this autumn. But, for now, the university wrote back that they hardly dared do my play—it had no women in it! And the ERA ladies on campus would descend with ball-bats if the drama department even tried!

Grinding my bicuspids into powder, I suggested that would mean, from now on, no more productions of *Boys in the Band* (no women), or *The Women* (no men). Or, counting heads, male and female, a good lot of Shakespeare that would never be seen again, especially if you count lines and find that all the good stuff went to the males!

I wrote back maybe they should do my play one week and *The Women* the next. They probably thought I was joking, and I'm not sure that I wasn't.

For it is a mad world and it will get madder if we allow the minorities, be they dwarf or giant, orangutan or dolphin, nuclear-head or water-conservationist, pro-computerologist or Neo-Luddite, simpleton or sage, to interfere with aesthetics. The real world is the playing ground for each and every group, to make or unmake laws. But the tip of the nose of my books or stories or poems is where their rights end and my territorial imperatives begin, run and rule. If Mormons do not like my plays, let them write their own. If the Irish hate my Dublin stories, let them rent typewriters. If teachers and grammar-school editors find my jaw-breaker sentences shatter their mushmilk teeth, let them eat stale cake dunked in weak tea of their own ungodly manufacture. If the Chicano intellectuals wish to re-cut my "Wonderful Ice Cream Suit" so it shapes "Zoot," may the belt unravel and the pants fall.

For, let's face it, digression is the soul of wit. Take philosophic asides away from Dante, Milton, or Hamlet's father's ghost and what stays is dry bones. Laurence Sterne said it once: "Digressions, incontestably, are the sunshine . . . the life, the soul of reading!" Take them out, and one cold, eternal winter would reign in every page. Restore them in the writer—he steps forth like a bridegroom, bids them all-hail, brings in variety, and forbids the appetite to fail.

In sum, do not insult me with the beheadings, finger-choppings, or the lung-deflations you plan for my works. I need my head to shake or nod, my hand to wave or make into a fist, my lungs to shout or whisper with. I will not go gently onto a shelf, degutted, to become a non-book.

All you umpires, back to the bleachers. Referees, hit the showers. It's my game. I pitch, I hit, I catch. I run the bases. At sunset, I've won or lost. At sunrise, I'm out again, giving it the old try.

And no one can help me. Not even you.

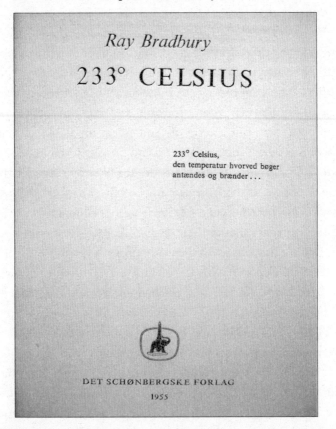

Ray Bradbury

233° CELSIUS

233° Celsius,
den temperatur hvorved bøger
antændes og brænder...

DET SCHØNBERGSKE FORLAG
1955

"Celsius 233: the temperature at which book paper burns." The 1955 Danish translation, with the title converted to centigrade, represents one of the first foreign language editions of *Fahrenheit 451*. All other Latin alphabet foreign language editions (including subsequent Danish editions) have been published with the *Fahrenheit 451* title restored.

Part Two
Other Voices

I have now read the book and found it powerful. The sort of future society that he portrays is only too possible.
—Bertrand Russell, March 13, 1954

Nelson Algren (1909–81), whose best-selling novels of social realism propelled him into the ranks of America's most popular midcentury authors, received an advance copy of *Fahrenheit 451* from Ian Ballantine's senior editor Stanley Kauffmann in early September 1953. Both Algren and his wife found *Fahrenheit 451*, as well as the two companion stories "And the Rock Cried Out" and "The Playground," absorbing and relevant cautionary tales. Algren's September 30 reply was incorporated into Ballantine's fall 1953 advertising campaign.

From a Letter to Stanley Kauffmann, Ballantine Books

Nelson Algren

Mr. Bradbury can bring the future closer to the reader than most writers can bring the present. This is because, no matter how prophetic, he is always topical: like Orwell, his fantasies are never so remote but that we see their beginnings all about us. His understanding of our own times affords a special force to his portraits of man's future, and a humor not possessed by any other science-fiction writer.

Orville Prescott (1907–96) was the lead book reviewer of *The New York Times* for nearly twenty-five years. His influence spanned the middle decades of the twentieth century, and his October 21, 1953, "Books of the Times" review provided a crucial endorsement for *Fahrenheit 451* that raised the novel's plea for intellectual responsibility and independent thinking above the conformist pressures and political polarization of the early 1950s. Prescott's assertion that Bradbury was already "the uncrowned king of the science-fiction writers" reflected Bradbury's emergence as one of the most recognized names in a field that was rapidly expanding its readership into mainstream American culture.

BOOKS OF THE TIMES

Orville Prescott

Throughout history, in times of crisis and disaster, men have looked to the future, if not with confidence, at least with hope. It would be better than the unhappy present. There would be plenty to eat. The enemy would be defeated. The Messiah would come. The heathen would be converted. Education, universal suffrage, scientific discoveries would usher in a brave new world. But in the mid-twentieth century all this has been reversed. One of the characteristic aspects of our time is that we fear the future. We fear the unholy powers unleashed by science. We fear the absolute power of states more tyrannical than the tyrannies of the past because they strive to rule men's minds as well as their bodies. And writers, who can imagine the dreadful details of such a future more vividly than the rest of us, write books capable of troubling our sleep indefinitely. . . .

Ray Bradbury is the uncrowned king of the science-fiction writers, a young author whose fanciful imagination, poetic prose and mature understanding of human character have won him an international reputation. This is his fifth book and, alas, the first I have read. It contains one short novel, "Fahrenheit 451," and two excellent short stories. One of these is a gruesome fantasy about the barbarous world of childhood. The other is a grim and exciting thriller about two American tourists stranded somewhere in Latin America just when most of the white race is exterminated in an atomic war.

The title of the short novel refers to the temperature at which book paper burns. This is the story of a fireman whose job was not to put out fires, but to start them. In answer to alarms put out by informers, fire companies burned books and the houses of the lawbreakers who concealed them. Books were false, useless and only made people unhappy. It was eccentric to think, psychotic to enjoy the beauties of nature. Normal people doped themselves with synthetic entertainment.

Mr. Bradbury's account of this insane world, which bears many alarming resemblances to our own, is fascinating. His story of the revolt of his fireman, who refused to burn any more books and actually wanted to read them, is engrossing. Some of his imaginative tricks are startling and ingenious. But his basic message is a plea for direct, personal experience rather than perpetual, synthetic entertainment; for individual thought, action and responsibility; for the great tradition of independent thinking and artistic achievement symbolized in books.

Gilbert Highet (1906–78), a distinguished literary critic and classics professor at Columbia University, was also an influential adviser for the Book-of-the-Month Club who spent a lifetime promoting the values of literature for general reading audiences. Throughout the 1950s, his radio program *People, Places, and Books* was widely syndicated in America, Canada, and Great Britain, but it was as chief literary critic for *Harper's* that he wrote one of the first reviews of *Fahrenheit 451* to appear in a major-market magazine. His December 1954 review, "New Wine, Old Bottles," led to a long friendship; in his 1965 introduction to *The Vintage Bradbury* story collection, Highet would place Bradbury among those rare authors whose work "can be instantly recognized by any sensitive reader, and once recognized can never be forgotten."

FROM "NEW WINE, OLD BOTTLES"

Gilbert Highet

The finest living American fantasist, Ray Bradbury, has produced another wonderful story, called *Fahrenheit 451*. . . . 451° is the temperature at which paper catches fire. The book is a meditation on the theme of book burning. But it is much more than an assertion that we ought not to burn unorthodox books. Its hero lives in an epoch in which *all* books are burned, simply because it is a bore and a disturbance to think, and people are happier watching TV all day long and going to bed with a miniature radio whispering and crooning in their earholes. The danger (as Mr. Bradbury sees it) is not that the X group want to burn the Y books and vice versa, not even that a dictator wants to keep all the people ignorant, but (worse) that, moving down one of the slopes on which we are poised, we may reach the stage of hating literature because it is an effort to assimilate, despising books because they are beyond us, changing schools into "activity centers," and abandoning the search for happiness because we prefer soothing or exciting pleasures. All this is presented in a series of clearly described, superbly imagined pictures, part of a terrifying yet hopeful plot: the Mechanical Hound following silently, the City ascending into the air . . .

Idris Parry (1916–2008), an eminent literary scholar, was best known for decades of illuminating and engaging radio programs for the British Broadcasting Corporation. His March 25, 1954, review of *Fahrenheit 451* appeared in *The Listener*, the BBC's national broadcast publication, and provided one of the first influential assessments of *Fahrenheit 451* in Great Britain. It also marked the BBC's first interest in Bradbury's work, eventually leading to a number of dramatizations. Parry's fascination with Bradbury's novel emerged from his own deep interest in the totalitarian nightmare worlds of Franz Kafka, and from his attraction to all literature that explored the boundaries of rationality.

NEW NOVELS

Idris Parry

America of the remote future is the scene of *Fahrenheit 451*. We can assume that a novel set in the past or the present is an account of something that has happened, but of which we have never heard. But the writer who chooses the future does not have this advantage. He is making it all up; he must be. Ray Bradbury's short novel has all the ingredients of absurdity. Well, no, not all: nobody could get them all into one book, though many have tried. The title refers to the temperature at which book-paper burns. Guy Montag is a fireman, but in this machine state of the future the business of the fire brigade is not to put fires out but to start them; their hoses spout kerosene, not water. Possession of books is a crime against happiness, so the fire brigade is alerted only to burn down houses where books are found. Perhaps that prospect is not so absurd. Neither is the fact that people are psychoanalyzed if they walk alone in the woods and watch birds. But what are we to make of a mechanical hound, a contraption of wires and cells and steel, that can be tuned to hunt down any individual (everybody's 'wavelength' kept on file) and kill with poisoned fangs?

> Light flickered on bits of ruby glass and on sensitive capillary hairs in the nylonbrushed nostrils of the creature that quivered gently, gently, its eight legs spidered under it on rubber-padded paws.

This may be tolerable to comic-strip addicts or Yale University (which recently presented *The Tempest* set on another planet, with Antonio and Sebastian arriving by spaceship), but can it satisfy serious readers of fiction? It can, provided the theme is handled by a writer as capable as Ray Bradbury. He gives his impossibilities such vital shape that spiritual truth overwhelms rational disbelief. Montag begins to think, and, as everyone knows, this is disastrous. He steals a book; he begins to read; his treason is discovered and police and the Mechanical Hound pursue him across the city. This hunt will raise the strike, words per minute, of any reader who is not actually dead. I am afraid the book is so exciting that it stands little chance of being considered serious literature.

Ray Bradbury's style is something you will scarcely notice at the first reading. It is an organic expression of personality, pulsing—now fast, now slow—supple, incisive, so moulded into his tale that matter and manner are one and indistinguishable, a physical symbol, a structure of irrational truth. The symbol is valid because it compels us into itself. This is our experience as much as Montag's, not observed and accepted, forgotten as soon as the light dies in the screen, but suffered intimately, a tearing of old scars. So it ceases to be the terror of a particular man in the impossible future. This happens to us, today, in our eternal present.

Sir John Betjeman (1906–84) became poet laureate of England in 1972. As a youth he was taught for a time by T. S. Eliot before entering Oxford, where he was tutored by C. S. Lewis. By the early 1950s Betjeman was already well-known as a journalist, essayist, and poet, and his review of *Fahrenheit 451* in the April 2, 1954, London *Daily Telegraph* played a significant role in the successful March 1954 release of the British hardbound edition. Betjeman's strong praise of *Fahrenheit 451*'s cultural criticism was more openly received in Britain, where the Cold War climate of fear had less of an effect on publishing and the literary marketplace.

New Fiction

Sir John Betjeman

Ray Bradbury, an American, is by far the best science fiction writer. But it comes as no surprise to me to find *Fahrenheit 451* a betrayal of modern science and the false idea that "progress" can be reckoned in terms of scientific inventions. He is too much of a poet in all he writes, too full of imagination to be anything but a prophet.

He foresees an America living in cities and at war with the rest of the world. A war is a matter of sending out flights of bombers and is over in 48 hours. All houses are fireproof. Interior walls are huge television screens. Conversation is just mutual back-slapping. Education is just committing facts to memory. No opinions, no philosophy or sociology are allowed. Religion is run by advertising firms and Our Lord is used for toothpaste advertisements.

His hero is a man called Montag, a fireman. Firemen in his world are used to start fires, not to prevent them. They are a sort

of sanitary squad and rush out, at the command of the State
Police, to burn any secret hoards of books. Books are illegal.
One reads from State-selected books thrown on to the televi-
sion screen.

Montag is so foolish as to steal one of the books from a
pile he is burning and to read it. He also makes friends with a
young girl who is a rebel and subsequently liquidated. Montag's
wife betrays him to the police and he escapes in a thrilling chase
wherein he is pursued by an eight-legged Mechanical Hound.

I have left out of this description the powerful horror of this
unlikeable but compelling tale. I advise it for all worshippers
of speed, popular wireless entertainment, luxury flats and mechanical labour-saving devices. Once read it will never be forgotten, and should be in every laboratory and technical college
and atomic plant in the country—if those places are allowed
subversive books.

Adrian Mitchell (1932–2008), a prominent English poet and playwright, was a creative leader of the antiwar and antiauthoritarian movement in Britain for more than four decades. He was equally at home writing for the Royal Shakespeare Company, the National Theatre, and countless regional and fringe venues. Critics considered him the "shadow poet laureate" of Britain, and his early attraction to *Fahrenheit 451* testifies to the way that Bradbury's novel cut across political and sociological ideologies. Mitchell penned this early review for the April 28, 1954, issue of *Isis*, Oxford University's literary magazine, while serving as student editor; in spite of his youth, Mitchell's signature mix of carnival effect and shadowy terror is already evident in his dark and brooding praise of *Fahrenheit 451*.

1984 AND ALL THAT

Adrian Mitchell

Ray Bradbury is not in love with the future. For him it contains the already planned murder of the individual, an easy victim in a metal landscape. His first novel, *Fahrenheit 451*, is an attempt to prevent the crime by anticipating the moves of a delinquent civilization. Prophetic detection is no work for flatfoots; the private eye must have vision and intellect. Wells educated science fiction but left it skinny and uncertain, Orwell gave it strength and now Bradbury employs it to carry his fears.

His hero is a fireman; his job is to set fire to any house suspected of harbouring books, the contraband of a televiewing age.

"It's fine work. Monday burn Millay, Wednesday Whit-man, Friday Faulkner, burn 'em to ashes, then burn the ashes. That's our official slogan."

The plot follows his crippled progress, which leads to a vol-untary exile from the negation of his enemies: drug-headed hu-mans and intelligent machines. Mildred, his wife and traitor, is drawn in thick, vicious lines; she sits in her parlour watching the three walls, which are flat-faced television screens; her only misery is the absence of a fourth wall-screen. Outside the house, seasons change and murder wears a fine uniform. Inside, her senses are slack; she does not notice the smell of dead love, stale in the bright house. Only her television 'family' affects her pulse.

Bradbury's style weakens when he pictures his sympathetic characters. The fireman and his terrified professor talk and look like people, but the fey Clarisse and the exiles are half-obscured in romantic mist. Clarisse runs in the moonlight and drinks the rain; she might have been real, instead she is made up with cosmetic sentimentality. Fantasy should glitter like hard-frozen snow; it should have no patches of grey slush. Fortunately these patches are rare, but they stand out like pimples on a hard face. This looks like a temporary rash, for Mr. Bradbury's imagina-tion is in good health and maturing rapidly; the complaint is no more than a touch of the spring and should be easily cured.

The book could have been absurd; in the clever hands of its author it becomes a serious novel, not a heavyweight, but still a well-made and balanced body. The images of fire encircle a scor-pion civilization, which we watch as its tail stings its little head to death. For this is a hell that ends; the book concludes with the cremation of an era and the first word of its successor. At the death, large-scale horror is transformed into poetic narrative as the hero listens to the bombers screaming overhead, and in his hysteria knows what must happen:

> He felt that the stars had been pulverised by the sound of the black jets and that in the morning the earth would be covered with their dust like a strange snow. That was his idiot thought as he stood shivering in the dark, and let his lips go on moving and moving.

No man's vision is perfect, but Ray Bradbury has better second sight than most. The dry attackers of novels set in the future should drop the gaudy paperbacks to deal with a sterner man, and perhaps the Science Fiction label could be torn off; it has prejudiced too many careful readers already. *Fahrenheit 451* has faults, but it also has blood in its veins and nerves in its skin.

Sir Kingsley Amis (1922–95) was a lifelong reader of science fiction who developed a particular interest in the cultural commentary of dystopic novels. His 1950s breakthrough as a popular master of comic realism came during his years on the faculty of the University of Wales at Swansea, and led to a Princeton fellowship in creative writing during the 1958–59 academic year. The lectures Amis gave for his Gauss Seminars, presented during his year at Princeton, were soon gathered and transformed into *New Maps of Hell* (1960), a detailed study of the dystopian aspects of certain science-fiction writers. His lengthy and very positive analysis of *Fahrenheit 451* spreads across two chapters in *New Maps of Hell*, and remains the most extensive commentary on this novel by a major literary figure.

FROM *NEW MAPS OF HELL*
Kingsley Amis

From chapter IV, "Utopias 1"

Bradbury is the Louis Armstrong of science fiction, not in the sense of age or self-repetition, but in that he is the one practitioner well-known by name to those who know nothing whatever about his field. . . .

The suppression of fantasy, or of all books, is an aspect of the conformist society often mentioned by other writers, but with Bradbury it is a specialty. His novel *Fahrenheit 451*—supposedly the temperature at which book paper ignites—extends and fills in the assumptions of "Usher II." The hero, Montag, is a fireman, which means that on receiving an alarm he and his colleagues pile on to the wagon and go off and burn somebody's house down, one with books in it, under the regulations of the Firemen of America, "Established, 1790, to burn English-influenced books in the Colonies. First Fireman: Benjamin Franklin." In the expected central dialogue, the fire chief explains to Montag how it all came about:

Classics cut to fit fifteen-minute radio shows, then cut again to fill a two-minute book column, winding up at last as a ten- or twelve-line dictionary resume. I exaggerate, of course. The dictionaries were for reference. But many were those whose sole knowledge of *Hamlet* . . . was a one-page digest in a book that claimed: *now at last you can read all the classics; keep up with your neighbors*. Do you see? Out of the nursery into the college and back to the nursery; there's your intellectual pattern. . . . Life is immediate, the job counts, pleasure lies all about after work. . . . More sports for everyone, group spirit, fun, and you don't have to think, eh? . . . Authors, full of evil thoughts, lock up your typewriters. . . . We must all be alike. Not everyone born free and equal, as the Constitution says, but everyone *made* equal. Each man the image of every other; then all are happy, for there are no mountains to make them cower, to judge themselves against. So! A book is a loaded gun in the house next door. Burn it. Take the shot from the weapon. . . . Ask yourself, What do we want in this country, above all? People want to be happy, isn't that right? Haven't you heard it all your life? I want to be happy, people say. Well, aren't they? Don't we keep them moving, don't we give them fun? That's all we live for, isn't it? For pleasure, for titillation? And you must admit our culture provides plenty of these. . . . If you don't want a man unhappy politically, don't give him two sides to a question to worry him; give him one. Better yet, give him none. . . . Don't give [him] any slippery stuff like philosophy or sociology to tie things up with. That way lies melancholy.

One could offer plenty of objections to that, starting with the apparently small point that complacency about sociology, which Bradbury shares with his colleagues, is at least as bad as complacency about the tabloidization of the classics, and that what we ought to want is less sociology, not more. Further, there is about Bradbury, as about those I might call the nonfiction holders of his point of view, a certain triumphant lugubriousness, a kind of proleptic schadenfreude (world copyright reserved), a relish not always distinguishable here from satisfaction in urging a case, but different from it, and recalling the relish with which are recounted the horrors of *Nineteen Eighty-Four* and a famous passage that prefigures it in *Coming Up for Air*. Jeremiah has never had much success in pretending he doesn't thoroughly enjoy his job, and whereas I agree with him, on the whole, in his dislike of those who reach for their revolver when they hear the word "culture," I myself am getting to the point where I reach for my earplugs on hearing the phrase "decline of our culture." But in this respect Bradbury sins no more grievously than his nonfiction colleagues, whom he certainly surpasses in immediacy, for *Fahrenheit 451* is a fast and scaring narrative, a virtue hard to illustrate by quotation. There are at least two good dramatic coups, one when a creature called the Mechanical Hound, constructed to hunt down book owners and other heretics, looks up from its kennel in the fire station and growls at the hero; the other when Montag goes out on duty with the Salamander, as the fire engine is called, and finds that the alarm refers to his own house. The book emerges quite creditably from a comparison with *Nineteen Eighty-Four* as inferior in power, but superior in conciseness and objectivity. At the end, of course, Montag eludes the Mechanical Hound and joins a band of distinguished hoboes who are preserving the classics by learning them by heart.

Bradbury's is the most skillfully drawn of all science fiction's conformist hells. One invariable feature of them is that however activist they may be, however convinced that the individual can, and will, assert himself, their programme is always to resist or undo harmful change, not to promote useful change. It is quite typical that the revolutionary party in *The Space Merchants* should be called the Conservationists. Thus to call the generic political stance of science fiction "radical," as I have done, is not quite precise: it is radical in attitude and temper, but strongly conservative in alignment.[1] This, however, does not weaken its claim to be regarded as, some of the time and in some sense, a literature of warning, as propaganda, not always unintelligent, against the notion that we can leave the experts to work things out for us. Such is equally the impression given, I think, by our next topic, utopias in which the forces of evil show themselves in economic and technological, rather than political, terms. As I said at the beginning, these departments are not, and should not be, readily separable, but emphasis can be graded. In the next section I shall show how Mrs. Montag amused herself while

---

[1] "Negative" might be a better description. Such glimpses of the posttotalitarian future as we can glean show a society just like our own, but with more decency and less television. Nobody ever says how these reforms are to be brought about. Further, no positive utopias, dramatizing schemes of political or other betterment, can be found in contemporary science fiction. Modern visionaries in general seem to have lost interest in any kind of social change, falling back on notions of self-salvation via naturopathy, orgonomy, or the psychic diagnostics of Edgar Cayce.

Montag was busy on his incendiary routine of "Monday . . . Millay, Wednesday Whitman, Friday Faulkner."

From chapter V, "Utopias 2"

Without turning on the light he imagined how this room would look. His wife stretched on the bed, uncovered and cold, like a body displayed on the lid of a tomb, her eyes fixed to the ceiling by invisible threads of steel, immovable. And in her ears the little Seashells, the thimble radios tamped tight, and an electronic ocean of sound, of music and talk and music and talk coming in, coming in on the shore of her unsleeping mind. The room was indeed empty. Every night the waves came in and bore her off on their great tides of sound, floating her, wide-eyed, toward morning. There had been no night in the last two years that Mildred had not swum that sea, had not gladly gone down in it for the third time.

As regular readers will have guessed, Mildred is Mrs. Montag, wife of Ray Bradbury's book-burning fireman. It emerges, I think, that while it will not do for science fiction to characterize in conventional, differentiating terms, it can have something to say about human nature by dint of isolating and extending some observable tendency of behavior, by showing, in this case, how far the devolution of individuality might go if the environment were to be modified in a direction favourable to this devolution. The lesson to be drawn from the more imaginative science-fiction hells, such as Bradbury's, is not only that a society could be devised that would frustrate the active virtues, nor even that these could eventually be suppressed, but that there is in all sorts of people something that longs for this to happen. There are plenty of embryonic Mrs. Montags waiting for the chance to be wafted away by the Seashells, or to share her jolly evenings at the Fun Park, breaking windows or smashing up cars with the steel ball, to join with her in watching three-wall television and trying to persuade her husband to get the fourth wall put in. This eager denial of mind, this longing to abandon reality via mechanical wonders, is obviously relevant to the political thesis of Bradbury's *Fahrenheit 451* and of many other works: the deliberate use of technology to promote an unworthy quiescence is a familiar idea. Correspondingly, Mildred Montag is a victim of epidemic neurosis: a cleverly staged scene shows her being brought round after a suicide attempt by a couple of cigarette-puffing handymen who just have time to use the almost fully automatic evacuation machine on her before rushing off to the next of their dozen nightly cases. What is most important here, however, is clearly the notion of the Seashell jag, for this need presuppose no kind of political manipulation, whether malevolent or mistakenly paternalistic.

Harold Bloom (1930–), America's best-known literary critic, scholar, and anthologist, is Yale University's Sterling Professor of the Humanities. His abiding interest in creativity and literary traditions led to publication of *The Western Canon: The Books and School of the Ages* (1994), which promotes teaching an apolitical vision of the literary canon today in much the same spirit that Bradbury's *Fahrenheit 451* promoted the preservation of canonical literature in a darkly imagined future. Not surprisingly, Bloom's introduction to *Ray Bradbury's Fahrenheit 451* (Philadelphia: Chelsea House Publications, 2001) begins to define the novel's place in the literary tradition as well as its continuing relevance for the twenty-first century.

INTRODUCTION TO *RAY BRADBURY'S FAHRENHEIT 451*

Harold Bloom

While *Fahrenheit 451* manifestly is a "period piece," this short, thin, rather tendentious novel has an ironic ability to inhabit somewhat diverse periods. In its origins, the book belongs to the Cold War of the 1950s, yet it prophesied aspects of the 1960s and has not lost its relevance as I consider it in the new millennium. One does not expect the full madness of a new Theological Age to overwhelm the United States, despite George W. Bush's proclamations that he never makes a decision without consulting Christ. And yet, in time, there may be no books to burn. In the Age of Information, how many will read Shakespeare or Dante?

I resort to a merely personal anecdote. A little while back, the New British Library wished to celebrate its grand instaura-

tion, and invited me to show up to help close a self-congratu-
latory week. At a Friday afternoon symposium, I was to make
a third, in conjunction with the leading British authorities on
software and on "information retrieval." After I protested that I
did not know what the latter was, and knew nothing of software
(having not yet learned to type), I was told that my function
would be to "represent books." I declined the compliment and
the invitation, while reflecting gloomily that a once-great library
was betraying itself.

Reading *Fahrenheit 451* after many years, I forgive the novel
its stereotypes and its simplifications because of its prophetic
hope that memory (and memorization!) is the answer. When
I teach Shakespeare or American Poetry I urge my students to
read and reread *Macbeth* and *Song of Myself* over and over again
until these essential works are committed to memory. Myself, I
have *eaten the books* (to employ a Talmudic trope), and I repeat
poems and plays to myself for part of each day. Bradbury, a half
century ago, had the foresight to see that the age of the Screen
(movie, TV, computer) could destroy reading. If you cannot read
Shakespeare and his peers, then you will forfeit memory, and if
you cannot remember, then you will not be able to think.

Bradbury, though his work is of the surface, will survive as a
moral fabulist. "The house will crumble and the books will burn,"
Wallace Stevens mournfully prophesied, but a saving remnant
will constitute a new party of Memory. In our America-to-come,
the party of Memory will become the party of Hope, a reversal
of Emersonian terms but hardly of Emersonian values. Is there
a higher enterprise now than stimulating coming generations to
commit to memory the best that has been written?

Margaret Atwood (1939–) is a celebrated Canadian novelist and poet whose international honors include a wide range of American, British, and European literary awards and award nominations. *The Handmaid's Tale*, along with other Atwood novels, are often regarded as science fiction, but she considers them speculative works or, at most, Earthbound sociological science fiction firmly grounded in projections of today's reality. Bradbury's sense of *Fahrenheit 451* as a sociological novel, projecting elements of the present into an all-too-possible future, strikes a similar chord that goes far to explain Atwood's enduring attraction to this novel; she expressed these views in "The Star's Our Destination," the (London) *Guardian's* May 13, 2011, survey of the favorite science fiction works of leading authors.

"FAHRENHEIT 451"
Margaret Atwood

As a young teenager, I devoured Ray Bradbury's *Fahrenheit 451* by flashlight. It gave me nightmares. In the early 1950s television was just rolling forth, and people sat mesmerized in front of their flickering sets, eating their dinners off TV trays. Surely, it was said, "the family" was doomed, since the traditional dinnertime was obsolete. Films and books too were about to fall victim to the new all-consuming medium. My own parents refused to get a TV, so I had to sneak over to friends' houses to gape at *The Ed Sullivan Show*. But when not doing that, I fed my reading addiction, whenever, however, whatever. Hence *Fahrenheit 451*. In this riveting book, books themselves are condemned—all books. The very act of reading is considered detrimental to social order because it causes people to think, and then to distrust the authorities. Instead of books the public is offered conformity via four-wall TV, with the sound piped directly into their heads via shell-shaped earbuds (a brilliant proleptic leap on the part of Bradbury). Montag, the main character, is a "Fireman": his job is to burn each and every book uncovered by the state's spies and informers. But little by little Montag gets converted to reading, and finally joins the underground: a dedicated band of individuals sworn to preserve world literature by becoming the living repositories of the books they have memorized.

Fahrenheit 451 predated Marshall McLuhan and his theories about how media shape people, not just the reverse. We interact with our creations, and they themselves act upon us. Now that we're in the midst of a new wave of innovative media technologies, it's time to reread this classic, which poses the eternal questions: who and how do we want to be?

FAHRENHEIT 451:
THE MOTION PICTURE

The finale, with the fine Bernard Herrmann score, shows the Book People moving in a snowfall through the woods, whispering the lines from all the books they have remembered. This ending has never failed to move audiences. The film ends on this high note, and one leaves feeling you've seen more than was really there.

—Ray Bradbury

Arthur Knight (1917–91) was a highly influential motion picture historian whose survey of movie history, *The Liveliest Art: A Panoramic History of the Movies* (1957) became a leading film studies textbook. He wrote regularly for *The Saturday Review* and *Playboy*, and taught in the film program at the University of Southern California from 1960 to 1985. Ray Bradbury was an occasional guest lecturer in these classes, and together Knight and Bradbury formed the core leadership of the Writers Guild of America, West, Film Society during the 1960s. Knight was a dedicated opponent of censorship, and his December 3, 1966, *Saturday Review* analysis of François Truffaut's adaptation of *Fahrenheit 451* demonstrates a deep understanding of the challenges involved in translating Bradbury's novel into film.

"Shades of Orwell"

Arthur Knight

Although Ray Bradbury is often described as a science-fiction writer, he himself tends to shy from that label, preferring to be known simply as a writer. There is more than ordinary justification for this view. Bradbury is enormously enthusiastic about writing, but not enthusiastic at all about the brave new world he fears the scientists and geneticists have in store for us.

Like George Orwell, he projects the more alarming symptoms of today's sicknesses upon a wall a few decades or generations away, where, magnified to super life-size, they scarifyingly dominate the entire landscape, blotting out the human spirit, exorcising our most cherished human values. But where Orwell in his angry works seemed to call for action now to prevent the world from slipping into *Nineteen Eighty-Four*, Bradbury often conveys the impression that already it is far too late. His nostalgia is for the small-town America of back porches and rocking chairs, of fresh-mown lawns and nearby woods in which to ramble. For him, science is no panacea, and he seems to embrace science fiction writing as a kind of "*Mene, mene, tekel . . .*" of things to come.

All of these qualities are abundantly visible in *Fahrenheit 451*, François Truffaut's vivid and imaginative adaptation of one of Bradbury's best, and best-known, works. It postulates a not-too-distant time in which books are outlawed enemies of the state: they stir dissent and unrest; they make people unhappy. For a placid, non-questioning, utterly passive populace, the books must be destroyed.

Montag, the hero of this story, is one of the destroyers, a fireman-in-reverse whose job is to *start* fires. (Fahrenheit 451 is the temperature at which paper turns to ash.) Meeting a teacher who reminds him disturbingly of his own wife, Montag begins to wonder about the job he has been doing so unquestioningly. If books are so bad, why do people jeopardize their careers to read them? If books are so dangerous, why are some people willing to give up their lives for them? For an answer, Montag rescues a copy of *David Copperfield* from the pyre, reads it clandestinely, and is denounced by his wife to the government. The fireman finds refuge in a community of subversives who read and memorize books to preserve them for the future.

This, of course, is Bradbury the humanist, the writer who holds that man truly exists only when he is exercising all his senses and exerting all his faculties. But the Orwellian strain is present as well in the omnipresent television screens with their uninterrupted flow of tranquilizing pablum, in the drab uniformity of the people's costumes and their responses, and in their dead apathy to news of war and disaster. Truffaut embraces Bradbury and Orwell with equal enthusiasm—which means that there is some ambivalence within the film itself. Logically, the book burners are quite right; and if happiness is to be equated with wall-to-wall television, soma pills, and (Bradbury's favorite panacea for transportation snarls) high-speed monorails, then indeed who needs books? On the other hand, because Bradbury lacks Orwell's political bite, the book burners remain peripheral to the theme of totalitarianism even while occupying screen-center; they are but one singular manifestation of a larger danger that is surely sensed but never shown.

As a film, *Fahrenheit 451* moves slowly but intriguingly, setting its intellectual snares for Montag, fashioning a world that we all know could exist but should not. Oskar Werner, his accent unaccounted for, makes of Montag a reluctant hero, a sensitive man drawn ineluctably, irresistibly to the world of books. Julie Christie, also unaccountably, plays the dual roles of teacher and wife—which, as it turns out, is neither a plus nor a minus. But Truffaut, working for the first time in color, continues his romance with the motion-picture camera, playing with slow motion, maskings and movements, and constantly keeping the screen as alert and aware as Bradbury's own sensibilities would dictate. The resultant film is highly original, thought provoking, and at the same time distressingly superficial. The dangers that lie ahead are not from the book burners, but from those who may direct them; and somehow *Fahrenheit 451* never gets around to this.

CAST

Montag	OSKAR WERNER
Linda	JULIE CHRISTIE
Clarisse	JULIE CHRISTIE
The Captain	CYRIL CUSACK
Fabian	ANTON DIFFRING
The Man with the Apple	JEREMY SPENSER
The Book-Woman	BEE DUFFELL
T.V. Announcer	GILLIAN LEWIS
Doris	ANNE BELL
Helen	CAROLINE HUNT
Jackie	ANNA PALK
The Neighbour	ROMA MILNE

TECHNICOLOR®

PRODUCTION STAFF

Director	FRANCOIS TRUFFAUT
Producer	LEWIS M. ALLEN
Associate Producer	MICKEY DELAMAR
Executive Associate	JANE C. NUSBAUM
Screenplay	FRANCOIS TRUFFAUT and JEAN LOUIS RICHARD
Based on the novel by	RAY BRADBURY
Additional dialogue	DAVID RUDKIN and HELEN SCOTT
Music	BERNARD HERRMANN
Director of Photography	NICHOLAS ROEG
Production and Costumes designer	TONY WALTON
Art Director	SYD CAIN
M. Truffaut's personal assistant	SUZANNE SCHIFFMAN
Assistant Director	BRYAN COATES
Film Editor	THOM NOBIE
Special Effects	BOWIE FILMS LTD. RANK FILMS PROCESSING DIVISION CHARLES STAFFEL

UNIVERSAL CITY STUDIOS

A Universal Release
An Enterprise Vineyard Film Production 1966
Filmed in Pinewood Studios, London, England

"fahrenheit 451"

Universal Studio's promotional bookmark was distributed for the 1966 release of François Truffaut's adaptation of *Fahrenheit 451*. This was Truffaut's first color motion picture as well as his first English-language production, and it took nearly six years to finance and film. The production credits on the reverse include Bernard Herrmann's acclaimed musical score, the innovative and influential cinematography of Nicholas Roeg, and the dramatic pairing of Oskar Werner and Julie Christie. Werner had recently starred in Truffaut's award-winning *Jules and Jim*; Christie, who portrayed two roles in *Fahrenheit*, had just finished filming *Doctor Zhivago*. *Fahrenheit 451* was entered and shown at the 1966 Venice Film Festival.

François Truffaut (1932–84) was an influential critic of the French New Wave cinema movement who would go on to become one of the movement's leading directors as well. He had a high regard for Bradbury's early works, and spent more than six years planning and creating his film adaptation of *Fahrenheit 451*. His comprehensive journal of the filming spanned the January to June 1966 shooting schedule and was serialized (in English) for volumes 5–7 of *Cahiers du Cinema* (1966–67). Many of the entries focus on the logistical challenges and the complex working relationships with the actors and crew, but a few passages combine to provide insightful commentary on aspects of Truffaut's vision for *Fahrenheit 451* and the evolving film experience as it related to the actual novel.

FROM "THE JOURNAL OF *FAHRENHEIT 451*"

François Truffaut

Friday, January 14, 1966

. . . *Fahrenheit 451* is the super-simple story of a society in which it is forbidden to read and to possess books. The firemen—who once upon a time put out fires—are responsible for confiscating books and burning them on the spot. One of them, Montag, on the point of being promoted to a higher rank, influenced by meeting a young woman (Clarisse) who questions the order of things, begins to read books and to find pleasure in them. His own wife (Linda) informs on him out of fear, and eventually Montag is brought to the point of literally burning up his own Captain. Then he runs away—and you will only need to buy a ticket to one of the better cinemas to find out where to.

When I was a boy at school and we talked on Mondays

about the films we had seen over the weekend, the two questions that always came up were:

(1) Is there a fight in it?
(2) Are there any naked women?

In respect to *Fahrenheit 451*, I can answer yes to the first question and no to the second, but without taking any special pride in it.

In point of fact, this film, like all those taken from a good book, half-belongs to its author, Ray Bradbury. It is he who invented those book burnings that I'm going to have such fun filming, which is why I wanted colour. An old lady who chooses to be burned with her books rather than be separated from them, the hero of the film who roasts his Captain—these are the things I am looking forward to filming and seeing on the screen, but which my imagination, tied too firmly to reality, could not have conceived by itself. . . . Ray Bradbury comes to my aid, providing me with the strong situations I need in order to escape from the documentary.

Sunday, January 16

. . . A science-fiction film makes everybody go creative, sometimes in the wrong way. Someone will say to me smoothly: "To show that the life of these people is dreary, I've made you a dreary what-have-you (a set design or dressing or costume)." The danger of these booby traps is enhanced by my own tendency to wave problems aside and say: "Leave it be—we'll look at it later on." I reckon that in this film we shall hit snags at every stage—a snag a day, a snag a set, a snag a scene; in short, a proper snag festival.

Three years ago, the concept of *Fahrenheit 451* was an SF film, set in the future and backed up by inventions and gadgetry and so on. Now that we've had James Bond, Courrèges, Pop Art—and Godard, by God, yet—I'll cut off at a bit of a tangent too, as when I made *Jules et Jim* a period film to bypass the danger—of Jim as a racing driver, Jules a fashion photographer and Catherine as a cover girl. Obviously it would be going too far to make *Fahrenheit 451* a period film, yet I am heading in that general direction. I am bringing back Griffith-era telephones, Carole Lombard/Debbie Reynolds–style dresses, a Mr. Deeds–type fire engine. I am trying for anti-gadgetry—at one point Linda gives Montag a superb cutthroat razor and throws the old battery-model Philips in the wastebasket. In short, I am working contrariwise, a little as if I were doing a "James Bond in the Middle Ages."

Wednesday, January 19

I have refused to authorize two writers to do a book about the making of the film. When they see this ship's log of mine, they will probably think it is the reason for my refusal. This is not the case. In fact, it is because whenever I work from a novel, I feel a certain responsibility towards the author. Whether it comes off or not, whether it is faithful to the book or not, the film of *Fahrenheit 451* should only favour the sales of one book, the book from which it was taken. A book about the making of the film would only create confusion with Bradbury's. To my way of thinking, the best idea would be to reissue the novel, illustrating it with stills from the film. . . .

Friday, January 21

. . . I knew that *Fahrenheit* had some shortcomings, as every film does. In this case it is the characters who are not very real or very strong, and this is because of the exceptional nature of the situations. This is the chief danger in science-fiction stories, that everything else is sacrificed to what is postulated. It's up to me to fight that in trying to bring it alive on the screen.

One very unfortunate thing of which I had not thought at all is the military look of the film. All these helmeted and booted firemen, smart, handsome lads, snapping out their lines. Their military stiffness gives me a real pain. Just as I discovered when I was making *Le Pianiste* that gangsters were for me unfilmable people, so now I realize that I must in future avoid men in uniform as well. . . .

Universal's Hollywood lawyers wanted us not to burn books by Faulkner, Sartre, Genet, Proust, Salinger, Audiberti, etc. "Stick to books that are in the public domain," they said, for fear of future proceedings. That's absurd. I took counsel's opinion here in London and was told: "No problem. Go ahead and quote all the titles and authors you like." There will be as many literary references in *Fahrenheit 451* as in all of Jean-Luc's eleven films put together.

Wednesday, March 9

. . . The subjects of films influence the crews that make them. During *Jules et Jim* everybody started to play dominoes; during *La Peau Douce* everyone was deceiving his wife (or her husband); and right from the start of *Fahrenheit 451* everybody on the unit has begun to read. There are often hundreds of books on the set; each member of the unit chooses one, and sometimes you can hear nothing but the sound of turning pages.

Wednesday, April 20

. . . Ray Bradbury gave me a free hand in adapting his novel, for he knew it would be difficult, having tried himself to make a stage play from it. Jean-Luis Richard and I worked on the construction for ten or twelve weeks, and, having finished the job at the beginning of 1963, we have often taken it up again since, tightened it, reshaped it, so as to get the story into 110 minutes and keep the budget down.

It will surely be an offbeat film, especially for an English-language production, but within its strangeness it seems to me to be coherent. . . .

Tuesday, June 21

. . . Although the adaptation of *Fahrenheit 451* was written a year before the screenplay of *La Peau Douce*, there are, strangely enough, a number of things common to both films, and if Montag's wife is called Linda—and not Mildred, as in Bradbury's book—it's probably because the Jacoud affair was already in my mind. For the rest, *Fahrenheit 451* will be more like *Tirez sur le Pianiste*, perhaps because in both cases we are dealing with an American novel, stocked with American material. I don't know what the film will look like; I know it will look only remotely like what I have written about it here, since, quite obviously, I shall have spoken only of what was unexpected or impressed me, and not of what was accepted long ago either in my mind or in Bradbury's. Now, on the screen you will see only what was in our two heads, Bradbury's brand of lunacy and then mine, and whether they have blended together well. . . .

It slept. It was not awake, it was only gently humming in
its great kennel in the far corner of the police station. The
dim light of three o'clock in the morning, the moonlight from
the open sky framed through the open window upon itx, touched
here and there on brass and copper and steel, on bits of
ruby glass and on sensitive capillary hairs in the nylonbrushed nostrils of the creature that quivered gently, gently.
Its eight legs, with the rubber-padded paws, were spidered
under it. It was like a great bee come home from some field
where the honey is full of poison wildness, of insanity and
nightmare, its body full of that kksk over-rich nectar, and
not it was sleeping the evil out of itself.

The sheriff of the small town lay on his cot, his deputy
on another cot across from him, something had kept them awake
for an hour now. They both discovered each other with their
eyes open. Then they both looked at the metal hound humming
in its kennel between them, and at last the sheriff said,
"I wonder, sometimes I wonder, what does it think, late nights,
or does it think at all? Is it alive, I wonder, or what?"
"It doesn't think anything we don't want it to think."
"Then, that's bad," said the sheriff, quietly, sadly, "for all
we put into it is hunting and finding and killing. All we put
in it is bad. That's a shame."

Bradbury's Mechanical Hound was originally intended to anchor an unpublished story about a small town where the sheriff and his deputy use the
Hound to track down criminals. Bradbury incorporated the story's opening
description of the Hound into his expansion of "The Fireman" into *Fahrenheit 451*. Only the opening page of this story has been located. From the
Albright Collection; courtesy of Donn Albright and Ray Bradbury.

CREDITS

A Note
about the Author

Ray Bradbury (1920–2012) was the author of more than three dozen books, including *Fahrenheit 451*, *The Martian Chronicles*, *The Illustrated Man*, and *Something Wicked This Way Comes*, as well as hundreds of short stories. He wrote for the theater, cinema, and TV, including the screenplay for John Huston's *Moby Dick* and the Emmy Award–winning teleplay *The Halloween Tree*, and adapted for television sixty-five of his stories for *The Ray Bradbury Theater*. He was the recipient of the 2000 National Book Foundation's Medal for Distinguished Contribution to American Letters, the 2007 Pulitzer Prize Special Citation, and numerous other honors.